inter alia:
terra

S. L. Guerreiro

First published in Great Britain by S. L. Guerreiro in September 2024

ISBN: 978-1-0685343-0-0

Front cover by Dee
Twitter/X: @duskidraws

www.slguerreiro.com
Twitter/X: @megabookdork
BlueSky: @megabookdork.bsky.social
Instagram: slguerreirolourenco

To all those who have had the courage to chase their dreams in the face of adversity.

Opening Statement

Begin Transcript 1.

I never believed in fate. Not until recently. Not until everything I'd ever known came to a standstill and waited for me to believe in it. Waited for me to acknowledge this new reality, to embrace it.

I look at where I am now, and I know that everything that has happened, every decision I made, every thought I ever had, led me to this moment. I've suffered losses and love, devastation and pure joy, and now—with only a few final nights ahead of me—I know it was all worth it. I welcome my destiny, as if I ever really had a choice.

As I lie on a thin mattress on this Verax ship, a sound system playing a song I haven't heard in a decade, I peer out the window and watch the stars. It's become somewhat of a routine, the music and the stars. I remember looking at them back on Earth with my dad. He and I would point out the constellations visible that night, while lying on a mossy hill, away from the invading town lights.

Watching the stars and listening to a song, it has become a reminder of what it means to be human. To enjoy the little things, to remember a song from a more innocent time and recall what it was like to hear it for the first time. The political climate, the new advances in technology, who I was friends with at the time, and, more specifically, what I felt in the exact moment the song was playing.

I always used to wonder what else was out there, among the stars. That's how humans used to think. Now, we're afraid. And, I believe, we always will be. Even if we survive what's currently happening.

I've been asked to write this down, as an example for forthcoming generations, no matter their species or home planet, no matter their history or their future. We need to share how our pasts can affect our present, and how our futures can affect the here and now. How it can pull us in a direction we didn't even know existed.

But to share this with you, I need to start at the very beginning. Just as First Contact had been initiated. Before the Verax and the tether. Before the war. And before the beginning of the end.

1

I sat in the boardroom of a space hotel, created by a billionaire whose guts I hated. The hotel had initially been created as an indispensable research station, orbiting Earth from a distance just below one hundred thousand kilometres. But only a few years after the launch, in 2039, the research centre had changed drastically, swapping out labs for boardrooms and observation decks for hotel rooms. It grew to three times the size it was when it first started, sporting a new cinema, a mall, and even an attraction allowing passengers to board a shuttle for a quick trip into space, for the cheap price of $500,000. These changes were happening as my father and I were claiming ration tickets from the local food bank. While my father was diagnosed with a terminal illness and requiring medical care that put you on a three-year waiting list.

In front of me lay a lengthy, polished piece of oak, serving as the boardroom table. Its rustic appeal almost alien in this high-tech station. It stretched out, accommodating for around twenty seats. Approximately the amount of people expected for this meeting. Oskar Hagen, the billionaire in question, had organised it. But I knew nothing of who was to attend it, other than a long-lost colleague of mine in the linguistics industry, David Flores.

Much like me, he was too excited to get any sleep in his hotel room, so when he walked in at 5:27am that morning, we stared at each other, unsurprised.

"Alex! Couldn't sleep, huh?" he said, dropping his books and loose papers onto the table next to me. His thin, pointed face, accentuated by cheap, rectangular, metallic glasses, always had an air of placidity. Even in the face of First Contact, he looked as thrilled as one would be after winning £5 on a scratch card. But maybe that's why I liked David as much as I did. His composure kept me grounded.

"Too much going on," I replied. A cold coffee sat before me, and I took a bitter sip before pushing it to one side.

"I know, right? I can't wait to hear it." His thick southern American accent dipped ever so gently. He reshuffled his papers in a way that didn't matter.

"What did you bring with you?" I asked, peering at the books, which covered a range of topics, including Theoretical Linguistics and Applied Linguistics Methods.

"It's just... Backup, mostly. I'm not sure it'll be of any use."

I nod, unsure how to add to the conversation in any meaningful way. After all, we didn't know what we were in for. General Frederikson, who had invited us to participate in this First Contact procedure, had been very quiet about what to expect. He had also sounded frustrated. Maybe this process was going to be a little more complex than anticipated.

We sat in silence, no engines humming, no clocks ticking. Just the scrape of David's papers, and the slide of the coffee cup I'd decided to pull back towards me.

The walls were covered in pictures of the station's history. The early stages of its construction, staff smiling during lift-off in Houston, Texas, as Ævi Inc., Oskar Hagen's company, had borrowed NASA's launch pad. There were portraits of important researchers, focussing on test tubes containing space dust; landscapes of Hagen himself cutting the ribbon to the touristic observatory, and announcing the name of the station as the Observer. A fitting name for a place hosting the most powerful space telescope made by humans, hoping to capture the first signs of alien life.

"It doesn't feel real, does it?" muttered David.

"No, I guess it doesn't."

And yet, here I was, sipping cheap coffee from a paper cup, in an empty boardroom, waiting for the most important event in my life since my father died six months prior. Outside of this room, mall shops were cluttered with plastic merchandise advertising Ævi Inc. as the next best thing since Tesla. Robots, imaginatively called ÆviBots, rolled around the fast-food chains, delivering spilt drinks and dropping knives and forks in the name of progress.

Was I angry about life back then? Maybe so. But I didn't realise I'd be mourning its simplicity only weeks later.

"Good morning, everyone." General Frederikson, the President of the Security Council at the United Nations, sounded weary, his voice dragging at a pitch he wished he didn't have to propel. He stood tall in his sharp, dark blue military suit, punctuated with medals and adorned with golden, military accolades.

All around me were a collection of faces I'd never seen before, some in military attire I didn't recognise, some in shirts and ties. Many of the faces seemed tired, like they had been hauled from their workplaces, put on the earliest shuttle to the Observer, and not slept a wink since they got here.

"You should all have tablets in front of you," continued the General. "The transmission we picked up is available there for you to listen to. Now, before any of you get carried away, that recording is there for our linguistics team to use, not for any of the rest of you to make assumptions."

In front of each of us were little placenames on which our full names and specialities were displayed in a seemingly professional manner. It looked as though Hagen would not be blessing us with his presence today.

"You were briefed about our goals through some of the documentation we provided you," said Frederikson. "But I will be going to each team today and making sure you definitely have all the information you need." His bottom lip pouted naturally, and his cheeks sagged; this was not a man that smiled often.

"Linguists, I'll start with you, seeing as we want to focus on decryption of the message first." Leaving the rest of the groups to chat amongst themselves, Frederikson approached David and me, shielding us from the others. "What's the plan?"

David cleared his throat and took charge. "Well, we'll need to listen to it. Maybe a few times, before we can agree on a way forward. But I think, knowing that all we have is an audio message, it might be best to use the IPA to transcribe it phonetically and then—"

"In English," said Frederikson curtly.

"Well, a phonetic transcription will... How do I put this? Interpret the individual sounds within a language. And phonemes—" He paused. "They're like units of sound, that humans produce; they help distinguish one word from another. The most common example of this, is with the words 'tab' and 'tap'. How does one determine the difference in sound between the 'b' and the 'p'? So, I think recording every individual sound they make may help to at least look at how they use phonemes and identify what noises they can produce. Maybe even how they construct words and sentences. But that's a long shot at the moment."

"I think the idea is to start constructing a database," I added, "or a dictionary of the language, but using only sounds, if that makes sense. The problem is that we're coming at this... dilemma, from the perspective of human languages. We don't know how their language began or evolved. We don't have common roots. We could be faced with sounds that are so far removed from anything we know. Using phonemes from human languages to record their sounds is already... not accurate. We'll probably have to invent new ones just to account for the noises they produce."

"I see," said Frederikson. "Is there a way to be more precise?"

"Not really. It'll be guesswork mostly," replied David.

"It's all about finding patterns. But I think we'll know more when we get started. Although, you need to know the truth: this is basically impossible." I sat back in defeat, even before we'd heard the message.

And for a moment, I wondered why I had even accepted this job in the first place. Deciphering a message from an alien species through sound alone was hopeless. Completely infeasible. Any linguist would agree with that. So, why had I accepted to give this a try? Maybe it was out of eagerness to step out of my comfort zone, or maybe I needed something else to carry me forward in my time of grief. But truthfully, I think fate was toying with me already.

"If we could find a Rosetta Stone type device, that would increase our chances of figuring this out," said David, a false promise in his eyes.

"I see. Maybe I could get someone to help with the pattern finding. Very well," Frederikson said. "Make a start and keep me informed." He moved to a group of military advisers further along the table.

"Shall we?" asked David, earphones in hand.

I nodded, and slid the earphones in. The message was immediately available upon opening the tablet, as if waiting there, begging to be heard.

The vocalisations unnerved me, the speech itself jarring and unrestrained; my hands had begun to shake. I covered my ears and blocked the murmurs around the room, attentively listening to the harsh language. It felt articulated, with strong stresses spiking through every so often. I felt my body drain, the blood rushing far away from my head until I felt light, my core falling, falling far into some obscure pit, a complete unknown. The combination included a mixture of clicks and sounds emanating from the throat and tongue, more so than the lips, or non-human equivalent. My mouth became dry. The transmission ended, and I was left with nothingness. Earphones removed, incomprehensible chatters around, everything was a blur. I felt myself floating above my body, separate, alone and confused. None of this was real. It couldn't be.

I stumbled out, abandoning the other bodies in the room. I ran until I couldn't catch my breath, until I suffocated on my own tears. An urge to move, to keep moving, to get away, to not deal with this… It was too much. All of it. I was not ready. No one was.

I found myself next to the fountain, sitting on a bench, in the central plaza of the Observer; its many shops and restaurants surrounding the park. The park extended to the size of two football fields side by side. Designed like a public garden, the greenery spread out like a contagion of grass. Smooth cobblestones trickled throughout, creating charming, intertwining walkways. Flowers and shrubs sprouted in a stunning array of colours and dotted the grounds. I had perched on one of the many benches in this area. The large fountain, made of a dark stone, sat at the centre. Tourists freckled the area, eating fresh sandwiches and playing on the greenest grass I had ever seen.

Across the entire top of this open space expanded a huge glass ceiling, a curved cupola, through which I could see distant stars. Out of one corner, I saw Earth, a blue edge. Had the station tilted a little more to the left, the view would have been spectacular. Looking up, I couldn't help but feel small, another minuscule being, on a hypocritical station, hundreds of thousands of kilometres from a pale blue dot.

Out of all the pale dots in the universe, the message had come to us. Surely, that counted for something.

Small droplets fell across my shoes. I let the rushing of the water quash my anxiety one drop at a time. Insecurities needed to disappear. I needed to focus. Even though there was no chance of us being able to decrypt this thing, I still felt like I needed to try. If not for me, then at least to keep David company in his false positivity.

Walking back, I felt my face regain colour little by little. The message had lasted a mere thirty seconds, so I sat back down and replayed it again and again to capture as many individual sounds as I could.

Peering at David, I realised he had been in a trance ever since we had first put our earphones in. I touched his arm. Teary eyes stared back at me.

We spent two days transcribing the message into a list of recognisable sounds. It took time to listen to a collection of noises, almost indistinguishable from one another to begin with. But when I listened attentively, I could tell there was more: tone, emphasis and repetition of phonemes. But, more importantly, sounds that were not too dissimilar from human syllables. It was fascinating to hear something so completely new and unknown and to start spotting the patterns and familiarities. These were articulate creatures. No matter the difficulty of this task, there was promise in the air—even if the message could never be translated, we were on the edge of change. Something was happening, and we were going to be on the front line.

"We're meeting in five. You ready?" asked David. We had walked together from the seminar room in which we had been working, heading for an end-of-day meeting, which always took place at five o'clock. Fredrikson had expressed wanting to know every little development; he even took time to go on a twenty-minute rant about good communication between teams. Unsurprisingly, Hagen had not shown us the same respect, having not attended a single meeting since this whole ordeal started. The man was a ghost on his own station.

Together, David and I marched across the plaza, its lights flooding the park in a sunset-orange and pink glow. I had just dipped into one of the many shops lining the outskirts of the park. All I had needed was a new notebook, but the only one I could find had "Why believe in Heaven, when you can believe in Hagen?" inscribed across the front.

I carried it with me into the boardroom in embarrassment. I should have packed more notebooks when I was told I'd be up here.

I turned to David. "Want to lead?"

He nodded, but before he could reply, Hagen, the man himself, stormed into the room, a team of assistants at his tail. He gripped a tablet between his fingers, his eyes piercing the screen. Every muscle in his body had direction, control.

I glared at him. The man had orchestrated this team, hand-picked each specialist for specific reasons only he knew of. His station had received the very first message from an alien species, and he had manipulated everything from day one: keeping it hidden, not only from the press, but from the United Nations and world leaders, controlling who had access to it and who to involve in the matter. His ties to the political world, and his pressure in the economic sphere, all enabled him to do whatever he liked, in whatever fashion he thought was best. His allegiance was to himself and his company, alone. The rest of us were to muck around in the mud until he decided to show up.

And now, finally, he had decided to reappear from the shadows of his offices. Hagen had adopted a corporate manager look from the 2010s: dishevelled, greying hair, an old polo shirt and beige chinos. Something that screamed "I'm just like you", but with an air of "Look how busy and important I am".

"Maybe that's for the best," concluded David, seeing the scowl that had grown on my face. "If I miss anything, just jump in though. I wouldn't want them thinking you're not a hard worker." David delivered a gentle smile.

"We'll make this quick," said Frederikson. Turning to David, he continued, "Run us through what you've got."

David stood up. The group, made up of around twenty people, all turned to face him. Not the greatest public speaker, David struggled to keep his hands steady.

"We've, uhh, managed to transcribe the whole transmission phonetically. With a combination of phonemes — um, sounds, that are human, and some new sounds, that we've had to adapt to. This allows us to see how they use vocalisations in their language and culture." He took a moment to steady himself. "Our next step is to look at where the sounds break off, what we would call word boundaries. To locate full words and ends of sentences, and things like that. From there, we could start to look at prosody, which are the patterns linked to intonation and stress in a language."

"Very well. Small progress but progress nonetheless," Frederikson interjected.

"Once we've located the patterns, we'll be digging into the heart of it. That may take some time, and, honestly, it'll be mostly conjectures." David's hands dropped by his side, his head bowing, a look of defeat, but also of sincerity.

"We'll get to it when we get to it. You and Alex have been doing great so far. Hagen here has pulled some strings to get you the latest pattern recognition A.I. His assistants will get you set up."

Hagen threw a quick smirk towards us. My skin crawled.

"That's very generous, thank y'all for that," said David.

One of the biologists leaned forward to make himself known. "Is it worth us answering in a human language for them to decipher ours instead?"

"It's not a bad idea, but I would like our linguists to try their hand before making that decision. We need to understand what is being said to avoid a faux-pas. But it's a backup plan if we need it," replied the General with a nod.

"Well—," started David.

Hagen scoffed. "You are right though. The longer we wait, the worse the pressure will be. Sending an initial reply in a human language may be the best solution to ease tensions."

Someone at the back raised their voice. "They could be dead for all we know. It might have taken a million years to get here, that message!"

A man in uniform pointed a finger at Hagen. "Didn't you wait two weeks before saying anything to anyone? And now, you're putting pressure on us to get this done faster?"

The room erupted into a frenzied discussion, growing louder by the second. I watched as I saw human beings unravel in real time.

A loud bang sounded around the room, leaving everyone quiet. A small man in a suit and glasses perched on his nose had been the one to slam the table with a folder. Someone from Comms.

"What is it with you people? Are we not all here to help each other? Are we not all specialists in our own fields, to be listened to when we give valid information? Or are we all talking into a void? The message was sent over two weeks ago. The transmission itself is two weeks old. It's crystal clear because that's when it was sent, not just when we picked it up. We checked." He sat back down with a huff.

"Thank you for your clarity," replied the General. "Maybe we can hear from the other departments before we call it a day. Now, I value all your opinions, but there is no room for panic and spontaneous reactions. Tomorrow, I want everyone that comes into this room to arrive with a clear and open mind. We're not here to argue, we're here to make progress. Carry on."

David and I stepped outside, pausing near a set of elevators that led down to the hotel rooms. The station's tourists had lessened since we had first arrived, leaving it bare and muted. Maybe Hagen had restricted access to non-essential visitors since the work on the message had begun.

"Oof, that was a rough one," muttered David, away from prying ears.

I smiled sympathetically. "I get it though. They're terrified, the thought of being in danger, of not acting fast enough."

"You're right..." He paused. "I need to get some rest; I'll catch you tomorrow." David gave a half wave and walked into an elevator, the doors shutting behind him.

It was past 6 p.m., but most of the shops were still open, the odd person coming and going with bags of junk they had bought. I scanned some of the restaurants—I had avoided them with all my might. The last thing I wanted was to put another penny in that man's pocket. But after a few days of eating the same, mediocre cheese sandwiches, the more I leaned into putting my futile, anti-consumerist values to one side. The Mexican place nearby smelled incredible. Maybe it was okay, just once, to enjoy the little things.

"Hey, you're one of the linguists, right?" said a voice behind me, in a thick Australian accent, and a young, energetic tone. I turned and faced one of the engineers on the team, a man in uniform, a badge under his name tag: N. Hoang embroidered in capital letters. His face expressed delicacy and gentleness, and there was a softness in his eyes, contrasting against his steady, firm stature.

"Yes, that's me," I replied.

"Fantastic work in there. It was a bit of a shitshow that last bit, but hey, who can blame them for losing their minds." He laughed, and I smiled in return.

"Thanks. I'm sorry, I didn't catch your name?"

"Nat. Or, *Nhat* Hoang, officially. But people call me Nat. Alex, right?" he asked, and I nodded. "I'm with engineering, but I do a bit of everything."

"A bit of everything?"

"Yeah, I'm not going to bore you with details. Look, I don't know if you're up for talking more work, but I don't feel particularly useful at the moment, so I'd like to offer my help. If you need it, of course?"

I hesitated. Was there anything an engineer could help a linguist with? I doubted it. But he seemed enthusiastic enough that a bit of positive encouragement would be welcome.

"I saw you checking out that Mexican place, would that sweeten the deal?" He gestured to the restaurant I had been scoping out.

"Go on then, you've convinced me." I grinned, unconvinced this was truly about work, but I admired his boldness and cheek. Something told me his heart was in the right place.

We walked in together; the sweet smell of cumin and oregano filled the air as we found a seat.

"So how did you get to be here, in this mess?" The chipotle sauce was stronger than I had expected, but I covered my temporary discomfort by asking Nat more questions.

"Well… I went into the military when I was a kid. Seventeen, I think…" replied Nat, between mouthfuls. "I mean, I know, looking back, that it was because of some shitty propaganda scheme they had going on, back in Aussieland, where—my parents were refugees from Vietnam—where they would tell all the refugees, and kids of refugees, that if you went into the military, you would be defending your country and stopping wars like that one from happening again."

I had been well aware of the growing tension across the globe, more specifically China's invasion of northern Vietnam in 2026. It had caused a flood of refugees; Australia was among the many countries close by, like Malaysia and Indonesia, to open their borders, as requested by the UN.

"Well, it was all bullshit, but in the end," Nat continued, "the military offered to pay for my education. So, after a few years, I managed to get my engineering degree completed, to work on aircraft. By then, I had figured out that that's what I wanted to do with my life, so I pushed on and got my master's and PhD. I did some work on some of the newer aircraft and spacecraft with NASA, and um, I guess that's where Hagen got me from anyway." He paused. "Wow, I really rambled there."

The fire in my mouth had calmed down—that, or I was getting used to the everlasting blistering heat.

"No, no, that's okay. It's interesting to hear where people come from. To see the journey from where you started to where you ended," I replied.

"Ended, huh? That makes the whole thing seem very terminal."

"What— No, I didn't mean it like that—"

"I'm just messing with you." He grinned and took another bite out of his quesadilla. "I'm not like those other idiots in there. I mean, those guys are on edge. Well, anyway. What about you, where did you start?" His eyes gleamed, and it struck me that he was genuinely interested.

"Well, umm…" I hoped he would stop me, tell me I didn't need to reply if I didn't want to; tell me it was okay to be introverted, to be quiet; tell me that my past didn't matter. But, instead, he stayed silent, and let me figure out exactly what I wanted to say. "I grew up in France. My mother was French, my father was also a refugee. But my mother died when I was a kid. Too young to remember." This part was easy. I took a sip of water, swallowing the nausea creeping up I usually felt when someone asked me to open up. "And I did well in school, so I got a scholarship and went to the US, to Harvard, to study language and linguistics. I worked part-time to support myself and kept studying until I got an MA in Linguistic Anthropology. From there, I found odd jobs that tied in with my studies, until someone took me seriously." I chuckled to myself. The road had been much harder than that, but it was easier to simplify things. "And I released some research on language decryption that attracted some attention." Then, my father became ill and changed my life. "So, that's me."

I pushed the anxiety down, repressing all the grief I had felt since the funeral six months ago. And all the pain prior to that, prior to—

"A hard worker," he said. "I bet you were the little nerd at the front of the class, huh?" His grin widened.

I pushed it all back some more, focussing on the here and

the now. This conversation. "I was, yeah. And I bet you were the one at the back always cracking a joke."

"You got me there."

My heart warmed, but I wasn't sure if it was the company or the food. The food, definitely the food. "So, you mentioned you wanted to help?"

"Right. My team's a bit dead at the moment. Not much the engineers can do without a vessel to look at. I thought the guys doing the hard work might want a spare hand?"

"Well, you're right, it would help. But I'm not sure there's much to do right now. A lot of the work is about listening and knowing what to listen for. It's kind of hard to explain how to do what we do to someone who's not done it before."

"I totally get it, don't worry. But if you need someone to..." He rolled his head around, trying to think of things... "print stuff out, or write things down—"

"You have no idea what we do, do you?" I stifled a laugh.

"No, I have no idea." He snickered to himself, his cheeks going rosy.

"Thank you for asking, though. I'm sure we'll need more help in the future. You'll be the first person I ask."

I glanced at him and recognised the keenness in his eyes, accompanied by a softness that I had learned not to expect from strangers in this day and age. An ÆviBot rolled over, its treads squeaking against the glamorous floor tiles, and we ordered another drink each.

OBSERVER DIGITAL ARCHIVE
Conduct, Safety and Security Rule n.1:

"Respect and comply with the alarms."

Red Alarm (possibility of immediate danger): Please make your way to your nearest Hub Bunker

Blue Alarm (small breach in oxygen): Please make your way to your nearest Suit Station

Orange Alarm (possibility of smoke or fire): Please make your way up or down one floor

All visitors and staff members are required to comply with the station's alarms. Please follow the guiding lights on the walkways. For your safety and the safety of others, please act quickly and calmly. Should any alarms sound, please leave your belongings behind and assist any passengers, should they require it, ensuring you do not put yourself in danger first.

Hub Bunkers are located on every other floor. Please see the guidance below for exact Bunker locations. If the guiding lights are not directing you, please observe any signs with a red background and follow the arrows to safety.

Hub Bunkers are designed for your protection. Equipped with its own generator and tech kits, a Hub Bunker has the capacity to seal and isolate itself from the station, securing its oxygen, and keeping the comfort of its passengers at the core of everything it does. <u>Please note</u>: you may be required to find your nearest Hub Bunker for your safety; it will ONLY seal should it be absolutely necessary. Hub Bunkers are designed to create their own artificial gravity, their own supply of oxygen and provide enough food and water to cater for up to thirty people per Bunker for approximately thirty days, whilst maintenance is being carried out on the station. You may be required to find another Hub Bunker should the first one you come across be full. Instructions on how to use Hub Bunkers are located in each Bunker.*

Suit Stations are located on every other floor. Please see the guidance below for exact Suit Station location. If the guiding lights are not directing you, please follow any signs with a blue background and follow the arrows to safety.

Unlike Hub Bunkers, Suit Stations do not have allocated resources for survival; they can only provide space suits and environmental suits. <u>Please note</u>: there are enough space suits for 150% of the maximum population allowed on the station at all times; there are enough suits for all passengers. When the blue alarm rings, you will be required to suit up. Please leave all loose belongings, including jewellery, accessories, and loose-fitting shoes (such as high heels), outside the suit. Once in the suit, please follow any other given directions by either staff or monitors. Instructions on how to use the suits will be available at all Suit Stations.*

**Numbers are for guidance purposes only. Actual allocated resources may vary dependent on stock. Terms and Conditions may apply.*

2

We had been set up in one of the dozens of seminar rooms—a large educational area with a few circular tables scattered around the floor. Each department had claimed a workspace at the beginning and had stuck to the layout since. Comms and engineering had created a computer area, where they monitored radio communications and came up with interesting spacecraft hypotheses, based on the distance and time it took for the message to come through. Meanwhile, David and I had a collection of whiteboards, each with a variety of symbols and letters identifying different sounds.

Together, we continued to work at a decent pace, searching where the breaks in sentences could be, looking for full stops, commas, or alien equivalents. Nat had helped with the setup of the A.I. on one of the computers; a program solely built for this purpose.

"I think we have enough information to start the A.I., Alex. Can you input that data—you're better with this new tech stuff. I'll see if there's another iteration, another way to find these word boundaries."

I sat down at the desk and input the settings into the A.I.

program. I hadn't used software like this before, and I'd always done this kind of stuff by hand, but we were pressed for time, so exceptions had to be made. My mind zoned in and focused, only the work ahead of me mattered. I ran the software—it found a small number of patterns, but nothing significant. Saving the data, I got up again to look at the boards. Something wasn't adding up.

"I'm not sure that was it," I said in David's direction, as he read, muttering the sounds to himself like someone practicing a poetry recital. Grabbing the earphones, I listened to the message using an enhanced audio spectrum analyser. The thick, intricate, aggressive voice clamoured into my ears once more as I altered the calibre of the sounds. Turning the dials and changing the frequency, something caught my attention. Rewind. Start again. There it was: a faint click. It hadn't been there before. I turned the dials all the way down, and it was gone. Turned back up, it became clear, imperceptible to the natural human ear. Starting the message from the beginning and running the A.I. software at the same time, I got up and approached another board and marked each click. The software flared up—each click occurred after a few phonemes. Could these be word boundaries? Every space between words, every clause, every full stop, or paragraph break?

"David. I think I've found something."

He turned, his attention undivided.

"There's a small click that we didn't hear; their frequency is too low." My heart had begun to race—there was an excitement in these kinds of projects you just couldn't deny. We were deciphering something the human eye and ear had never seen or heard before.

"Incredible. Tell me, did you notice a change in frequency or decibel between them? If they differ, there might be more to this."

"I'll check now." Back at the computer, David hovered over my shoulder. I played it again and monitored the decibel and frequency count. They fluctuated, but certain ones stood out more than others. Ends of sentences? Could that be it? Or was it related to tone?

"Make a note of that," said David. "Input that new condition into the A.I. program." I did as he said. The program loaded the information, the progress bar mimicking our anticipation. These turned into the longest seconds of my life—each moment dragging out longer than the previous one.

"Yes!" I heard David shout before I had fully understood. The patterns remained regular. They used repeated syllables. They had sentence structure. They had grammar and punctuation.

The room became quiet as each department watched our next moves. Some came up behind us, not knowing what they were looking at. Hagen loitered amongst them.

"What has happened here?" he asked, his hand on David's shoulder. I could feel the threat of him even though it wasn't me he was touching.

"We've discovered something significant." I could hear the smile on David's face, the pride, the honest and childlike excitement. "We might have complete sentences."

Hagen nodded. He didn't seem to understand the enthusiasm for small discoveries. Yet, this was probably one of the biggest achievements in modern linguistics. Something the history books would write about in years to come.

"Excellent work. When do you think you can decipher the rest?"

"Oh, not for a while yet, but—"

"Alright, keep it up," interrupted Hagen before meandering away.

David's face had hardened, but when he turned to me, he flashed a quick supportive smile. No amount of pressure could take this away from him.

Past midday, Frederikson entered the room and without hesitation walked towards us linguists. He took a chair and sat opposite David and me. His pitiless demeanour could be felt as he slumped down.

"We need to start talking options," he said. "Hagen has spoken to me about picking up speed. Although I understand you've made progress today, we need to start thinking about moving this forward faster." He looked towards David before continuing, "Are you able to construct something, a response, in a human language, to send out soon?"

"I mean…" started David, staring at me, "No." He shook his head, a look of utter bewilderment in the creases on his forehead. "We can't do that without knowing what they said. When Columbus arrived in North America—"

"I'm not here for a history lesson, Flores," snapped Frederikson.

"And I'm trying to prevent another one from being made." David's breath caught in his throat; confusion had turned to anger. The two men glared at each other.

"He's right, and you know it," I intervened. "No amount of pressure from Hagen should push us to compromise our work. I thought you were in charge here." A frown formed on my forehead; I could feel its creases digging into me.

"Well, then you have misunderstood the situation," replied the General. He stood up, pushing the chair under the table, and he continued, "Write a suitable response in English. You will have my approval before it gets passed to Hagen. The faster, the better." And with that, he disappeared amongst the other teams.

David and I looked at each other, disbelief and frustration across our features. We were under no illusion that Frederikson had limited power here. But this was Hagen's show, and no one else was ever going to run it.

Despite not wanting to do this, I saw no other option. I seized the tablet and formulated a response. The first human words to be uttered to another species. They would be cautious words; I'd make damn sure of it.

"We are human beings of planet Earth, of the Sol System in the

Milky Way Galaxy. We have heard your call. We offer you a peaceful welcome. We invite you to communicate with us." David's voice cracked through the meeting room; his gaze fell upon an empty space on the large oak table. Simple phrases, no conjunctions, repetition of a single pronoun. It was the best we could do in the half-hour they gave us.

"That is what we have so far," stated David. "If there are any changes y'all wanna make, we can make those now. Obviously, it's quite general and doesn't refer to their mess—"

"Sounds perfect," interjected Hagen. "We should send it."

"You can't be serious?" I said, standing up. "We need to make sure their message was at least along the same lines."

Surely, he had lost his mind. Yes, the message was as conflict-free as we could make it, a relatively simple list of words for them—realistically, a more advanced species—to translate. Would we ever be able to translate *their* message? Without any meaning behind the sounds, I'm not sure we ever could.

"Mr. Hagen, we can't send this off—" David tried to add, but the table had grown rowdy and restless once again.

"We've waited over two weeks already—" said someone at the far left of the table.

"Two weeks is nothing. What the hell do—" added a man whose name I had not caught yet.

"That response is shit. We need more—" The voices kept multiplying.

"It's an invitation for them to come over here and—"

"It's done."

"I can't believe anyone would write—"

"What do you take us for, you fucking—"

"I've sent it."

"What if their message mentioned nuclear—"

"I've sent it!" Hagen's voice was distant, passive, while his smile was not.

My heart sank. My fingers clung to the edge of the chair like I was going to pass out.

"You did *what*?" The General's quiet demeanour diminished like a flame, whispering, disbelief incarnate.

"I sent it."

Everyone turned towards Oskar Hagen.

General Frederikson took a moment, then raced up to the man in charge and shoved him against the wall, a deep thud as Hagen's back collided with the metal surroundings. Frederikson's fists clumped around the hem of Hagen's polo shirt.

"What the fuck did you do?! You son of a—"

"I am the future. What are you going to do about it?" The stillness in his voice disturbing. Hagen knew he was untouchable.

I couldn't keep my eyes off them, my mind fading, dissociating from the angry outburst, finding solace in a quiet peace somewhere in another reality where none of this was happening, but returning in time for…

"Sir…?" A small voice came from the other end of the boardroom. "Sir!"

"We've got something." Comms, headphones on, frantically tapped away on their tablets.

"Tracking…" said one.

No.

"Recording…" said another.

This can't be.

"What do you *mean* you have something?" Frederikson let go of Hagen and turned, his face the purest depiction of everyone's fears. They all rose and opened their tablets. I did so too, with great hesitation, fitting my earphones in.

"We only sent it… How did they…" Frederikson looked around, finding the nearest tablet to him. Sweat grew on his forehead; the tablet shook in his hands.

The rambunctious voice scraped through my ears once more. The tone in this transmission grew harsher, stricter, or more… aggressive. This was it; we had fucked up. *Hagen* had fucked up. I perceived the familiar sounds, a sea of unidentified phonemes amongst some recognisable clicks. And a word I did not expect to hear… *"Earth."* In a thick accent, an imitation, a shattered reflection. But I had heard it. They understood every word we had said to them. They had translated it immediately. *What was going on?* How was this possible? Space was so vast, messages were supposed to be delayed, yet they had replied as fast as… As face-to-face contact. Were they close? Was their tech so superior that they had picked up on transmissions immediately? Where the *hell* were they?

Silence around the room. I took a deep breath. Closing my eyes, I let my mind drift to a familiar, voiceless place. A space where I could regain my composure and calm my heart rate. I missed that reassurance, that stillness and comfort I would feel when I finished work anywhere else. Where I could retire to a hotel room and forget everything that had happened. But here, the fear, the anxiety, it metastasised. My father would have told me to… He had spoken to me in a similarly aggressive tone. Particularly towards the end, when the frustration and anger had chewed him up and spat him back out. The man I had known and relied on my whole life, a man I did not recognise in the end. The one who had drained me of everything I had.

No, I didn't need to think about that now. I couldn't let my predisposition to human emotions and signs of aggression corrupt my work. I placed a hand on David's shoulder: a cursory reminder that we were in this together.

"Can you send a high-quality, enhanced version of the recording?" I said, addressing Ashvik Jayasinghe, leader of Comms. He tapped away and nodded to me. My tablet pinged with the new file.

"Come on," I said to David, who subsequently got up and followed me. We departed, leaving the room full of speechless, careless men. David and I had work to do.

When we entered the seminar room, I went straight to the whiteboard, erased previous debunked theories, and started afresh with the new message.

"Did he record me saying it?" Disbelief in David's voice. "It's audio only. I'm the one that said it. He gave them *my* voice," he said, getting lost in his own words. Utter and complete heartbreak, a betrayal of an unquantifiable nature. "He used it to propel his own agenda... He threw it at them like a bone to a dog..." He sat, rubbing his hands across his five o'clock shadow and towards the back of his neck.

Abandoning the whiteboard, I crouched in front of him. "It's not your fault. It's Hagen," I said, placing a hand on his shoulder. "We have more lines to transcribe. We can get this right, and then, there won't be any pressure, or any coercion. Push through it."

He nodded. That was all he could do.

"We can't find where the message was sent from. Their technology must be incredible: to be able to send a message from a great distance, and to do it so stealthily. Their response time was less than a minute, though. Whether they understood us or not, we'll have to see..." Ashvik sat down after revealing his insubstantial findings.

Three days had passed, and we had all worked without much repose. Three days of trying to find answers, of trying to find *them*, with nothing to show for.

"I'm afraid we won't find them unless they purposefully show themselves to us. We've tried everything. We just don't have the technology," he continued.

I fiddled with the ends of my ponytail. There was nothing more unsettling than throwing a message into a void, not knowing *who* you were talking to or what they looked like, just to get an eerie message back seconds later.

"Keep scanning, that's all we can do." Frederikson had worked up a habit of wiping his brow when he was out of ideas, a mannerism I had witnessed many times in the last week. "Hagen, any news on the new scanning equipment you mentioned?"

"We're still on the prototype stage. It may take some time yet," he replied. Hagen and his assistant had been whispering to each other during the meeting. A discreet yet irritating habit they had begun since the incident three days ago.

I sat quietly—my mind rummaging for what Hagen's next move would be. If we weren't careful, this could end in disaster. When I pulled my hand away from my hair, it found my pen, which I twiddled between my fingers, pressing the edges of it in the space beneath my nail. The pain grounded me.

"Okay," continued Frederikson. "Well, we look forward to that aid. In the meantime, we need to keep advancing. David, you're next."

David stood up to address the room. His suit had crumpled, and the bags under his eyes told stories that everyone here, except Hagen, could relate to. "Well, deciphering the language at the moment is being done using our best knowledge of human languages, which... Well, it doesn't work that way, but it's all we have. We're... We're making progress." David's defeatist tone was deafening.

"Using the patterns found with the A.I. program, we're trying to identify what the recurring syllables mean. In the last message, they clearly pronounced the word *'Earth'*. Therefore, it is our interpretation that they understand our language and have responded accurately to our reply. So, there is sense and meaning in the message, and the patterns we are looking for *are* important. We also have a theory about their way of separating words and sentences. It's going to take some guesswork and some luck to figure this one out."

My eyes shifted around the room; the departments had lost interest in what David had to say. The progress was small, insignificant to them. The stress of the situation was enough that even minor advances were not a reason to be appreciative of the work; they needed answers. Answers that came with reassurance. In the background, the distant hum of the air conditioning and ventilation system could be heard.

"Hm, hm." Frederikson nodded. A kind motion but a disappointed one. "I'm not going to lie to you, we were all hoping you had made more progress than that."

Not far from the General, Hagen released a heavy sigh, an echo of the sentiment shared across the table. "Do you need a larger team?"

"Umm... No, I don't think that's the issue," hesitated David.

"What's the issue then?" blurted Hagen, leaning forward. He drummed his fingers on the table.

His bitterness irritated me. Did he really believe this blunt manner of addressing the team would magically make us understand a language we'd only heard twice?

David paused. "Well, having a conversation with them would be more efficient," he said, when he had found the confidence. "But that should happen after our initial introduction. What I'm saying is, it would be easier if we jumped to the part where we could all be friends, introduce a linguist from each side, and start working more pro-actively." He chuckled, but the room did not mirror his nervous laughter.

Hagen stood up and leaned in closer. "What you're saying is you're finding it too difficult. That you're not up to the task?" He turned his eyes to me and continued, "Maybe *she* should take over. That would be easier for you, wouldn't it?" Eyes back on David. "Take a step back, let someone else do the hard work, is that right?"

I frowned. I felt the anger bubble up from my core.

"N... No. That's not what I'm saying," replied David.

Frederikson glared into the back of Hagen's head.

"It's Alexandra, right?" said Hagen, his teeth sharp. I nodded. "Write another reply in English. If we have nothing in four days, we send it. Make it a good one."

Another response in English or a partial translation in four days. Another impossible task. Another completely irrational demand.

"We can't do that." I straightened up, my voice stern. No man-child was going to bully me.

"You can't or you *won't*? Because I'm capable of doing just that by myself. But I thought I'd give you the benefit of the doubt and the opportunity to figure out some of the shit they've said to us before writing it. But if—"

"I'm not risking everything just because you said so. We *need* more time."

The faces around the room glanced away. No one else would stand up to this prick.

"*You* need to understand," he replied sternly, "that you're not in charge here. You can be replaced in the blink of an eye. You can be on the next shuttle back, and we," he traced a circle with his finger, indicating the rest of the team, "we will not stop here. We will pick up where you left off and go in whatever direction we choose. *If you want to give up, that's on you.*"

And there it was, the image of my father, of me using those exact words.

"*If you want to give up, that's on you.* But you can't keep acting this way!" The tears had coated my cheeks. My father had stood there, in an old, musky dressing gown, in his dilapidated living room, panting like a dog. The outburst had occurred, but the anger had rested on his chest like a disease, changing him from the inside out. Junk had lain strewn around the room, dust coating even the most mundane daily items. "I can't keep doing this. You... you mope around, like there's nothing to *live* for. Like everything is over! And you lash out at me... I'm still your daughter. I'm still me!" I had felt my heart break once more as I had uttered those words. His diagnosis had stung him, had broken him from the person he once was, into one I could barely recognise.

"You don't know what it's like," he said, the poison still on his breath; a voice so old, raspy and exhausted yet so full of anger. "To have done everything. *Everything!* That I have. To have seen your mother die, to care for you, to have lived the life we lived, always breaking even, never getting quite enough, and this… This is the repayment I get from life?" He had shouted those last words. "When you understand this, when you have suffered the way I have suffered, and lost all your memories, you can yell at me all you want. Until then, get the *fuck* out of my face. Get out of here!" He had grabbed a chair and flung it across the dining room in my direction. I had lowered myself, cowered out of the way. The chair had smashed into a cabinet. Glass and wired electronics came clattering to the floor. A photo frame landed in the debris: a faded picture of my mother and father together, her arms around his shoulders, at a long, distant beach, somewhere lost in time and space or in another universe, where they were both once happy and healthy.

I had scrambled to my feet, grabbed my bag off the kitchen table, and ran out the door. Only when I had sat down on the bus did I manage to stop crying, shrivelling up inside.

I crumbled. Here. Now.

"Dismissed," said Hagen, gesturing to the group. He stormed out, his assistant and the team following suit, leaving me to sit with my dismantled memories. Was it giving up? That's not how I had intended it to sound, but that's how he had taken it. I was not someone who *gave up*. If Hagen needed an answer in English or a translation in four days, I would deliver that. I had to. For the sake of proving to myself that I was nothing like my father.

ALEXANDRA GAUTHIER'S DIGITAL ARCHIVE

<u>From</u>: Emmanuel Gauthier

<u>To</u>: Alexandra Gauthier

<u>Date</u>: September, 25th 2034 09:56

<u>Location</u>: Favourites Folder

<u>Subject</u>: YOU CAN DO THIS!!!

Hey baby,

When we spoke on the phone yesterday, you seemed to be having a tough time. University is a time for self-discovery so I want you to get out there and go find yourself! You'll make some friends soon enough, I promise. But in the meantime, keep your chin up. You've made it this far, haven't you?!

Look, when I started Uni, back in… 2004! God, I feel old, haha! Well, I wasn't the most outgoing person either. But things change when you get into the groove. You meet YOUR people and you stick together for the rest of your life!

And if you ever have another crappy day, where your self-confidence is shot, well you can always read this email again. I'll be here. Forever and always.

Love you,

Dad xx

3

After a warm shower, I left my hotel room and bought a sandwich and a coffee from the mini-Walmart. It was going to be a long night. David and I had agreed to work through it and come up with any possible translations as fast as possible. Working together could enable us to, maybe creatively, devise a solution.

I reached our usual table in the seminar room, a clipboard in one hand with the printed-out pattern notes for both messages. Two whiteboards stood in front of me, each one depicted the phonetic transcriptions of both messages. Below the transcriptions, between the lines of text, were dashes indicating the supposed word boundaries. We needed to work immediately, and fast.

'*Earth*' stood out on the second whiteboard. It had been said with a hint of human disdain; something I couldn't rely on to measure the aliens' true feelings. I put that thought to one side and focused on the facts.

'*Earth*' was a good place to start. I knew its place in the sentence. I knew its meaning. The first phoneme—the first sound—from '*Earth*' *was* repeated in the transcription. But not the '*th*'. The voiced dental fricative was unique to that word in the message. The fact that they could replicate that sound was ground-breaking enough, and something the biologists were using to advance their research. Did it guarantee these aliens had a tongue and a set of teeth? I shook my head; too many random thoughts popping in and out. I needed to focus on what was accessible to me.

'*Earth.*' I looked at the pauses surrounding it: one harsher click before, and a softer one after. It could be the beginning of a sentence, or the first word after a comma. I made a note of that. The following word erupted in a short and punchy manner, followed by a longer word boundary. If I had to make a guess, an almost necessary step at this stage, I would have said 'people', 'persons', or even 'citizens'. I wrote that down too.

I jumped when I heard the door shut behind me. Nat stepped in, wearing a loose t-shirt and sweatpants. Not a bad idea, considering the hours we were going to put in this evening. I regretted wearing office attire and pumps; my feet were going to be sore in a few hours.

"Sorry, didn't mean to scare you," said Nat.

"What are you doing here?" I asked.

"I thought you might need support, or help, or something…" His eyes glanced over the boards, taking in as much of the transcription as possible. His voice had been quiet and softly spoken. He continued, "I'm not sure if I can be of much help really, but you guys seem to be stuck in the middle of it. It's not fair." A genuine smile on his lips, he grabbed a seat and stared at the board some more.

It would feel inappropriate to express how much this meant to me—with the pressure on us linguists, and Hagen's looming gaze hanging over us at all times, Nat was putting himself on the line here.

"It's kind of you to be here. I won't hold it against you if you leave in ten minutes." I wanted it to be funny, but the humour had left the sentence as I had spoken it.

"I promise, I won't."

I turned my face so he wouldn't see me blush.

"And hey, if you think I've missed something, give me a shout," I added.

"It looks like you got most of it covered," he said with a slight smile. "Those dashes, they're pauses, right?"

"Yes, the lower the frequency, the bigger the pause. At least, that's our first guess." I took a sip of my coffee, the bitterness stuck to my tongue.

"Tell you what, I'll grab a piece of paper and write it all with actual full stops and spaces so I can look at it clearer. I'm just getting lost between dashes and slashes right now." He chuckled to himself, grabbing a piece of paper and a pen.

"That might help actually," I replied, looking at the patterns from a different angle.

"And, I will be on coffee duty this evening," he announced, with the same passion a kid would declare what he wanted to be when he grew up.

"Well then, that makes you the most powerful person in this room," I said with a grin. The sight of his toothy smile sped my heart up just a fraction.

"So, talk me through it. I might not understand a damn thing, but if you say it out loud, it might help you."

The door slammed shut, and David rushed in with a pile of papers between his arms. He had made a habit of bringing notes with him that he thought would help, but never did.

"Sorry I'm late," he said, and spotting Nat, "Oh, we have a visitor! Mr. Hoang, nice to finally meet you." He dumped his papers onto a nearby table and offered his hand.

"Call me Nat. And David, I presume?" They shook hands.

"Yes. Yes, that's right. Nat, as in Nathaniel?"

"Kinda. My parents couldn't decide between the traditional Vietnamese *Nhat*, and a more anglophone Nathaniel. Turns out when you move to an English-speaking country, they just butcher it anyway," he replied with a shrug.

"Y'all know, I couldn't believe it when I first saw you at

the meeting." David turned to me. "One of the youngest engineers to join NASA, this one!"

I glanced at Nat, who was now looking a tad embarrassed.

"Ah, stop it! You're making me go all pink."

We all shared a laugh, a brief respite from the sweeping stress sinking deep into our shoulders.

"So, uhh," started David. He rummaged through his many papers. "This is what I've come up with so far. I was gonna go for food, but I ended up writing a bunch of notes about the possible words following..." He stared at the whiteboard. "You got that too! *'Earth'* people—people of Earth! We both came to the same conclusion then."

"Surely that means you're on the right path," said Nat.

"Let's hope so," I replied, but I knew we were a long way off from accomplishing anything.

It was useless. My eyes ached, and my stomach growled. David and I had spent most of the night making notes, writing hypotheses, and coming to incorrect conclusions, to no avail. Nat had left at around two in the morning, his own knowledge exhausted. *'Earth'* remained the only word that held true meaning, a certainty in a sea of silence, screaming trustworthy letters amongst the chaos.

I dropped my head in my hands. "We're going to have to be honest," I said. My voice had started cracking, deep and sleepy, my throat scratchy and dry.

"I know... Maybe, this is where things go wrong, huh?" His laugh echoed around the otherwise empty room. He was right, though. This was dangerous territory. He had been correct to bring up history, out of fear of it repeating. Language presented a barrier, one that could be misinterpreted, misunderstood, and could cause, well, anything to happen. It demanded caution, but Hagen was not a cautious person. Why be vigilant when you have a cushion of wealth to protect you?

"We need to start thinking about the reply in English," I said. I didn't like to admit it, but there was no other solution.

"I'm not sure I want a say in that, to be perfectly honest."

"Because he used your voice last time?"

"I don't want to be responsible for whatever happens next. And neither should you. This wasn't our idea—this… replying whatever it takes. That's not us. We shouldn't have to abide by everything he says…" His voice trailed off. Linguists were not familiar with *'quick'* work. When we researched a language or decrypted an ancient tongue, it took decades to make significant breakthroughs. So far, we'd had two weeks to look at a language not even from our planet.

"That's fine; I think I know what I want to write," I replied.

"You don't have to, though. That's what I'm saying. It's okay to step away."

"No, I don't think it is. There's too much tension in that room. Someone's going to mess this up, and I have an opportunity to stop that." That wasn't the truth, and I knew it. It was my own desire not to screw up. I scratched my arms, willing the sensation to wake me up. "I want to control the message we're sending out," I concluded.

"What would you say to them if you could?"

"In this context, I would—"

"No. I mean, if you could say *anything* to them, what would you say?" he added.

I looked out of a nearby window. It took a moment for my pupils to focus and adapt to the dark. "Umm, I don't know… I think I'd start with a hello and uhh…" I stopped myself; I had never thought of it this way. It had always been in the context of my job, never my own personal beliefs or wants.

"I think," started David, replacing the silence and resting his head on the flat of his hand, "I think I'd tell them to come back later."

I chuckled at that idea. The concept of telling an alien species—the first living creatures we'd met outside of Earth—*"No, sorry, I'm busy. Come back later."*

"I'm serious," he continued, and I saw the sincerity in his features. "I'd tell them to come back later. We're not ready for this. We're not ready for interstellar travel, for galactic democracies, or universal languages. We're not. We can't compromise. We can't keep our own shit together on our own home world. We have wars and climate issues. We've never been able to band together, as one species. And they decide to show up now? When we've ruined the planet; when we're making tiny steps into space, so small that we shouldn't even have been noticed. Yes, we may be noisy, and we send out probes on planets we haven't set foot on, but we're *far* from ready." His eyes clouded over and shifted to the large windows. "The worst of it is that we think we *are* ready. People *want* to be ready. This is life-changing; the planet will never be the same again. But the truth is, we're corrupt creatures. We're greedy. We ruin things, even things that we should respect, things that bring us life. But we don't care, we only think about the next big event, the best innovation, the newest discovery. We don't look at the soil beneath our feet and cherish it. We look for ways to use it until it gets all muddy, and then we leave it behind to rot.

"If aliens truly have come here to start a friendship, they need to look elsewhere. They won't be getting any love or respect from us."

We sat in silence for a moment. Maybe he was right, but I needed to try—I would never be able to live with myself if I didn't try to start this relationship with some understanding, some genuine patience and kindness. The response in English needed to be inviting, friendly and compassionate.

I regarded the blank note on my screen. It was waiting to be written, enticing me to scribble my own personal message. And maybe some of that now included David's theory: come back later.

The lights on the station would shift soon—the equivalent of a sunrise, dragging us into the next day.

"Why do you think they've come?" I asked.

"My heart tells me they were lonely. My head says they want something." He paused. "Truly, I think they want something. There's no other reason to cross an ocean of emptiness, to risk yourself, your culture, your future generations, to approach another species. If they are anything like humans, they are here to conquer." He let the idea sit with me, and I'd be lying if I said it didn't terrify me. It brought back the idea of history repeating itself. Of this Darwinian concept of survival of the fittest. Those who conquer, those who win, will be the strongest. They are the ones that get to survive. "What about you? What do you think?" he asked.

"They sent a direct message to the Observer, the most powerful space-station and communication tool we have. But not Earth. I think they need help. Which is why..." I got up and straightened my shirt, which had rumpled throughout the night. "The reply in English should be about offering assistance. A helping hand, nothing more, nothing less. We owe them the benefit of the doubt."

Maybe I was being hopeful. Maybe a part of me believed that an advanced civilisation could move past the notion of conquering. When a stranger approached you on the street, it was often because they wanted something: money, food, medical assistance, or some other resource they didn't have. Even if they complimented the way you dress, more often than not, it was because they wanted to see what was underneath. In my thirty years of living, no stranger had ever approached me and asked me to be their friend. But I needed to remain optimistic, so I put my money on assistance, and hoped for the best.

"... and this is why we're unable to proceed with our research. If any new information arises, we will, of course, be happy to help advance the project, but there's nothing more we can do at this time."

Frederikson regarded David with patience; yet the vein thumping on his forehead thickened by the second. Had we let him down? Probably, but honesty was the best course of action. Giving the team any more hope of us transcribing this message within the given time frame would only let them down further.

"Thank you for your... integrity, David. I admit this will not be easy for Hagen to accept, but we will make do. For now, could I request you both attend each of the meetings as usual? Please ensure you keep working; maybe Hanni and the rest of the biologists could use your help. I'm sure you can come up with some decent information about vocal cords and things of the sort."

"Yes, of course," replied David. "Thank you for your understanding. I know it's not easy managing a team of this... temperament and diversity in beliefs."

"To say the least. Every now and again, I think of my old office. Don't tell Hagen this, but I appreciate the fresh air you get when stepping outside. You don't get that here." He chuckled. For the first time, I glimpsed his more personable side. He was right; the air smelled stale and fabricated, eternally recycled and perfumed to give the appearance it was fresh. But anyone with a good sense of smell could detect the dusty filters.

David smirked. "I know what you mean... The days last longer here."

Frederikson nodded and added, "They never seem to end. Very well. I have some more work to do. Don't stray too far." He departed, heading to his next meeting.

David and I stood in silence a while longer before I spoke. "Why does it feel like we've given up?" I couldn't shake that feeling, but I also knew the task had been impossible from the beginning. Yet, if the aliens had replied to our message with some kind of understanding, then maybe there was hope for us after all. Once a solid line of communication was established, David and I would have our hands full.

"Because you work yourself too hard. It's healthy to know when to stop. Come, I'll treat you to a drink in that bar across the plaza."

I followed him, a nagging feeling in the back of my head.

A deep, tired voice with a French accent, one I had heard all my life, and it kept asking me why I wasn't trying harder. Why I had given up. Why I wasn't fixing the problem. I tried to squash it down, to pull a curtain over it, to lock it away, but any time I did, it screamed louder still. Even as David talked, a beer in one hand, gesticulating with the other, that voice still scolded me for abandoning my duties. My father had always been a hard worker; he had always pushed me to work to the best of my ability. And sometimes, I had worked beyond that ability. Maybe this was one of those times.

I dug my fingernails into the palm of my hand. The pain helped, but even so, as I went to bed that evening, a little bit tipsy from the drinks, my father still criticised my every move.

"Thank you for your message. We cannot understand your language. If you need assistance, we will help." My voice quivered as I spoke the words. In the back of my mind, a feeling hounded me. My voice could be exploited. Stillness. The smell of sweat burned my nose.

Another string of simple phrases. Easy to decrypt for them. With limited misunderstandings.

"Do you genuinely believe they need help?" asked Hagen with a snarl.

"I think it's a strong possibility," I replied. I did not break eye contact; today would not be the day I bowed down to Hagen. Biologists and engineers had both had passionate discussions this morning, interrupted by Hagen, whose opinions were negligible at best, and offensive at worst. "I think it should at least be something we offer them."

"You see, that's where I disagree."

I held myself from rolling my eyes. He had interrupted every conversation this morning, like he had woken with a fire in his soul, ready to burn down every argument or point of view he disagreed with.

"How about we take five minutes to think about this?" suggested Frederikson. "Take five. I want everyone to come back with clear heads." He shook his own head at the pile of papers sitting in front of him. The departments rose, and I joined them outside. Nat bumped into my side. His arm against mine.

"Hey."

"Hey," I replied. "How's it going?"

"It's going great. Apart from the fact that I can see every muscle in your body tense up and your head about to explode."

I stopped in my tracks, unable to respond to that, unable to change it in any way. Caution was the right way to go. I knew it. But most of the people in that meeting wouldn't stand up for what was right.

"You need to relax. You're doing great. You're challenging the biggest dipshit on the pla— On the station." He smiled at his own mistake, and I caught his contagious grin.

"You know, I can't believe I have to keep repeating myself with him," I whispered, cautious of our other colleagues around us.

"Well, look, keep standing your ground. I'm still here, still supporting you. Take a deep breath, come back with some fight in you, yeah?"

I felt a surge of adrenaline course through me once more and prepared to kick up my discourse another notch. If Hagen wanted a debate, if he had hired me for my professional opinion, that's what he was going to get.

"I'm getting a coffee; do you want one?" asked Nat.

"Why not." I tried to smile, but the tension from the quarrelling had tired me out. I paced around the plaza, my thoughts all over the place, jumping around from point to point, all of which I wanted to make. It felt so hard to be believed, to be trusted. Was it even about me, or was this Hagen's way?

I caught Nat's eye. He held up two cups of coffee and nodded in the direction of the boardroom. I joined him, grabbing one of the drinks.

"I've taken the liberty of rewriting your reply." Hagen reclined into his seat as he spoke. His assistant sat at his side as usual, tablet in one hand, earphone in one ear.

"May I ask what you've changed?" I asked. Although I knew whatever he came up with would be ridiculous. He had no filter when it came to expressing himself.

The team settled in, their eyes and ears glued to the conversation at hand.

"I took some time to reflect," he said as he looked towards Frederikson, "and decided we needed to be more assertive."

I took a sip of my coffee, the intense heat of the fresh brew burnt my tongue, but the pain felt good—another release of adrenaline. I turned away from Hagen. There was nothing more to add. Assertiveness did not scream a call for war. It was still worrying, still not right, but I needed to take it easy. I didn't want to sway him too far, annoy or berate, for him to act even more irrational.

General Frederikson waited until everyone was seated before starting. "Oskar Hagen and I have spoken, and we have agreed to sending the following message: "*We will happily meet with your leader. Please be aware that we are armed and will use our defences should the case arise. Once we have discussed a peace treaty, we may talk more liberally.*" Does anyone—"

"Are you fucking kidding me?!" I shouted, slamming my cup on the table. The coffee had got my heart racing, and now that the unutterable words had been spoken, I felt I couldn't stop. Not only had he mentioned being armed, but his wordage could also confuse. Adverbs and subordinating conjunctions, imperatives and compound-complex sentences. My own words came to my mouth faster than I could think them through, "How is that more assertive?! You are openly suggesting we could defeat them in some imaginary war! Do you not think—"

"Calm down! I won't have some woman shout like I don't know what I'm doing," Hagen retorted. Although he appeared angry, he was also, somehow, on the brink of laughter. It made me feel small, like a peasant among royalty, like no matter what I said in my defence, it would be mocked.

"You *know* what you're doing? Have you spoken to aliens you don't understand before?" I folded my arms under my chest, the presence of my own body like a weighted blanket coating me against whatever rage would come next.

"No, and I don't suppose you have either. These are creatures that live, ones you *can* talk to, not a dead language to decipher in the depths of your isolated apartment. Between the two of us, I do believe I have more experience in deals and negotiations to be talking with these beings."

Isolated apartment? How could I ever respond to that? Was there a hint in there that he knew my life, knew I *had* isolated myself since my father's death, knew I had so few friends? Could it be *that* personal? How could he have known that? Had he vetted the people on this team, stolen private information so he could push the right buttons at the right time? The anger in my chest lessened and would soon turn to tears. I spun to Frederikson.

"You can't do this," I said to him; every part of my being was pleading with him.

"It has been agreed, Alex. Take a seat and we can keep talking about this. Calmly."

"Alex is right. We need to rethink this," said Nat, tension on his face, but confidence in his tone. He was going to keep his cool, even if I didn't.

"Says the dude that is literally banging the hormonal chick—" said a voice at the other end of the table.

"Hey, there's no need for—" David interjected.

"No, man, she's right. That message is way too aggressive," one of the biologists spoke up.

"We need to collect ourselves," said Hanni, chief biologist.

"Shouldn't we get someone with more authority to okay this? What about the UN?"

"Dude, think about it. What would you think if you got that reply?" said someone else.

"I mean, it says *'peace treaty'*, what more do you want?"

I turned my gaze to Hagen once more. A fictitious emperor disregarding the squabble from high above. But he paid no attention to the argument at the table; he only spoke to his assistant. After a quick mutter, they pointed towards the tablet in front of them. Frederikson had voiced the message out loud; nothing could stop them from sending it now.

I felt like getting up, grabbing the tablet, and smashing it, anger slipping through my fingers. If I did that, I would lose all the professional integrity I had accrued over the years. All the hard work and respect I had earned. How badly could this go if I let it slip? What were the chances this reply would cause an issue? Would the aliens not prefer peace talks themselves? No, surely, I was being a little too dramatic. Another thing they could throw in my face, the same way Hagen had said *'some woman'*, like I had turned into an abstract object or an animal to be tamed. No, I didn't want to be known as the person to have thrown one of Hagen's private advisers' tablets onto the floor and smashed it. I would never get another job.

"What does she know if all she works on is dead languages?" a man jabbed.

"I can't believe you would treat this like it's some business meeting. These are aliens, guys!"

"No, he's right though! How many business deals has he agreed to? Surely that stands for something."

"This is *not a business deal*!" shouted a biologist.

"It's not an ancient language either!"

"Y'all need to calm down now." David's voice had not been confident enough to interrupt the debate. He sank further into his chair as the voices grew louder.

"You can't be serious, Flores, you guys barely did anything!"

"Mate, you have no idea how hard it is to decipher this stuff." Nat.

"Of course, *you* would say that."

My eyes darted back to Hagen. The two of them had

agreed something. This was it; they were going to send it. Maybe I still had time to say something? To do something? The anger in my chest demanded I slap the tablet out of the assistant's hands. I rose, unsure what to do next, fists clenched. Hagen smiled and met my eye once again. He had done it. He had sent it.

A sudden whoosh, air slipping out of the room, and the temperature dropped. I couldn't breathe. I looked to my right. A deep red coated my vision. David sat still, a mixture of shock and peacefulness on his face. Blood poured out a gaping hole by the side of his head, syphoning out towards the window. My heart dropped. Gasping for air, I held onto the table. Across from me, a military advisor bled out. The open gash across his chest, or where his chest *had* been, seeped blood, which coagulated into floating bubbles in the air, and caught into the draught escaping the room. To my right, at the window, I saw it: a metallic creature, a droid-type construct, only the size of a dog. A small flat head sat atop four metal legs, clamped or suctioned onto the window, strong enough to be leaning in through the opening it had created. Lifting its front two limbs, the clamps snapped into spikes and flung, its legs extending like an unending wire coil. A limb struck Frederikson through his back as he got up. The clamp opened up and retracted once more, leaving a hole the size of my hand in the middle of his gut. I tried to breathe, the air still escaping my lungs. It rushed around my ears, papers flying in all directions. Another fling of the metallic coils, faster this time, hit a woman in the side. On the retraction of the wire, her body, screaming in pain, flew towards a wall and bounced off, smashing her skull into the table. I saw David. His eyes tranquil, his head fell to the left. No, not this. Not again. I couldn't shake the imagery, so similar to my father's own corpse.

As fast as I could, I dropped to the floor and scrambled, grabbing onto random objects that passed me by, the air pulling us all towards the gaping hole into space. Touching things, solid objects, meant this was real. The cold polished floor. The hard oak table. The cooling, wet blood.

The sound of the metal swinging kept thrashing the air. Heavier objects fell towards the opening in the window; a window that would crack under too much pressure. A small side table hit the opening, blocking most of the air seeping out. I caught my breath. Turning to face the reality of the room. Blood, bodies, furniture tossed around. Among the screams, the whining, the moaning of dying bodies, of souls trapped in never-ending agony, the clicking of more droids along the window. Another hole. Another whoosh as a metal coil flung towards another woman crawling on the floor, hitting her in the back. Another guttural scream. The window cracked and the glass fractured, threatening to give in. I froze. David still sat, calm, his head to one side. A single, immovable point in the room, eternal. No, I would never make it out.

But a hand grabbed my arm and dragged me backwards. I scrambled to my feet and looked up to see Nat, hunched over. He had a scratch across his face, a deep bleeding wound that would scar. Only then did I feel the fresh tingle of a cut on my own arm. I caught my breath. We needed to get out of here. I struggled, but we got to the door. The crack in the window spread, splintering, a growing web, seconds away from snapping. Another fling towards Hagen's assistant, whose leg was trapped under the collapsed oak table. I heard the gurgle of him drowning in his own blood just as Nat opened the door.

Pulling me through it, Nat looked around, trying to spot any survivors to drag to the exit. Hagen, halfway across the room, crawled on all fours, blood pouring from his mouth. Another metal coil flung in through the window, striking him, pulling him up, his feet off the ground, his whole body held limp in the air, as if his blood was too adhesive, too viscous to be dropped. The coil retracted, pulling his body towards the window. Hagen smashed into the glass, the final force shattering it. The air dragged both Nat and me towards the gaping nothingness. But we slammed the doors shut in time, and Nat reached for a panel by its side, sealing the area with airtight metal shutters. Everything and everyone inside had been lost.

OBSERVER DIGITAL ARCHIVE
Conduct, Safety and Security n. 2:

"Respect and comply with all staff members."

All staff members are required to wear and display their watches and wristbands at all times. You can identify a member of staff by their department using the colour code scheme below:

Black Wristband: Upper Management and above

Red Wristband: Middle Management

Orange Wristband: Lower Management and Seniors

Yellow Wristband: Employees (incl. Seasonal)

Blue Wristband: Security and Safety Team

Green Wristband: Engineering and Technical Team

All non-staff will also be required to wear and display their white wristbands. VIPs are eligible to wear golden wristbands, providing them with exclusive access to restricted areas. To find out more about our VIP packages, please visit our website, or use the My Observer app.

Wristbands are on display for a variety of reasons:
- *to allow passengers and guests into allocated areas;*
- *to make sure every person on board is accounted for;*
- *to help passengers identify who may best help them, should*

they require assistance.

*In an emergency, please remain calm and listen to your staff members attentively; they are equipped with knowledge of the station you may not have, and will be able to direct you to safety, should you require it. Abuse, disobedience and disrespect to our personnel will not be tolerated.**

**We are not responsible for the behaviour and attitudes of our staff. All beliefs and comments are their own. Should you wish to speak to someone about this, please visit our Guest Relations Team, located in section B7 by the Central Plaza.*

4

All alarms rang—a trio of loud, high-pitched sirens accompanied by red, blue, and orange flashing lights. Turning away from the metal shutter, I stumbled forward, dazzled by both sound and sight. I couldn't find my breath. There was oxygen here, I knew that, but it felt too thick, too stubborn.

In front of us, the short hallway past the lobby, leading back to the plaza, was also lit up. Desperate screams cut short echoed down the corridor. Loud thuds of bodies collapsing to the ground. Swift motions of the coils flinging through the air. Glass shattered. Cobbles cracked. And the tap of metal legs on metal floor felt almost rhythmic amongst the chaos.

I felt Nat's hand tightening around mine. I hadn't even realised he was holding it.

He turned to me and mouthed, "Ready?"

Ready for what? Survival? I didn't know what that looked like anymore. But, I nodded anyway.

We crept through the door and pressed our backs against the side of the nearest shop, eyes on the ground. None of those creatures were in sight, but they had clearly been here not long ago. Crying and groaning persisted in the background, far enough away that we couldn't see them, accompanying ear-piercing alarms.

Nat paused, holding up his other hand to stop me, his chest heaving against his t-shirt, muscles tense. The click-clacking of metal on metal continued but moved further away. He looked around and, dragging me behind him, stepped into the shop we stood beside. We hunched over now, slipping towards the back of the shop—a tech store that displayed the latest phones and tablets. Pristine consumerism in the midst of chaos. We hid behind the various counters until we reached a back door, an odd iron-like smell in the air. Somewhere, a man screamed.

I sat behind one of the registers, my back pressed against a cabinet. My mind was in a daze, as I tried to recall the moments before it had all gone to shit: the argument about sending the defensive message back, the look on Hagen's face, the feeling of needing to stop it and not getting there in time. I had hesitated. That's why this had happened. That's why they had died. Why David had looked so peaceful. He had wanted no part in this, didn't want to be associated with whatever message was being sent back. And we had left them behind. It was all my fault. Tears formed in the corners of my eyes, and I tensed up. Why hadn't I stopped them? I could have tried harder.

Beside me, Nat scoured the drawers and cabinets. He stopped when he picked up a keycard, which he then slotted into a panel on the back door. He crawled his way inside, dragging me with him—the alarms still blaring in the background. Nat closed the door, locking it behind us, and turned on a light.

A moment of respite, where we could gather our thoughts. But I didn't want to. I didn't want to do anything. After all the pain and grief I had gone through recently, this... *This* was the final straw. I wanted to lie there, to let them take me. To give myself the death I deserved. Full of pain, metal ripping my body to shreds, blood spilling out of me. I deserved it.

"Hey," said Nat, pulling me back into the moment.

Stacks of shelves, full of various tech equipment, cables and tablets, stared at us, as if none of this had just happened. Only a few hours ago, a retail worker would have come back here and restocked the shelves out the front.

Whatever noises were coming from the plaza had been vastly turned down in this little back room. We were shut away from reality.

"We shouldn't stay here too long. I just thought we should get to safety first before we keep going." His tone strained.

It took some effort to find my voice. "Keep going where?" I lacked the energy or desire for any kind of positivity; I was too focused on keeping my heart from breaking my ribs.

"Hub Bunker, probably. That's where the alarms are telling us to go."

Yet, even in times of tension and renunciation, my logical thinking kicked in. "I thought blue was for Suit Stations?" I asked.

"They're all blasting, to be fair. The only guy that could understand which one to listen to is the one sitting up in Command."

"So, we go to Command?" I inspected my arm. The blood had smeared across my forearm and had dried up already. Nothing to be concerned about.

Nat frowned for a moment. "We try the Hub Bunker first. It's only a few doors down. And it might be our only shot at getting back to Earth."

We sat in silence for a moment, catching not only our breaths but an instant to accept what we had both witnessed. Our teams were gone; our work destroyed; our lives threatened, and we had no way to protect ourselves and no idea what would happen, or why those creatures were doing this. I thought back to all the things I had left in that room: my phone, most of all. I'd lost my emails, my work, my contacts, and all the last pictures I had left of my father.

"David was right," I said. "They want something."

Nat considered this, his eyes on me. "I'm sorry. About David."

"He thought they wanted something." My mind ticked now. If I thought about this, I didn't need to think about— "They attacked the station though, not Earth. So maybe the resource they want is on the planet. Too valuable to destroy. The station was in the way. An annoying construct that didn't reply the way they wanted it to."

"Alex—"

"I should have done something. I knew he was going to—" My face crumbled as fresh tears coated my cheeks. "I should have—" I closed my eyes and caved in. I hadn't tried hard enough, *again*. Nothing was worth it. Life. The pain we feel. The agony of daily difficulties. The torment of change. The trauma of loss. It wasn't worth it.

Nat pulled me in, and I fell onto his shoulder. We stayed a while, my breath catching between sobs, but my inhalations smoothed out eventually. Once the cries had lessened, he grabbed my hand.

"I think they might have moved far enough away. Shall we?" he said.

Did I have the strength to do this? Probably not. But Nat pulled me up anyway.

We made it back to the front of the tech store without a problem, and, for the first time, through the front windows, I saw the carnage that had been left behind. The alarms still rang, the flashes accompanying the beats. The bodies on the ground had piled up; blood had poured and stained the cobblestones. None of them moved or moaned anymore. Death stood still. A stagnant silence among a myriad of other sounds: the restaurant's prosaic radio station, the fountain splashing water, and the wheels of an ÆviBot spinning as it tried to get itself off the ground.

"I can't see any of those creatures," said Nat. He seemed calm, but his eyes told me he wouldn't sleep for days after this.

If we survived that long.

"Maybe they've finished destroying what needs to be destroyed."

"I wouldn't count on that. Come on, follow me."

He grabbed my hand once more and pulled me from this shop to the next, still crouching down, avoiding any more noise. We slid from shop to shop and arrived at the central point of the plaza. The nearest Hub Bunker sat around the corner, out of sight.

"Wait there," said Nat. His attention focused on something I could not see.

Around me, the stillness of the carnage made me feel nauseous. The smell of iron wafted to my nostrils and enhanced the queasy feeling in my stomach.

He stepped further back into the restaurant. I followed his form shifting between tables until I spotted a body lying on the floor. Pausing there, he moved about, shuffling, but my eyes couldn't make out what he was doing. When he returned, he had a handgun strapped to his waist.

"What the hell do you need that for?" I said, a little angrier than I had intended.

"Protection."

"You think you can take down an alien robot with a gun?" I pushed the irony in my tone a little more.

"It's worth a try, isn't it?"

I hesitated. We each had our own way of coping, and Nat came from the military. Maybe that was enough. Maybe it made him feel a little safer.

We waited a while longer before making the final turn into the corridor. And when we did, we stood in silence. The Hub Bunker appeared at the end of the corridor, its doors wide open, what was meant to be a welcoming invitation to safety. But leading up to it, dozens of bodies lay scattered, pooling in blood: a coagulation of broken frames and disordered body parts. Nat pushed forward, planting his feet in the spaces between the bodies, the soles of his shoes picking up the perfect bloody footprint.

As I filed along behind him, I took in the various faces, some looking up, some leaning against the floor. A familiar face stood out from the bundle… The receptionist that had welcomed me aboard the Observer a week or so ago. The girl's perfect hair had become unkempt during her runaway. Red lipstick smeared.

Inside the Hub Bunker, an older man and a woman lay splayed out, their clothes soaking up whoever's blood was left on the floor. Nat glanced at the control panel.

"It malfunctioned," he said. Pressing a few buttons, he shook his head. "If it didn't work for them, I doubt it'll work for us…"

Fucking Hagen. Had he taken safety shortcuts to cut down costs? All this bullshit about the passengers' safety being the number one priority…

"Shit…" I muttered, still staring at the bodies. They could have survived. They *should* have.

"We can't stay here." He looked around, attempting to find another solution.

"What if we called for help? Where's Comms or Command?" I suggested.

He looked at me. I knew what I was suggesting. Instead of fleeing and saving our own lives, we would call for help. Maybe even help others. We could still go to another Hub Bunker, but *this* felt like the right thing to do. And we'd potentially be sacrificing ourselves in the process.

Nat nodded. "This way," he whispered, his gaze shifting away from me, something clearly on his mind, but I was too afraid to ask. It would have to wait.

As Nat stepped over the bodies, he paused once more, and leaned over.

"I don't really know how these things work. But we might need one to get in." He grabbed at people's wrists, looking for different coloured wristbands. He picked up an orange one and a red one, then decided he had touched enough dead bodies.

We hid behind the corridor wall before stepping out towards the plaza. Nat's military training kicked in, and he held the gun ahead of him, stabilising it with his left hand, and we moved forward with caution. We approached the far-right side of the plaza, where another reception desk appeared. A vibrantly lit sign held above the desk said 'Guest Relations'. To the side of it, a couple of elevators were tucked away. I read the signs along the elevator wall: 'Command', 'Communications', 'Fire Crew', 'Security', 'Engineering', 'Mech Suites'.

"Nat," I said softly. He turned to me. "Can we talk?" He had been particularly quiet as we searched for a way up.

"Don't you want to get to Command first?"

"I want to know what's on your mind," I said, but I realised then that it was selfish, to demand answers at this specific moment.

He looked down to the ground; his thoughts faded, his eyes glazed over.

"Look, I just want to get off this station."

He approached the elevators, waved a wristband in front of the sensor, and then selected the 'Command' floor. A red cross appeared on the panel. He tried the other wristband, same answer. He did the same for Comms, and we both heard the elevator making its way down to them. At least the power was still on.

"You know I want the same, right? Going to Comms doesn't stop that. We can see which Hub Bunkers are working from there," I said to breach the unsettling silence.

"I know you do. But…" His pause lasted longer than I had anticipated. Did I *truly* feel the same way? I wasn't sure. The instinct I had in the back of the tech store was real—that desire to give up, it had been calling me for a while. Before I had been called to the Observer. Hell, if I was being honest, it had started festering before my dad had died. It slid into my mind every now and again, an insect burrowing into my brain, trying to make a permanent home, scratching at the inside of my skull, trying to unhinge me, to make me lose all self-respect. *Amour-propre*, as my dad would say—what makes you value yourself as a human being. He'd reminded me towards the end of his life that I had none. And here I was, trying to convince Nat that I did.

I thought of my apartment in London, a small, dingy little place not too far from my current work site—or, my *old* work site, I should say. I had taken a sabbatical to be here. Thinking of that flat, of the memories held within, I found nothing of worth there, nothing worth making new memories for.

"But I *have* to get home. My— Someone is expecting me," he added.

He did, it seemed, have something worth returning to. And as we stepped into the elevator once it arrived at our floor, I wondered how different that made us. Nat had worth in his life, had desires and wants. I still didn't know that much about him, and when I glanced at him, I saw the tension in his jaw. There was something else going on in his life. And that was more than I could say for myself.

I felt the dried blood of my arm pull at my skin and scratched it off.

As the elevator doors opened, I witnessed the utter disruption of the Communications area. Desks and chairs had toppled over; equipment lay strewn along the floor—a display of the pure panic felt in the moment the station had been attacked. A man had attempted to crawl towards the exit, his hand reaching towards them in an eerie cry for help. But he lay in a pool of his own blood instead.

Nat and I stepped around the corpse, taking in the rest of the room. Alarms still rang, but on top of the bellowing were various warning beeps and sirens from different computers dotted around the room.

I approached the closest screen to us.

'*WARNING: Oxygen low. Level 2, Sector 3B, 15F, 24A. Level*

9, Sector 19L. Level 22, Sector 1A, 1B, 1C, 1D…'

The message flashed repeatedly, a bright orange caution. Nat hung over my shoulder. There were too many sectors for it to display the message in its entirety.

"Jesus…" he said, before moving to another computer. "This one says there's no power in some areas."

I moved to a different screen.

"There's a whole portion of the station that is just… gone…" I said as I stared at the digital replica of the Observer. Nat came back to look at the evidence—the diagram's lower levels had been severed from the station and floated away into space.

"What if there are still people in that area?" I studied him, trying to find the same fear in him that I found in myself.

"There's nothing we can do…" he replied. "We need to send an SOS, that's the only way we can help anyone…"

I nodded and searched for a radio or a computer that might serve as a communication method, but all the desks had a set of headphones. I sat down at the closest and attempted to find the right software or… I ran my fingers over my face; I had no idea what I was doing. This was too far out of my depth.

"God damnit!" Nat shouted, but it soon turned into a muffled, nervous chuckle. "Why didn't I study comms instead?" He stood in front of another screen, pushing buttons and clicking the mouse. "I can't get this to work… I think I need some kind of security clearance. Would you mind looking for a manual or something?"

"Sure," I replied.

This area abounded with desks and computers, but it sat on a mezzanine overlooking other screens at the forefront of the room. Straight ahead of me, I saw the large window overlooking the staggering darkness of space. The stars had no idea, no feeling towards what our few insignificant life forms were going through. They remained unshakeable, uncaring, sedentary. Perpetually impassive of the things happening around them. Why should they care? They were larger than life. And life would survive somewhere, even if not here.

I followed the steps down the mezzanine, arriving in an area designated to be a discussion space. Not quite command centre, but not too dissimilar. For a moment, I wondered what the actual Command looked like. What purpose did that serve if all the station's most crucial functions could be performed here? Was it Hagen's office space? Only a cold desk in an empty room for him to feel important in.

Behind command centre, under the mezzanine, I could see a few more bodies lying on the floor, their faces hidden. They didn't look real from where I stood—nothing but another corpse, somewhat pretend, somewhat real, perhaps sleeping, perhaps dead. I turned away from those thoughts and continued my search for the files.

Beside the sleeping corpses, large stacks of servers towered, lights flashing and a low hum emanating from them. I made my way towards them, seeing at the far back, against the wall, a series of old metal file cabinets, some at hip height, some almost reaching the ceiling.

A metallic clunk cut me short. I stopped breathing. Another smaller clunk, coming from one of the cabinets. My heart dropped, and my hands shook.

Was this it? The moment everything ended? Had we pushed through the last few hours only to fail now? My breathing laboured, but I managed to catch myself. Those droids had metal coils, so even if it had gotten itself stuck, or pushed into a cabinet, it would be able to get itself out. Maybe? Or had it been disarmed? Now curiosity was getting the better of me. I stepped forward, one foot at a time. The metallic clunks were only small, like it had shifted in place, to get a better angle. I approached it still, turning my ear to the cabinet. Weren't the clunks too deep? It didn't sound like one of those droids anymore. Only a few feet away now. I paused. Was that... breathing? I moved up close, my eyes peering at the vent. In between the slit, a hazel eye stared back at me.

The cabinet door opened, smashing into my face. I fell back, clutching my lip, and looked up as a woman fell out, her robotic leg collapsing under her. Wide eyes stared back at me. I had crawled backwards on my hands, separating myself from this stranger.

"Oh my god, I'm so sorry," uttered the woman. She attempted to crawl away from me on all fours, but her leg refused to budge.

I gathered myself and rose from the floor. She looked defenceless and coated in sweat.

"Are you okay?" I asked and gave her a helping hand. "Who are you?"

"Joana," she replied. When she had steadied herself, I saw her features a little clearer. Her Mediterranean sun-kissed skin glowed under the bright LEDs. A small, dipped nose rested delicately between her wide hazel eyes, and a full head of dark, shoulder-length, curly hair bounced with her every movement.

"Alex. I'm here with a…friend." The word didn't sit well in my mouth—is that what we were? We barely knew each other, but also, I felt something deeper than friendship. Something that made my heart race when he was in the room with me. And, in this moment, a deep relief that he was the one that survived the boardroom incident. "Nat. He's upstairs."

"Aren't those creatures around?" said Joana, her gaze darting around, looking for signs of danger.

"Not here, no."

I paused for a moment, trying to imagine what could have happened here. A fight, but where had they come from? The windows looked intact. "We're looking for a way to send an SOS—do you know how the systems up there work?" I gestured with my head to the mezzanine.

"Sure, but…" Joana looked down to her leg. "I can't…"

I swept up Joana's arm, a yellow wristband dangling

loosely at the end, and helped her hop on her other leg. I felt her shaken body around me, possibly fear or exhaustion. As we reached the stairs, Nat looked down at us.

"Are we adding a new team member?" he asked, feigning a smile through his fear.

"Nat, this is Joana." I helped her up the stairs. "Could you take a look at her leg? Something's not right."

Nat swooped in, taking Joana's hands, and found a seat for her.

"You a cyberdoctor?" she asked.

"Nope," he replied. "But I'll give it a go. Can I…?" He hesitated, hovering his hands above the prosthetic.

"Of course," she replied. Eyebrows furrowed, her discomfort was clear. I imagined myself, back in that boardroom, with only one working leg. A shiver slithered down my spine at the helplessness I would have felt. A shit time for something like that to malfunction.

"I take it you were hiding down there?" I asked, leaning back against one of the desks.

Joana gave a jittery laugh. "Didn't want to die, so…"

"What happened?" asked Nat, his hands fiddling with a wire around Joana's ankle.

"I have no idea. I was," started Joana, seemingly interrupted by sensitive memories. "I was checking a file at the back when I heard some… screams. I ran out, and Maxim, my colleague, he was just there, b… b—" The words caught in her throat. Joana stared at the floor, escaping the embarrassment of crying in front of strangers. "And that thing… It was going around… Anyway, I managed to hide back there. I didn't dare come out until…"

Nat had ceased his tampering, hanging on her every word.

"Well anyway, getting into that cabinet knocked out my fucking leg, so I'm not sure it was worth it." She tried shrugging it off, but her distress overshadowed any dismissal she attempted to show.

"You're alive, aren't you?" said Nat.

Joana's smile grew. She nodded. "What are they anyway? Another one of Hagen's pet projects gone wrong?"

Nat and I looked at each other first.

"Aliens," I said.

Joana chuckled, and stayed silent, waiting for us to give her another, more realistic answer. And when we didn't, her eyes flitted from Nat to me.

"Shit. You're not joking, are you..." It wasn't a question anymore, just a statement from a terrified woman who almost lost her life.

"Do you know how to get Comms working?" asked Nat, busy rewiring something behind her ankle.

"Yeah, shouldn't be a problem."

"What do you do here?" I asked, looking around, trying to find signs on various desks as to which was hers.

"I'm a Cyber Security Analyst," replied Joana. "What do you guys do? Are you new?"

"We don't work here..." I started. "We're technically guests. Hagen had a—"

Hagen. His face. Blood pouring out of his mouth, reddening his teeth, staining the collar of his polo shirt. I blinked the thought away. I hadn't said his name yet. And if I thought of any other names, any other people in that room—

"He had an event—the Observer received a message, from these... aliens. We were working on that."

"Oh..." Joana looked away, like there was nothing more to be said, nothing to understand. It was still unbelievable, even to us.

"Try that," said Nat.

Joana's leg moved up and down, the ankle twisting in circles.

"It's not my normal gig, so you might want to get it fixed by an expert at some point."

"Thank you," she said, getting up. She did a few jumps, lifted both legs up, one at a time. "Right, let's see about that SOS."

She made her way to the nearest computer. Within seconds, the alarms stopped blaring in this room, although the individual beeps from other screens still screamed for attention.

"Something's not right," she said. Her eyes surveyed the screen, hopping from point to point. "The connection is not going through. Let me run diagnostics." She tapped and clicked away.

I still sat perched on a desk, wondering what possible difficulties we'd have to face next. Like an incoming attack from an alien species was not enough.

"Okay, I figured it out, and you're not going to like it." Her lips pursed.

Nat and I moved in behind her. Live camera feeds displayed the grey and grainy footage from outside the station. Cameras that had been out and affected by radiation for too long and clearly needed a replacement. Another thing the man in charge hadn't been willing to spend the money on.

"There should be an antenna here…" said Joana, pointing at a specific area outside the station. "… and here…" She pointed to another feed, where a substantial amount of the station's carapace was missing, as if torn away by a powerful grip. "And here." Another camera feed with a missing antenna.

"I take it some of those were the backups?" said Nat.

"Yeah."

"They don't want us to send an SOS," I said out loud. My mind raced with potential reasons for this. Did they take out the station, sacrifice all these people as a display of their force? To teach humans a lesson? To make the ones left on the Observer suffer? Did they not want us panicking a planet they had some use for? If they knew humans had nuclear weapons, would they be nervous about us taking down our own station to protect the planet?

"Let's not think about that," said Nat. "How do we fix this? If there are no backups, the only option would be to get another antenna and slap it on until the SOS gets sent, right?"

"Right," confirmed Joana.

"I don't suppose you know where Hagen keeps his spare antennas?" asked Nat.

We made our way to a nearby storage unit, still hidden away in the left wing of the Observer along with Comms and Command, which harboured some extra electrical equipment.

Advancing with prudence, we descended a set of stairs, that led us to a larger room with low hanging flickering lights and an endless amount of shelving. Electrical and mechanical equipment lay scattered around—shaken up in some of the commotion. The dark aluminium walls echoed Nat's footsteps as he did a perimeter check. Once he gave the all clear, we breathed a collective sigh and began our search for a spare antenna.

"What is all this junk doing here in the first place?" I asked. I could understand some spares for station emergencies or radiation damage, but this looked far too large.

"Some of it is junk, but, this here," replied Joana, as she tapped the sides of the plastic containers, "these are all spares. It's a storage space; if you go looking in the right places, you'll find stock for some of the shops here too. Bed linen for the hotel rooms. Spare bulbs for every single light source. All kinds of stuff. Definitely enough to make another antenna."

"Seems... excessive," I added.

Nat had been rummaging through boxes impatiently, leaving things piled up and boxes askew. He had not been subtle about the noise either.

"Hey, you okay?" I asked as I approached him. My hand traced the shelving—the feeling of something solid between my fingers kept me grounded. As much as dissociating would feel good, a safety for my mind to harbour in, it would not be productive.

"Yeah, I'm just..." he trailed off, dropping a large box back onto a shelf.

I flinched at the thump.

"I'm looking for the right cable. Otherwise, none of this is going to work." His brow had furrowed, his voice harsh.

"We'll find it. What does it look like?"

"It's a… coax cable; it's…" His eyes combed the area. "It's usually black, covered in a poly coating. Probably on a drum." He shuffled some more boxes, dropping them with a thud onto the shelves when he'd finished with them.

"Take a moment," I pleaded.

"The sooner we do this, the better."

"You're not going to get it done faster by slamming shit down."

He paused, his hand still on one of the plastic tubs, his grip firm.

"I'm sorry." He pulled the next one down and inspected the insides. "I just… I need to get home."

"What's this about?" I asked.

Memories took shape in the back of my mind, of my father getting stressed, frustrated, irate at inanimate objects. Throwing them around, breaking things. Hitting me. Sometimes accidentally, sometimes on purpose, especially towards the end.

"Life!" he said with an anxious laugh, covering his dismay. "Survival. I don't know what you want to call it, but I have things to live for back home. So." He put the lid back on that tub and pulled the next one down, with less noise this time. "I need to get back."

"Tell me more," I pushed. I felt I needed to understand his anguish for some reason. To be a part of it. It was selfish, but it felt like I could fight for survival with him, like it would give *me* a reason to try harder too.

"My little sister; she's pregnant. I promised I'd be there for her."

"What's her name?"

"Mai. She's having a girl, but they haven't found a good name yet." His lips stretched into a smile, that soon disappeared. "She's had issues with the pregnancy. Her partner works abroad, so they're not always around. So I said I'd be there." His head dipped. "This whole thing has gone to shit. I was only supposed to have been gone for a month max, but now, I don't know how long we'll be stuck here, if we'll even get out. What the hell is even going on?" He tried to laugh it out but bit his lip in an attempt to hold the tears back. "It sounds stupid. That after all the death we've seen here, that I would want to fight for this one life. This call for help, it could save the lives of everyone left on this station. So, I should be trying to do this for them. But, that little, unborn girl. She's my blood. My niece. And I *need* her to be okay. And for that to happen, I need to be back on solid ground."

"It's not stupid," I said. "It makes sense."

A pang of guilt struck me, that I had been so selfish in trying to coax this out of him. My hand slipped up his back to his shoulders and rested there, a warm and reassuring presence, I hoped.

"It's going to be okay," I lied.

"We need to keep moving." He pulled another tub and kept looking.

I nodded and began the same process with another set of shelves.

"Hey guys," said Joana, a few minutes later. "I hacked into the database—antennas are in sector 6, cables in sector 2, boxes 34 to 45."

"Thank God," said Nat, stepping away from the mess he'd made and towards the other sectors.

Shortly, we had all the individual pieces we needed, and Nat had begun working on connecting them all.

"What I don't understand," started Joana, "is, what do they want? Why disable a station, kill the people inside? What's their end goal here?"

Nat lifted his eyes to Joana but was too focused to reply.

"At the beginning," I started, "it felt to me that they

wanted to communicate clearly with us. Maybe they wanted help, maybe they were telling us they were coming close and not to panic, I'm not sure. Now, I feel like they want to know who's in charge. They could be showing us what they're capable of." My head swam with ideas. One idea in particular played on my mind: maybe the attack hadn't been instigated by the message. It had happened seconds after. Had the robots been crawling all over the station before it was sent out?

Above us, the lights flickered once more.

"Right now, I think they know where we are, and they're just fucking with the lights to scare us," said Nat stoically.

Joana peered at me, fear in her eyes.

"That was a joke," I reassured her.

"Oh, hah," said Joana, clasping her hand to her chest. "He's a funny one, isn't he?"

"You don't even know the half of it," he replied, still focused on the makeshift antenna he was putting together. A slight grin appeared on his face. He seemed to be forcing his way out of his anxiety. And maybe, humour was the way to do that.

Joana stepped closer to me and whispered, "I wouldn't trust that smile if I were you." She winked and moved away.

I grinned. Butterflies flickered deep in my stomach. I couldn't help it. Nat had that certain charm that I couldn't resist. I turned away from them, the small of my back pressed against the table.

My smile faded though. How could I, after everything that had happened, find happiness now? When my father had died, I had not smiled or laughed in months. In fact, one of the most enjoyable moments since the funeral had been that evening with Nat in the restaurant. How had I allowed that to happen? It had only been six months since the man's death. The guilt shrivelled me from the inside out.

I knew the pain was still there, heavy on my chest. And now that our lives were in danger, could I really afford to be distracted like this? No. And not only that, I simply didn't deserve it. Not after what happened in the boardroom, when I had the capacity to stop it all.

ALEXANDRA GAUTHIER'S DIGITAL ARCHIVE

From: Mathilde Guérin

To: Alexandra Gauthier

Date: January, 11th 2048 19:11

Location: Social Folder

Subject: Go for it!

Hey,

I know you said you didn't want to talk about it, but I still had some things I wanted to say.

The way you talked about this, it felt like a once in a lifetime opportunity. Take some time off work, accept the offer and go for it! You'll regret it for the rest of your life otherwise!

I know things have been shaky since... Well, you know when, but this seems like the first step of many. The first moment you expressed interest in anything for a while. If you think this will make you happy, I would never tell you to do anything else but this.

You said it was going to be far away and that we wouldn't see you for a while, so I guess you'll be in the US or maybe in Asia? Either way, let us know when you land. We worry about you, yeah?

Don't be a stranger.

Mathilde

From: Mathilde Guérin

To: Alexandra Gauthier

Date: January, 15th 2048 09:45

Location: Social Folder

Subject: [Re:]Go for it!

Hey again,

We haven't heard from you yet… I didn't hear of any planes crashing or anything else, so I'm assuming you're just crazy busy.

Please call or something?

Mathilde x

5

"It's… well, it's home-made, but it should do the trick." Nat showed off his rough and ready version of the antenna. Loose wires were tucked in and held tight with duct tape. As he held it, it shook from side to side.

I stood by them, looking at its frailty with concern.

"As long as it sends out the SOS, that's all we need," replied Joana.

And she was right—it just needed to survive a short while. Although part of me wondered if those droid creatures wouldn't just rip it out as soon as they noticed it sending a message. That was a risk we would just have to take.

We journeyed back to Comms, cautiously avoiding any noise, Nat at the front, guarded, gun in front of him. The staircase very softly echoed our footsteps. We still didn't know what attracted the droids: was it sound, or some infrared vision? Either way, we didn't want to take any chances. The cold steel walls surrounding us looked impenetrable. And yet, as I climbed the steps, my gaze found the cracks, the designed chipped edges giving it that desired rustic, superficially flawed look.

Back in Comms, Joana set up all the external cameras to display the path Nat was going to take. Her finger traced a route from the airlock door, up a series of ladders to what could be considered the top of the station, from a gravitational perspective.

"Ready?" said Nat, turning to me.

"What do you mean?" I asked.

"As in, ready to suit up?"

"Wait... You think I'm going with you?" The ground shifted under my feet. There was *no* way.

"I need an extra pair of hands, and Joana knows her way around stuff here."

"What?" I repeated. I shook my head. I couldn't. Not now, not with my present state of mind. The weightlessness would be too much, too tempting. I could drift off if I let go; I could forever fall in a darkness I would never understand, endlessly seeing the stars until I closed my eyes for good. My hands grew clammy, and with my index finger, I picked at the skin by the nail of my thumb.

"I can't," I muttered to him. That's all I could say. Because if I said anymore, he'd realise what a liability I was. A danger to myself, let alone to others.

"We'll take it slow, yeah? But I can't do this by myself." He was raring to go, to get the job done. This *needed* to be done if we wanted any hope of getting off this station. I couldn't see any other option.

"Okay," I said, but the disassociation still sucked all reality away.

By the elevator, we began undressing in the Suit Station. Nestled into a corner, circular in shape, with bolted down benches and changing facilities, it showed no distinction or privacy for any gender. The suits lay neat and folded in each of the lockers, waiting until their time came.

We swapped out of our clothes into a jumpsuit each, averting our eyes from each other's bodies. The suits were a dark blue in colour, unisex and unisized, thus too large on me and perfect on Nat. The Observer logo had been embroidered on the front left pouch, a delicate, threaded depiction of the station in a silvery white.

"That suits you," said Nat, finally taking me in. The cut on his forehead from the incident in the boardroom had dried and swollen.

I delivered an awkward smile, my mind lost in every single possible outcome that could occur on the outside of this station. I already felt the need to jump ship, in every sense of the term.

"Hey," he came closer, standing near enough I could feel his breath on the tip of my nose. Was it irrational of me to want to pull him even closer? To feel his warmth on my skin, to channel that into something worth returning to? "I promise you it will be fine. We'll fix the antenna, send the SOS, have a sandwich, and be home very soon."

Was he convincing me or convincing himself? Did he also have the same urge, to let go and be done with this mess?

I nodded.

With our jumpsuits on, we reached for the spacesuit itself: a white and navy-blue atmosphere suit with numerous belts, buckles and straps. We helped each other into them, and soon enough we walked out of the changing area and towards the airlock, helmets in hand. Joana had waited for us outside.

"You look about as ready as you're ever going to be," she said to me.

"I'm not sure this is what I signed up for when they sent me up here," I replied with an attempted laugh. But my chest had been thumping, an incessant drum, loud in my ears, my breath catching any time I remembered what I was about to do. This was so far from reality I didn't know how I hadn't passed out already.

"You and me both," said Joana. "I'll be watching from the inside, guiding you every step of the way. I know exactly where you need to go, so just follow my directions, and we'll be done before you know it." Her smile was tentative, but she gave a nod of her head as well, to emphasise her empathy.

Nat and I stepped into the airlock, between both sets of doors. He keyed in commands into a side panel, swiping the red wristband in front of the sensor for clearance. The first set of doors closed. Silence fell.

"Helmet on," said Nat. We secured our helmets and checked each other's to make sure they were airtight.

"Can you hear me?" asked Joana; her voice had croaked through the internal short-wave radio in our suits.

"Loud and clear," replied Nat.

My heart raced faster. There was no turning back.

"Good. You'll have to depressurise the airlock first, then open the doors. When you've done that, make sure you grab the harness clips just inside the doors. They are your lifeline." Between Joana's words, I could hear my breath bounce back off the walls of my own personal fishbowl, trapped and suffocating.

"Quite literally," continued Joana. "No life if you're not attached to that line."

"Not helping, Joana," said Nat. His own breathing had picked up; I could hear it through the radio.

"Sorry, sorry…"

Nat looked in my direction. I couldn't see what he was looking at due to the reflection in the glass, and no matter how hard I tried, I couldn't find his eyes, his face kept secret. I regretted in that moment having not touched him before sealing myself in this contraption.

As the air changed, I kept trying to find his gaze, but I never found it. I felt my weight shift, gravity slowly releasing my grip from solid ground, unburdened by my own body, but cumbersome in the suit. I couldn't reach for anything, couldn't move, just floated. My panic stretched out, my arms lashing at the air, until I felt a comforting hand pull me down. My feet back on the ground, I saw Nat's eyes. They held strength. I nodded to him, and, with one hand, I held on to a barrier on the inside of the airlock. With the other, I held him.

The airlock doors opened, and my breath escaped my lungs. Outside, the scene was pitch black. Off in the distance, the stars sprinkled across my entire vision. I could see the side of the station—thick metallic limbs hanging in the void above Earth. Nausea crept up my throat from the lack of gravity.

Everything felt so far away, so untouchable. Behind the big bubble of glass in which I was hiding, everything felt immaterial, unreal. I touched the side of the station, but at this stage, I wasn't sure those were my hands in front of me. The air from my lungs bounced back in my face, hot and moist.

Nat, his movement slowed to a crawl, tapped my shoulder. In his other hand, he held his interpretation of an antenna.

"You alright, Alex?" he asked. He seemed to be taking this much better than I was, and I wondered how much of that confidence was misplaced.

"Umm… Sure."

"I'll take that as a '*no*'", he said, laughing. "We'll be done real quick, okay?"

Joana's voice croaked through the helmets. "Alright, guys. Make sure you latch on to the harnesses. Then, when you head out of the door, there'll be a ladder to your right."

After securing a harness to each suit, Nat swung his arm out and grabbed hold of the ladder and pushed himself out of the airlock.

I approached the edge, sweat forming on my temple. The abyss below never ended, although, technically, there was no drop. Only an idling silence. I checked that the harness was still attached to me, before taking a wide step to the right of the airlock and clinging to the ladder. I looked down, past the edge of my toes, into an infinite nothingness. In my helmet, Nat's breathing matched my own exhausted puffs of air as we both struggled up the steps. Above me, I saw him advancing, holding onto the antenna tightly with one hand and using his other to go up the ladder. My eyes focused on the façade of the station—boring whites and greys in a sea of darkness. Heart thumping, my nerves crept up, close to reaching boiling point.

No one would believe I had ever done this. A spacewalk. My father would have— He wouldn't have believed me either. I didn't have the time or the energy to think about him right now, but for some reason I wanted him to know I had done this, to make him see I was doing everything I could.

"Keep going, Alex. You're doing great," Nat's voice came through my helmet. I gasped and panted until we arrived at the top of this ladder. He reached out his hand, a thick white glove, and I grabbed onto him with all my strength. We had come to an intersection: two ladders met like a crossroads. One would take us down, and the other would take us higher up the station. The peak looked far, a few hundred feet still. Nat pulled me to the top of the first ladder before grabbing onto the next.

"Make sure you shift your weight when you come to this one," he croaked.

"Go straight forward from there, Nat," crackled Joana in our helmets.

Nat moved up, continuing the long journey upwards.

The second ladder seemed out of reach for someone of my height. I'd have to leap to reach it. I hopped and grabbed a hold of it and pulled myself over, bouncing too hard. My weight deviated. My body flung now perpendicular to the ladder, my fingers hanging on tight. I let out a light gasp, panic flying through me. The harness kept supporting me, and so I took a breath. Nothing could go wrong; that's what the harness was for.

"Bring yourself in, Alex," said Nat, his chunky suit staring down at me.

Using my core strength, I pulled myself to the ladder.

"That's it."

My knees bashed into the metal, but I hugged the ladder tighter still, my cheek crushed against the neck brace inside the helmet. Breath slowing, I looked around—the space around us hadn't changed. I had briefly hoped it had all been a dream, that I would wake up in my own bed, in my flat in London, that I would go to teach at the Linguistics Institute, and fill my day with an activity that was less adrenaline-fuelled, less terrifying. But I was still here. Space was unforgiving.

"You've got it," said Nat, and I realised that I relished any bit of positive feedback he offered me. Maybe he knew that too.

I pushed forward, a fresh fire in my soul, a desire to achieve something, to not let anyone down. I climbed the ladder, following in his footsteps.

"You're both doing great," Joana said. The quality of the connection dipped as we moved further and further away.

We climbed, our harnesses tugging at our belts. To me, it was a pleasant reminder I was still attached to the station, a security line, the safety of my life in the hands of a thin cable.

The bulkiness of the suit in this environment slowed me down; beads of sweat formed across my forehead and neck, dripping down onto my jumpsuit. I could hear Nat's breathing straining through the radio; even he struggled, I reminded herself. This job would have taken years of training, but here we were doing it out of desperation and sheer terror.

"Once you reach the top, you'll be at the antenna. Or, at least where it *was*…"

"I see it," said Nat.

"You see it? The broken one?"

"No," he breathed heavy. "I see where it should be." He gasped once more as he pulled himself over the top and out of my sight.

Left alone for a short moment, I wondered if I *had* been dreaming this whole time. The disassociation got worse, yet I couldn't help but let my mind explore it every time. None of this felt real. My eyes hazed over, an idea that unless I felt, touched or sensed something, that it couldn't exist. The pain in my muscles should have been enough to ground me, but it wasn't.

I had four more steps to climb before seeing Nat again. But I didn't know if I wanted that reality. If I stayed here, looking at the grey shell of the station, I could ignore it all. If I closed my eyes tight enough, I would stop existing. It would all end. I would fade into the nothingness and not have to deal with any of it. I could forget, and be forgotten. The same way my father's memories had faded and strayed, lost to time. I felt that sinking vertigo once more, but the feeling in my feet returned, and I felt the pressure of the metal pushing into the palm of my boots, the weight and density of the suit in my arms, and the inside fabric of the gloves on my fingertips.

"Alex?" I heard Nat say.

"Coming. I just needed a breather," I replied and forced my muscles to move once more. Another step, another push in the bulky gear. I peered over the edge. Nat had immobilised himself, the antenna still held in one hand.

Pushing myself over, I felt like I had climbed to the top of the world. We both clenched the handrails at the top of the Observer, a wide angle of all the stars around us and Earth below. How far had humans actually gone? Were we the furthest people from the world right now? I looked at the big blue circle below us, and there was nothing, no words that could express how small and, simultaneously, how big I felt. I looked at the planet and saw everything: its oceans, its continents, the weather afflicting its land. I saw all the colours that made this planet unique: its blues and greens, of various shades, giving it life. If I reached far enough, I might be able to touch the colours themselves, change the weather by brushing my hand to one side. A fictitious God, capable of moving mountains and oceans with the tips of my fingers. Is that how Hagen had felt when he made this place? Had he placed his hand in front of his eyes and pretended he could eliminate the planet, or move things about the way he wanted to? Did he believe he could stop wars by flicking his finger, or catch the nuclear missiles between his fingernails?

To my surprise, when I turned around, Nat remained fixed in place, mesmerised too. He was silent, but he caught my eye, and we both realised we had shared this moment together. Just the two of us.

Turning back to the task at hand, Nat approached the panel where the old antenna used to be.

"Don't unclip your other harness, use a new clip on here," he said as he pointed to a built-in restraint for the harness. "That way you don't have to worry about flying away."

I did as he had suggested, limiting it to no more than a metre and a half, and lingered opposite him, the broken panel between us. He gave me the makeshift antenna to hold and moved his helmet closer in.

"Looks like it was ripped out," he said, still catching his breath. His fingers traced the scuff marks where the screws had been. His hands then moved to other marks: metal on metal. "They were out here. Not sure why they took the time to stop any communication."

"Maybe they don't know that we can't see them," I said, thinking out loud.

Nat pondered the reply for a while, his eyes sharing my fears.

"Can you attach the new antenna?" asked Joana.

"I should think so. I'll need a couple of new wires, I think. It looks pretty damaged." He unclipped some wire cutters from his belt and asked me to hold them. He cut the old wire clean and shimmied the poly coating off. Taking the new wire, he did the same and intertwined the same colour wires together, a bond that would last until this fixture would also be ripped from its holding. He reached out for the antenna, and I passed it to him.

"Hold it still," he said, and I placed my hands on it and held it down. Our breathing was the only sound I could hear. Nat unclipped a small drill from his belt and drilled the base of the antenna back into its original space. Once he had finished, he tried to rock it about; it stayed put.

"Not sure it'll hold if one of those robots tries to yank it out," he said to himself, clipping the tools back onto his belt. "Just need to finish the wiring... Anything yet?" he asked

Joana.

"No," she replied. "No, wait…"

Nat and I looked at each other, waiting for a response.

"Yes! It's working!" she said, her voice cracking with excitement.

"Great—send an SOS out immediately. We can't risk waiting until we get back."

"Done—it's a pulse signal at the moment. Get yourselves back in, and we can see if we can contact someone more directly."

Nat and I both sighed with relief.

"Told you we would be done in time for a sandwich," he said, presumably with a grin on his face.

"I think I'm going to need more than a sandwich."

"I'm sorry, but that's the limit to my cooking skills, I'm afraid," he replied.

I scoffed.

"I'm joking, I can actually make a mean phở when I want to."

"You'll have to show me some day. I'm not very versed on Vietnamese foods."

"It's my go-to comfort food. I'll make it for you. As soon as we get out of this hell hole."

Going back towards the ladder had confused me; there was no up or down, no feeling of stability in my body, no blood rushing to my head as I climbed the ladder the opposite way. The strain in my muscles felt real now; I could only imagine the genuine physical preparations it took to get a job doing these tasks daily. Covered in sweat, my hands felt hot and clammy in the gloves; I slipped every now and again, catching myself with plenty of time. Nat continued ahead of me, keeping his pace, panting into his helmet.

"Up ahead is your second ladder, about five meters from you, Nat," said Joana.

"Okidokie, artichokie," replied Nat, his good humour

possibly disguising his tiredness.

"Jeez, what are you? Like sixty-five?" said Joana with a chuckle.

"And looking good," he said, with a grunt as he approached the second ladder. He swung his arm down to grab the first step, but immediately retracted it, losing his balance, and rebounded off the station, catching himself in time.

"Oh my god—" Joana crackled over the radio.

The recognisable flat head of the droid peered over the edge, its bright white eye following their movement. Nat scrambled to his feet, panic rooting through him. I stopped in my tracks. The droid's legs carried it forward, facing the two of us head-on. One jab at our suits, and we would die.

A metal coil flung towards Nat, slower now, without the aid of artificial gravity. But the deep silence of space aided it, the coil sifting through the vacuum, with only our vision to rely on. Nat managed to swing his arm in defence, pushing the sharp end away from his helmet, but grabbing the coil to stop it from retracting. I couldn't stay here, waiting for another death, another grieving period. I looked around; I had nothing on me that I could use. Nothing immediate.

Nat yanked the droid towards him, grunting and wheezing in his helmet. It fell towards him at a greater velocity than he had expected.

"Nat!" I shouted desperately.

It fell towards him—no—on top of him. I needed to act fast, but I felt disoriented.

They scrambled, Nat grabbing its front two limbs, stopping the snapping motion aimed at his helmet and suit.

"Alex! Try to—" I heard Joana say, crackled, muffled.

He tried kicking it away, but the suit was too stiff. I rushed towards them. I couldn't— I didn't know what else to do, and I had no better ideas. I propelled myself further with my hands and feet, bouncing off the ladder. I ricocheted in a way I hadn't meant to, but my body launched at a decent speed in the right direction. I grabbed hold of its metallic body, dragging it off the edge of the Observer and into the depths of space with me.

"Alex?! Alex!" Nat's voice bounced around in the helmet but hadn't truly reached my ears.

I fell; I knew I had fallen. There was no way back now. But before I could fully accept my death, the droid had clung to me, not trying to kill me anymore, just trying to survive. It had life, a will to live, and I wondered if, somewhere under that hard shell, there was a living organism.

We tumbled, spinning together into a never-ending chasm. Eyes open, I could see the station appear every few seconds in the corner of my helmet. I pushed the droid away, but it clung to my suit, scrambling to reach… My harness. Keeping me attached to the station. It tried to crawl back. Grabbing one of its legs, I pulled it back down. These things were strong, but I managed to tug it a little, enough to get some purchase. Heaving it closer, I realised I couldn't kill it outright here. There must be some other way to get rid of it. The station retreated further and further away.

Somewhere, at some time, there had been shouting in my helmet. Nothing real. Just voices in an abyss. I scrambled some more, keeping the metallic legs as far away as I could. An idea had come to me, but I didn't know when it would take effect. And as soon as the thought had come, the moment had arrived. The tightness in the cord. The pull of the harness. It had reached the end of the drum. My neck snapped back. With the droid in hand, I used the bounce back and flung it. As quickly as it left my gloved fingertips, I felt something snap. The harness clip broke, the wire retracting into the drum.

No breath. I swam, hands grasping at the vacuum, unable to move forward. My fingers brushed something. I grabbed hold of it. The harness. It was real; I felt its presence in the palm of my hand. It was tangible. I gripped it with all my might. Looking down past my feet, I saw the droid squirming for purchase. It flung its wire coils to grasp at something, but the distance between us was too great now.

I hung there, in the darkness, unable to find the strength to reattach the clip, unable to find the resolve to let it go once and for all.

My name was being screamed into my helmet, on repeat, for the end of times. If I let go now, what would I find? Somewhere out there, somewhere I couldn't see, something was hiding. To my side, Earth sat still. Stagnant, here and now, even though every living creature on that *fucking* planet was busy, running around, catching trains at the last minute, late for work, babies crying, children playing, couples shouting. But when I looked at it, I didn't just see human beings. I saw the blue whales swimming in the oceans, the coal tits sitting on dark tree branches, and the worms digging underground. Everything moved yet stood so still from this distance. Why was it, hanging from the end of this harness, pure serenity in my body, muscles frozen, breath slowed, that my heart screamed at me? I looked at the harness in my hand. It would be easy to let go. I would just need to unfold my fingers, one by one, and leave the carabiner clip behind. It would return to the station, and I would stay, here, to look at Earth until my oxygen ran out.

Would my death be worthy though? Would it be meaningful? Would it matter? Did any life matter if humans kept rushing around the way they did? Does one cog in the machine stop the machine from working altogether, or does it get replaced with another dispensable cog until the end of time? Why was any of this worth it? I gripped the clip harder, feeling the rigid metal through the glove. Looking down, the droid had disappeared. If it was a living creature, it would die, but if it was an algorithm trapped in a box, it would live eternally. I had left it to exist, forever falling towards something it could never obtain. Could I live with that death myself? I wasn't sure. Looking up, I saw the Observer, a despicable creation of enduring beauty. The thin wire, the sole thing giving me a lifeline to a potential future. I kept trying to imagine a future. What would that even look like now, with these creatures trying to kill us?

Looking at the detail in the wire, the individual fibres had been twisted into place to create a strong cable. I had seen those twists previously, on a strong rope, that I had had to cut down. I remembered the fibres, each splitting as I had cut through them, ruffled at the end. When I had pulled the rope down from the ceiling, there had been nothing attached to it, only an emptiness where something had hung. I couldn't imagine being hung at the end of a similar rope. Maybe that was enough? Maybe that was something.

I gathered whatever strength I had left and pulled on it a bit. My body drifted towards the station. I clipped myself back onto the harness.

My name was still being shouted, bouncing off the walls of my glass bubble.

"I'm here, I'm here..." I uttered.

"What the fuck was that about?! Where is it?" Nat's fear had turned to anger.

I could hear the shake in his voice, on his lips. "Gone. It's gone," I whispered.

I took in the vastness one more time, letting the void eat my thoughts and feelings alive. Had I made the right choice, I asked myself. Would I regret living, when I had nothing to live for?

"Bring her in. Bring her in!" Joana sounded far away, her voice a distant mumble.

A second later, I felt the tug at my waist, the wire drum pulling me closer to a different doom. Was one death any different from another? Even in this emptiness, I felt trapped. Trapped into a life I didn't choose, trapped into feelings I didn't want to feel.

As I closed in, I watched the peacefulness of Earth. The clouds had covered a portion of the Caribbean in a swirling motion. Life never ended. Things were always happening. I felt tired. Life never ended. Until it did.

"—and did you seriously think—" Nat had been talking

this whole time, and I hadn't heard him.

My eyes felt scratchy. I wanted to sleep.

"Nat. Maybe give her a moment?"

I inched forward, the belt around my waist dragging me in. Maybe this had been the right call. Maybe something, somewhere still needed me.

As my body approached the airlock, I saw Nat, patiently waiting, hand on the harness control. He hadn't said a word, and even now, as I got close, he looked past me, not at me. Maybe he had read my mind while I had been out there. Maybe I had said some of my thoughts out loud. No, I didn't recall doing that. But I had been so out of it, maybe the words had left my lips, unnoticed.

I pulled myself in, grabbing handrails where I could. We unclipped our harnesses, the airlock sealed. There was a moment's respite as the air pressure regulated and artificial gravity returned. I gawked at the floor, numbness hugging my mind. My weight pulled me down, the soreness of my muscles deeply apparent now. The suit slumped me even further towards the floor.

Past the inner airlock, through the glass pane, I saw Joana resting by the side of a wall. She had a solemn air about her; an unspoken restlessness. It was quiet. With the inner airlock open, Joana stepped in as Nat and I removed our helmets.

"I'm sending a pulse SOS out at the moment. But our best bet is to speak with someone directly." Joana's eyes darted between the two of us. She hesitated, before continuing, "I'll set it up. You might want to get changed out of those." Her eyes shifted to the heavy spacesuits.

I didn't have the strength to nod.

Back in the changing room, through the unstrapping of buckles and unzipping of suits, thick silence invaded the air. Thumping along Nat's forehead was a vein I had never seen before. I didn't know what to say, but I felt the words slip from my mouth.

"I'm sorry," I whispered.

He folded the suit back into its previous space, popping the boots in the cubbyhole, but he left the jumpsuit on.

"I don't think you need me to tell you how that made me feel. It's obvious, but I…" He hadn't looked at me yet.

Anguish grew in my chest. I hadn't realised he cared about me. That he felt the same way I did about him. I wanted to touch him, make sure his presence was real. To give a reality to these emotions.

"I'm sorry," I repeated.

"Don't you think we've had enough death already?"

The words clung to me. Of course there had been a lot of death. What was one more?

"If you did that…" He shook his head, incredulity in his mannerisms. "If you did that because you think your life is not as important as mine…" He stared at me now. "Well, you'd be wrong."

I lowered my gaze, fiddling with a string from the waistband of the jumpsuit I had also kept on. A slight ache developed in my chest. Was it the pain of being alive, or was it guilt for how I had made him feel?

"There was no need to throw yourself away like that. We could have found another way. And I think if there's one thing we *do* need right now, it's a bloody linguist."

Although I wasn't looking at him, I nodded. There was truth in what he had said. An alien race that no one could understand had attacked us, and I was now the only one to have begun deciphering their language. I had a purpose. Whether or not I wanted any part in it.

"For what it's worth, I'm glad you're still here," he continued. "You keeping the jumpsuit on?"

"I think so," I replied with a nod, barely able to look at him.

"Cool. We can be jumpsuit buddies." His smile held pain, but I could tell he was trying.

OBSERVER DIGITAL ARCHIVE
Conduct, Safety and Security n. 3:

"Respect and protect the station."

We ask that all staff and visitors respect the environment: bin any litter, keep communal areas tidy and put things back where you found them. We request that you respect your surroundings and others around you.

Refuse and recycling bins are both available throughout the station. Please make sure you separate your trash accordingly. If you see any litter that is not your own, please pick it up or alert a staff member. Although we do have cleaners on site, proper disposal of litter is a guest's responsibility. In accordance with the law, a fine of $1000 could be issued to anyone seen littering or disposing of their trash irresponsibly.

Communal areas are available to all and should be left tidy and clean for other guests. Please remove all your belongings once you have finished using a communal area. For the safety and cleanliness of the station, all belongings left unattended for longer than fifteen minutes will be disposed of accordingly, even if they do not provide a security threat. Leaving a clean and tidy space for the next guest is a top priority.

Communal objects can be used in different areas of the station. We offer a range of picnic blankets, courtyard games (such as soccer, tennis, and basketball), and experiences that use communal items. To hear more about our amazing offers, please visit our website or use the My Observer App. Once a guest has finished using said item, it* *is their responsibility to return the items from whence they came. Should a guest fail to return the borrowed items, the monetary value will be deducted from their bill.*

Should a guest notice anything strange or abnormal, including, but not limited to, unattended baggage or suspicious behaviour, please alert a member of our Security Team immediately. Should a guest act in a suspicious way or leave their baggage unattended, they will be escorted back to the station gates and be forced to board the shuttle to return home. We do not wish to force passengers back home but will not hesitate to do so to respect the station and the enjoyment of our other passengers. For the benefit of all, please be kind to your environment.

** Terms and Conditions apply. Experiences need to be pre-booked via the My Observer App.*

6

"Right… Somewhere we have an instruction manual." Joana talked to herself as she searched through the metal file cabinets. She pulled out a thick yellow binder and dropped it on the desk. "Sorry guys. This isn't my department."

"No one expects you to know everything," replied Nat, still relatively cold after what had just happened.

"Phew. It's a big relief knowing one of the last people I'm going to see in my life is putting *zero* pressure on me." A wide grin spread across her face. I appreciated her sense of humour in this situation. It was one way of coping. Maybe a better one than throwing yourself off a space station.

The binder between Joana's hands was hundreds of pages long, a large tome of indecipherable communications content. But she soon found the radio frequency for the nearest BioTech station.

BioTech had become a well-known company during the 2010s, involved in multiple scandals at the time due to their waste management, but who straightened out their act and became a leading biotechnology corporation, particularly in space. They had three or four small stations orbiting Earth, each working on their own projects in confidence, usually secluded from other stations. At this moment in time, it was the closest manned station, and our only hope.

Tapping the keyboard a few times, Joana pushed her chair away.

"All yours," she said.

I hesitated. Why should I be the one leading this? But I stepped forward anyway, grabbing the headset, seeing as both Nat and Joana stood still. Maybe they thought they were giving me something to do.

I had somewhat come out of my daze. The conversation with Nat had helped me put a few things in perspective. I *did* have a purpose, and somewhere, deep in the back of my mind, my father screamed that I should be trying a little harder. That I wasn't done.

"Just press this button when you speak," continued Joana.

I took a deep breath—this was it, the moment we had fought for. We were going to get help. "B-4250, this is..." I checked my notes again. "This is OBS05, do you copy?"

A pause.

"B-4250, this is OBS05. We have an emergency."

Silence.

"It's alright, give them a minute," said Nat, placing his hand on my shoulder. Warmth spread from my shoulder down my torso. Warmth, or stress.

"B-4250, do you copy?" I repeated, clearer this time. A strain in my voice. Were we all alone in this? I turned to Joana, "Are you sure this is the right frequency?"

Joana nodded, but continued to flick through the binder, her hands frantically searching for another page, another answer.

"B-4250, this is—"

"Copy, OBS05, this is B-4250." A collective sigh. "How can we assist?" The man's voice crackled through the headset.

"Thank you, B-4250. We have an emergency here on OBS05. We are under attack. The crew... M-most of the crew and guests have been killed." My voice shook. I hadn't realised how hard it would be to admit the truth. No one had said those exact words out loud as of yet.

"I'm sorry to hear that, OBS05. We'll notify the ground ASAP. Can you confirm if the killer is still on the loose? Should the rescue team be cautious?"

I wasn't sure how he would take the next piece of information. "The killer is not human. The station is under attack by... droids. We have severe damage, impacting—"

"OBS05, did you say... droids?"

"That's correct."

"Like ÆviBots? The ones at McDonalds?" His pitch, puncturing through the radio, had shifted.

I shook my head. "No. No... Not service robots. Alien... Droids."

"OBS05, if this is a joke..."

"B-4250, this *isn't* a joke. Hundreds of personnel and tourists aboard the Observer have *died*. We need assistance immediately." My words cut through the silence in the Comms room.

There was a brief pause before his voice started once more. "Roger that. Can you confirm how many *droids* are attacking you?"

"I'm not sure. It could be fifteen, could be fifty. It's hard to know exactly. They are ripping out electrical equipment across the station, so we might lose Comms again. Sections of the station are missing. We've got multiple oxygen leaks."

"And how many survivors?"

I looked back at Nat and Joana. "As far as we know, three, including myself. There may be more elsewhere."

Joana slammed the binder shut and jumped onto another computer. We hadn't even thought to check; so much of our focus had been on calling for help.

"Okay. Find a safe spot and hang tight. Help is on the way, OBS05," he replied.

"Thank you, B-4250." I removed the headphones and

turned towards the others. "We did it. We'll be out of here soon."

Although the words had left my mouth, I didn't feel as though we were any safer. The droids could come in at any moment.

Running his hands across his face in relief, Nat leaned back against one of the desks. "Thank God..."

"I'm checking if there are signs of life elsewhere on the station," said Joana. "Not really my department again, but I figure I could give it a try at least." Tapping away, multiple tabs opened and closed before Joana found what she was looking for. "Technically, there should be 702 people aboard — that's the number of active wristbands. Staff and guests. And looking at what Hub Bunkers and Suit Stations have been used... We have four bunkers that are fully locked down. That means people inside." Joana turned her head towards us.

We weren't alone.

"Can you get CCTV in the Bunkers?" I asked.

"Let me check. I think it requires clearance I don't have."

"Can you bypass it?" asked Nat.

Joana tapped at the keyboard. New tabs opened.

"There."

The screen showed three camera feeds, each with grainy live footage. Some people moved, some remained seated. An elderly couple, huddled together, clasping each other's hands. A group argument, anger and fear on each of their faces. A teenage boy, sitting, his leg bouncing up and down in anxiety. He wiped his cheek with the palm of his hand.

My heart sank. "Can we talk to them?"

"Not from here. From outside the Bunker, you can."

"Wait, I thought you said there were four?" said Nat.

"CCTV is down in one of them," confirmed Joana.

"We need to help them." My voice caught in my throat. Remembering the bodies laid out by the bunker Nat and I had tried to use, I had truly thought we were the last ones alive on the station. How blind and selfish had I been?

"If we go out there, they could find us. There's nothing we can do but wait for help," replied Nat.

And I knew he was right.

Outside, the faraway stars kept glistening. Somewhere aboard the station sat the most powerful digital telescope in human existence, taking stunning pictures of far-off galaxies and making the most of its privileged position. I stood by the window; the stars were endless.

"Hey," said Nat. He stepped up beside me. His presence alone filled me with something I wanted to hold onto for the rest of my life. "I just wanted to say I'm sorry about earlier. It was a bit much. Some of the stuff I said —"

"Don't worry about it," I cut him off. "I know where it was coming from. Enough has happened already. I was reckless."

The air felt stiff around us. My actions had been a representation of my mindset, a mindset I had adopted since my father had died. Maybe even before that. Heedless and negligent. Misguided.

"Yeah, a lot has happened. And, look... I care about you. I don't want you going around thinking you're dispensable. You're not."

I looked at him—his face was nothing but honest. He motioned to the stairs behind us, and we sat down on the lowest step, looking out the same window, into the infinite starry night. Somewhere on Earth, the sun would be rising. Just another normal day.

"Now, I don't know what's causing you to be so *rash* with your decisions. But you can't keep doing that. This is something you need to do for yourself. And if you can't, then at least think of us, or of the people you might love back home. Joana and I would be lost without you—not only because I would have had to do that whole thing out there by myself, but, what? Do you really think Joana and I would know what the hell to do here, particularly if we're talking about communicating with aliens?" He chuckled to himself. "Well, I guess what I'm saying is give yourself a break. Whatever's making you unhappy right now, that won't last forever."

I took a deep breath. The stiff, metal stairs dug into my thighs. Thoughts jumbled around in my mind in a cyclone of emotions. My father, his death. *'Forever'* was exactly how it felt. Everything had weighed so heavily on me. And a small part of me wanted to let that go. But it still wasn't the right time. Not yet.

"You know," I said. And it was only in that specific moment that I decided Nat deserved my honesty. "I didn't think I was doing anything wrong. For a while now, I thought I was just... coping. But you are right. I was being... thoughtless. Out there," I said, vaguely pointing to the top of the Observer. "But also, back home. I," I paused, and rubbed the back of my neck.

"My dad raised me by himself," I continued. If I was going to let it out, I'd have to start from the beginning. "I loved my mum, but I never really knew her. But my dad... He was pivotal in pushing me to become who I am today. He taught me to try hard, with anything, any problem I faced. So I did: I worked my ass off. I studied. I did everything I could to make him proud. And at the end of the day, if I still failed, he congratulated me on trying my hardest, and he'd say, "*At least, you were the best version of yourself in that moment.*" That's a rewarding thing to hear when you feel like shit for failing.

"So that was my methodology for the best part of my life. Try hard. Fail. Feel good about trying your best. Then try again. It got me good grades, good degrees, good jobs. But when he was diagnosed with Alzheimer's, a part of him felt like *he* had failed. He was angry at himself for not succeeding at being healthy. And maybe he knew he was never going to be the best version of himself anymore... That sounds messed up, but I think that's what changed him."

Nat's eyes hadn't budged an inch, heeding my every word. I could feel his attention digging into me. It just made me want to talk more.

"Over the course of months, I came to visit him more and more often. Doctors had said he had been diagnosed late—that, maybe, he had not admitted he was having issues. Maybe stubbornness runs in the family; I don't know." I scoffed at the irony. "But every time I saw him, his anger grew; his disdain for being ill, or knowing he would never get better. I saw him change; this man who had been my hero, someone I admired my whole life, someone who had taught me to be the best version of myself. I cared for him, picked up after him… I tried my best to look after him, but… He didn't see a daughter in me anymore. I was a stranger, invading his space, telling him what to do."

Tears formed in my eyes, but a wave of frustration hit me at the same time. "It sounds so stupid when I say it out loud. Why does this even matter right now?" Done with the conversation, I got up. "Why the fuck am I crying over my dead dad when we could be slaughtered at any second?"

"Hey," called out Nat. "No. It's not stupid—"

"But why do I *feel* this way?! Look at what's going on around us!" I waved my arms out, my anger and exasperation forming more tears, mingling with my depression, coupling into the same exhausting ritual of self-hatred.

"You can't help the way you feel," he rose and clasped his hands around my face. His touch sent shivers down my spine. "You just need to feel it."

I tried shaking my head. "I don't *want* to."

"You can keep pushing it down, or you can face it," he said, nearing my face, meeting my teary eyes.

Everything was closing in on me, those bottled-up emotions I had tried to repress for so long. Six months. Six months since he had passed, yet this had been going on for so much longer than I cared to admit. The abuse I had suffered at his hands towards the end. I had taken it all on the chin. It was my duty, as a daughter, to be there no matter what, wasn't it?

"It was my responsibility, to look after him," I muttered out loud. The words had slipped out without context, the weight of them now unbound. "I had to. I had no choice."

Nat's hand slipped down to my shoulder. The warmth of his palm pressed deep into my arm. "If you had another choice, I'm sure you would have taken it. But you can't resent yourself for what happened."

"He hated me. He hated me so much," I uttered, my tears slowing.

"I'm sure he didn't. But it sounds like he didn't know how to show you he loved you anymore."

I watched Nat with a scrupulous eye. I bathed in his words, soaking in his wisdom, and nodded. It felt like the pieces of those memories had rearranged themselves. They could fit into a clearer picture of the man my father was at the end. A man so broken by his illness, so tortured by the possibility of losing everything dear to him, he had pushed everyone away. *He didn't know how to show you he loved you anymore.* Maybe that was a truth I could stick by, something that could let me swallow the bitter pill that was those last few years.

I took a deep breath between tears and took a step back. My mind cleared a little, and I turned back to the window. It felt easier to talk when one wasn't face-to-face with another person.

"I couldn't get him the help he needed. The waiting lists were too long, and I didn't have the money to go private," I said with a sniff.

The darkness outside made this whole conversation seem pointless. But I respected Nat's point of view. It did feel good to let this out.

"So, I did the work myself. A full-time carer, with a full-time job. I cleaned up. I made sure he took his pills. And he'd shout his abuse, slam things, throw others." My voice quivered. "And I took it." I saw my reflection peering back at me through the glass. "No one else was going to look after him.

"If you're wondering why I'm reckless," I said, turning to

face Nat, "it's because I don't see the point in being anything else. I've been cautious with everything in my life, pinpointing all my faults, bettering them as I go along. My whole life was carefully planned, Nat. To excessive detail. Each diploma, each university, each job. To achieve the best I ever could. And when this illness came along, not only did it throw everything in the air, it took away everything my dad ever taught me. Every lesson. The *"forgive-yourself"* lessons and the *"try-your-best"* lessons too."

I paused to catch my breath. Nat was still listening, his gaze glued to me.

"Because none of it mattered in the end. And now, here we are, on this stupid, ridiculous-looking station, our lives in danger, and the possibility of something so much more serious going on. And the funny part in all this," I said, with a sarcastic chuckle, "is that I wouldn't be here if I hadn't started thinking that way."

Nat's brow furrowed. "How so?"

"I take it, when you got the call, that you asked all the important questions: for how long, how much am I getting paid, how *real* is this? But I answered the phone, and Frederikson said we'd be moved to the Observer for the duration of the job, and I just said 'yes.' No questions asked. Just get me out of here. Away from this reality. Whisk me to some other place, because I can't deal with this anymore. And look where that landed us."

"Alex. You can't seriously be blaming yourself for everything that's happened?"

"I *saw* him, Nat. I saw Hagen's grin right before he pushed the send button on that second message. I saw it, and I didn't do anything. So, yeah, you're free to stand there and tell me I deserve to live, tell me I did everything right. Tell me it wasn't my fault. But I won't believe you."

Nat stepped up to me once more. "You did everything you could, in the time given to you. And that applies to everything: your dad, Hagen, and outside this station." His shoulders dropped. "If you ask me, you're still living by your dad's philosophy. And I think that's a good thing. It means not everything of his was lost, and that, even though you were being reckless, you still *did* try your best, still trying to correct whatever faults you see. You just need to be kinder on yourself. And, at some point, you need to learn to put yourself first."

I stopped breathing for a second. In a way, I did believe him. It was hard to let go of such convictions. But there was still an underlying anger. Something I couldn't quite put my finger on.

"You know, I've been thinking..." Joana had been sitting and staring at the screens with the Hub Bunker CCTV, drumming her fingers on the armrest. "These 702 people aboard. That number is not in the least bit accurate."

"How so?" I asked, grabbing a chair and sitting by Joana's side.

Nat perched himself on a nearby desk. A sadness lingered around him, and I struggled not to feel guilty about the conversation I'd just had with him. Yes, a lot of the things he said made sense. But I know now, that it takes a long time to work through your beliefs. To *truly* change.

"Well, this is no secret, but Hagen often brought people aboard without permission. He has his own personal docking station near his apartment, his own rocket, his own spacecraft. Sometimes he brought his wife, or *then*-wife, I should say. His guests didn't always have wristbands. And when they did, they were allocated from Hagen's personal stash."

"And those weren't always accounted for?" asked Nat.

"No. And these were only rumours. But more importantly, there were also plenty of wristbands that were stolen and never disconnected. Kids under a certain age don't use them at all. The wristbands mostly help with customer purchases and accessing hotel rooms, not monitoring how many people are aboard or where those people are. So, the 702 figure I gave you may be completely inaccurate."

"What about the Ascension, the shuttle? Was it docked?" I asked.

"Let me see if I can find that info…" Joana's voice dropped as her attention focused on the screen. "It *was* docked. But they disengaged from the Observer shortly after the attack."

"With people aboard?"

"I don't know… I can't see that anywhere here, but I doubt they scanned their passport information before boarding, so we have no way of knowing until they land."

"In some way, that's a relief," said Nat. "At least some people managed to get out unscathed."

Their eyes drifted to me, and I felt a drop in my gut. But I didn't know what to add to the conversation. For some reason, they saw me as in charge. As if a linguist would know what to do in these situations. A linguist struggling with her own self-worth. I stopped myself from shaking my head.

The CCTV still remained on one of the screens. The group that had been arguing had now split into factions, each sitting on opposite sides of the Hub Bunker. The tension was palpable even through the screen. The boy with the bouncing leg now stared at his phone, scrolling endlessly.

Catching Nat's eye, I knew he had had the same thought whilst Joana had been talking: what if those droids had jumped onto the Ascension before it had disengaged? People on Earth could be fighting them off right now.

I walked away—it was all too much to think about. I didn't want to watch the few remaining survivors cry on CCTV, just like I didn't want to watch Earth crumble from the Observer. Patience was a virtue, as they said, but time was testing that.

Nat appeared behind me. "You could use this." In his hands he held a bottle of spiced rum, the decorative label intact but the screw cap unfastened. "Well, maybe we all could." The three of us sat on the mezzanine steps, and, between us, the bottle of rum was shared.

"I found these as well." Joana pulled out an elegant and decorated box of chocolates, a delicate bow placed atop. *"Happy Anniversary, Karen,"* she read, "I think they were meant for my boss's wife." She unfastened the bow and opened the box. Beside it, she placed bottles of water that she had pried from a busted vending machine.

I grabbed a chocolate from the box—dark in colour, with salt flakes sprinkled atop. "These remind me of the ones you could get back home," I said. "I grew up in this little French town; they had a chocolatier on the high street. They'd always pack them in little boxes like this." I popped it in my mouth—the first thing we had eaten since this whole mess had started, and it tasted like home.

"Does your boss usually keep alcohol in his desk?" asked Nat.

"Yeah. And to be honest, you can smell it on his breath most days. Well, the rum anyway. I didn't know the chocolates would be there. That was just a nice surprise." Eyes lowered to the ground, Joana took a moment to reflect before continuing, "Odd to think he's dead now. His wife will never know..." Her voice drifted off as the collective guilt settled in. Another reflection on how much life could change by the time we'd touch soil again. The chocolatier might no longer exist. Funerals could be in high demand. People you knew could be gone in the fraction of a second.

We had spoken to B-4250 only an hour ago, but it had felt like several had passed. How was Earth reacting to the news? Would they hold an emergency UN meeting and send up troops to deal with the carnage? Would they even be able to defeat all the droids, or would there be a large human cost? I wasn't even sure the UN would get involved, with all the issues happening on Earth at the moment. Severe droughts, extreme heat, flooding, rising tensions in East Asia, and multiple wars: they had enough on their plate, without adding an alien invasion to the mix.

Alien invasion... it felt odd to think of it that way. Was it an invasion? Or were they defending themselves from the threatening message sent by Hagen? Had they even understood it? They had reacted so fast, maybe they were already on their way and hadn't even listened to the last message. What were their intentions? They wanted to disable the Observer, but why?

It was useless to think of these things at this time. We had no answers. All we had was the station beneath our feet, and the lives huddled in Hub Bunkers to try and look after from a distance.

"How do you think they're feeling in the Bunkers?" I asked. For some reason, I couldn't shake the image of the boy checking his phone, his leg bouncing up and down. The sheer terror that teenager was facing. He might never see his school friends again. Might never graduate or get the job he's wanted since he was ten. Had he ever experienced love or had his first kiss?

"I wouldn't worry about that, right now," replied Nat. "There's nothing you can do." He took a sip of the rum, before passing the bottle to me.

"I'm sure they're waiting for help, like us." Joana raised a smile and placed her hand on my shoulder.

"Tell us about this town you grew up in." Nat's interest was clear through the tone in his voice, but I was well aware he had changed the subject on purpose. And perhaps it was time to think of something other than death.

"There's not much to tell, really." I thought back to the sleepy place I had called home. Where my father had brought me up. "It's quiet, not that remarkable."

"So, you're telling me there was *nothing* special about it?"

I pondered it for a moment. "There was this little street you could walk up, old cobbles, no pavement, only the houses and the stone under your feet. If you kept walking, you'd go through an iron gate. It would open up, and you would walk into a small park. Just a bit of grass and a wall, really. By the edge of the greenery, there's this wooden bench that overlooks the valley below." Remembering that sunny afternoon so many years ago, my friend, Mathilde, and me, sitting on that bench, rollerblades on our feet, ice cream in our hands. It had been a good time, before life had gotten too difficult. At an age where fun and innocence still reigned and the pains that come with growing up waited at the crest of the hill. "That was my favourite place."

"Sounds quite quaint. There's lots of little hidden gems like that in Funchal too," said Joana.

"Is that where you're from?" I asked.

"It's where I've been my whole life. My home. I went to Aalborg University, in Denmark, for a while, but it was never home."

We sat in silence for a while, revisiting past memories and happy places in our minds.

I stood up, walked a few feet to the window once more and watched the stars glow in the dark. My eyes hopped from star to star, imagining the planets that could surround them. Countless worlds existed out there, with an infinite number of Earth-sized rocks. Was there a planet, somewhere, suffering a similar fate to ours? A world entering their next mass extinction, being threatened by an alien species? Were the survivors hopeful, or using their last few minutes alive to relate and connect and empathise with their loved ones?

I felt a sudden emptiness under my feet. Although I stood on solid metal, pulled down by artificial gravity, there was nothing after that. An emptiness so vast, I could die within seconds if it was somehow pulled from under me. Like the team in that meeting room. Like David. My heart weighed heavy, but my eyes kept fluttering from star to star. My dad had taught me the major constellations, not with a telescope or anything fancy, only what could be seen with the naked eye. Sometimes I would make up my own constellations, in my childlike wonder. Trying to memorise them had been hard, and so I had often forgotten them the next day and would start again from scratch.

I tried to bring myself back to that level of childhood innocence, of guilt-free imagination. Of eating an ice cream on a bench at age ten, or looking for patterns in the stars where there were none at age seven. But the harder I peered at the stars, the more I saw things I didn't like: a dead body, hanging; the shape of one of those droids; a huge ship, steadily making its way over. I blinked and inched closer to the window. *A huge ship.*

"Guys, can you—" I started.

Alarms blared out all through Comms. Joana jumped to her feet and up the mezzanine. Standing in front of a screen, her eyes fell on Nat as he followed her up.

"There's something out there," she said, peering over her screen towards me.

I turned and faced the distortion of light outside, the reflection of a thousand stars bouncing off this massive structure, moving at considerable speed towards us.

"They know we're here. That we're still alive," I said, a shake in my voice.

Its size grew as it got closer—sizeable enough to carry thousands of humans. Although difficult to see, it seemed to be shaped like a traditional blimp, but covered in a dark, mirror-like substance or metal. Camouflaged and blending perfectly in the darkness. A ship that size should have appeared on the Observer's radar system.

"You think they caught our transmissions to B-4250? Or the pulse signal?" asked Nat.

I couldn't keep my eyes off it. "It's our fault... We sent it out." I spun around to Nat and Joana. "What if they got to B-4250 because of us? What if they slaughter the rest of the people—"

"We need to get off this station," continued Joana.

"We could use one of the Hub Bunkers for safety," said Nat.

"Where's the nearest one?"

I didn't have the heart to tell them that a ship like that

could blast us into oblivion faster than we could make it to a Bunker.

"One floor down, but I saw a bunch of those things last time I checked the CCTV," said Joana, grabbing whatever she could, bits and pieces of tech. Nat grabbed his gun off the side, checking how many bullets were loaded.

"Let me try something first." I threw myself up the mezzanine stairs and towards the computer we used to speak to BioTech. My heart raced, but I needed to *know*. "B-4250, come in. This is OBS05." A crackly line.

"OBS05… I see it… What the fuck is that?" The man's voice crackled and grew unsteady.

"B-4250, you need to evacuate immediately."

"Oh my g—" Pure terror.

Scraping, a scream, and then nothing.

"B-4250? B-4250, come in." I hesitated. But I knew what it meant. Turning to Joana, I asked, "Do we have a view on them?"

"We could try a telescope, but we've taken a lot of damage to our equip—." Her voice stopped as the lights went out. The distant thrum of engines and servers slowed to a standstill.

"We don't have time, Alex. I'm sorry. We need to get moving." Nat waited.

Tears formed in my eyes. This was on me. This was *my* fault. Why the fuck did I get in touch with them? Everything kept going wrong. I slammed the headset down.

"What if they cut the air next?" asked Joana, her hand clenched up to her mouth, not quite covering the quiver on her chin.

"Come on," said Nat, directing both Joana and me to the door, the emergency exit sign guiding his way. "Stay behind me, okay? We'll get out of this."

ALEXANDRA GAUTHIER'S DIGITAL ARCHIVE

From: Brooks & Curtis Funeral Directors

To: Alexandra Gauthier

Date: December, 11th 2047 14:32

Location: Bills Folder

Subject: Money claim submitted for Ms. Gauthier invoice 019-256

Dear Ms. Gauthier,

Regrettably, the long overdue invoice 019-256 has not been settled despite many attempts to resolve the issue of the missed payment. Therefore, the money claim for the amount due has been submitted to HM Courts and Tribunal Services by our team at Brooks & Curtis Funeral Directors.

The court fees have been added to your debt, and the amount due is £8,968.36, as is evident via the attached invoice. Every stage in a money claim process incurs extra fees. Please make the payment as soon as possible. We understand that grief may delay this process. However, this postponement has endured too long, as per our previous correspondence with you.

The next stage of this claim will result in a judgement issued against yourself, Ms. Gauthier, and this will impact your personal credit rating. You can avoid this by settling the amount due before the case progresses. Should the claim progress beyond a judgement being issued, a warrant will be provided, and bailiffs will visit your premises to collect the outstanding amount.

Thank you for your attention. We hope for an amicable resolution to this issue; it isn't too late.

Best regards,

Steven Brooks

Funeral Director at Brooks & Curtis Funeral Directors

7

"Wait." Joana had stopped at the unopened door. Nat and I halted in our tracks and waited for Joana to continue. "I don't think this is wise. If we make any kind of noise... What if it attracts them?"

"Wouldn't it be better to get somewhere that has thicker walls? Like a Bunker?" asked Nat. The impatience in his voice rose with every second we stayed in Comms.

"No, she's right," I added. My thoughts raced. There was a solution here, somewhere, if I could just put my finger on it. Turning from the door, I took in our surroundings once more. Although the darkness encompassed us, the exit lights shone enough that I could make out the layout of the room.

"We need to go," pressed Nat.

The carnage in the space around us became a little clearer to my eyes: the loose wires, the broken tech, the thin metal walls keeping us somewhat safe from the vacuum outside.

"Joana, how did they not spot you?" I turned to my new friend as I spoke these words, my brain ticking, thinking of a solution.

"I... I don't know..." Joana released a half-panicked shrug

with her response.

"You were hiding in the metal filing cabinet. But they can clearly see or sense people behind metal. Or maybe they couldn't hear you. Or maybe..." The bodies of retail workers had been behind workstations, cheap chip-wood desks and battery-operated tablets in their hands. People walking around the park had been slaughtered on sight. But the people in Hub Bunkers hadn't been spotted or chased down. My mind swirled with ideas, but they were not formulating, so I spoke out loud once more. "So metal isn't what hid you. I think they operate mostly on sight. They saw us... in the boardroom, through the window. But I think there's more to it than that. If the Hub Bunkers provide safety from them, and *you* found safety here, then what connects you to them?"

We all took a moment, silence filling the air as we thought through possible options.

"Heat detection? Are the Hub Bunkers warm, like the servers downstairs are?" said Nat.

"They came right up to the cabinet I was in," replied Joana. "I thought I was— They didn't find me though." She tore her gaze away from us.

"Look, I don't think we have time for this." Nat's hands fidgeted.

"Joana, how much wiring is in your leg?"

"I'm not—"

"A lot," interrupted Nat, now on the same wavelength. "It needs to imitate the nervous system as close as it can, to replicate feeling and movement." He stared in Joana's direction. "Sorry, Jo."

"I don't understand..." she started.

"How much electrical wiring around a Hub Bunker?" I asked.

She caught on. "Enough to provide oxygen, food, and water, to recycle it all for a period of thirty days. They have their own backup generator if the power fails. Heat generator, all that stuff."

"So—" I started, but the ground under our feet shook at that instant. The whole station shifted to one side, throwing us all against the wall. Bolted furniture lifted and flung to one end of the room, smashing and falling towards us. I felt crushed, a sudden stinging sensation across my head. Everything turned to black.

My eyes darted open to a dark room. My head throbbed; a thick pulsating heat radiated around my skull. My face felt wet. I reached to touch it but couldn't move my right hand. Using my left, I wiped two fingers across my forehead. Blood, smeared across my hand. Nausea crept up from my gut. Something had happened. The taste of blood coated my mouth.

Where was I again? Taking in my surroundings, I tried using my right hand to move something in front of me, but I couldn't even budge. There were things on top of me, small things, like loose cables. I couldn't tell what exactly; it was too dark. Was that a desk in front of me, centimetres from my face? Was that why I was bleeding? My eyes darted around once more, but I couldn't take it in. What were those? I focused my eyesight, but everything was blurry. Desks, chairs, screens, tech, cables, maybe? Definitely cables. The Observer, that's where I was. The attack. The wiring that was going to save us from being detected. My hand remained pinned—too dark to see what was trapping it. Something had hit the station. Had it been shot? Were we being boarded?

We needed to get out of here. I moved my left hand to start pushing the furniture. Something moved in the darkness. My hand rested on the desk. Eyes staring back at me, a glint of light reflection. Movement—just one hand, one single finger, resting atop a set of lips. A tear going down a cheek. I froze. I quietened my breathing, but my head swam, and the quieter I tried to be, the more my body told me things were not right. The pain in my right wrist howling at me. My lip quivered; could I hold the pain in? I felt like screaming, wailing, crying.

But I saw the two eyes staring at me and realised they were Nat's. He stayed still. And finally, I realised why. The sound of metal-on-metal, clicking and clacking faintly through the room. I looked down; cables covered a good portion of my body. They had moved around as I had woken. How long had I been out?

I waited. Staring at Nat's eyes in the dark, not sure where the droids were. Was he in pain? I couldn't tell. We waited for what felt like twenty minutes before the metal-on-metal tapping disappeared. Nat waited another five to be sure before I heard his movement. The cables covering him fell to the floor, and he scrambled to my side.

"I can't move... My hand," I whispered between sobs. My head pounded with every sound. He grabbed the desk and moved it. Other pieces of equipment shuffled out of place, and soon I could move my arm freely. It throbbed at the wrist, an obvious sprain.

"Where's Joana?" I whispered.

"I don't know," he replied.

Together we looked for signs of life. The shake must have been of significant force to have displaced furniture that had been bolted to the ground. After moving some more of the debris, we found Joana lying unconscious. She looked peaceful in her sleep. I tapped her cheek with my good hand.

"Hey. Joana. Wake up," I whispered.

Joana's eyes fluttered open. A sharp frown formed across her brow.

"What happened?" She grabbed for her neck and rubbed it.

"I don't know."

"It seems a bit too early for the help we called for..." said Nat.

"We need to barricade ourselves until they get here. It's the only way we can stay alive," I suggested, my eyes still refusing to adjust to anything in front of them.

"We could try the Hub Bunkers?" Nat added.

"I'm not sure we'll make it," replied Joana. She perched herself up, and a look of despondency crossed her face.

A faint nod from Nat in the dark. "Barricade it is."

We found a cramped meeting room under the mezzanine level, sitting at the back, past the towers of servers, and decided this was the best place to hold up until help arrived. We pushed heavy furniture into the room to secure the barricade from the inside. I grabbed as many cables and loose wiring as I could. The idea seemed to have worked when Nat threw the wires over my unconscious body. If those creatures did have a heat sensor, then this plan wouldn't work for long. The Hub Bunkers would work better — the cabling and heat surrounding the entire structure to provide safety from space elements for a long period of time could have confused them, maybe even hid the bodies roaming inside. So, we needed to create a similar environment here, in this tiny room. A shiver ran down my spine at the idea that the people in the Hub Bunkers may not be safe for long. What if the electrical wiring had only confused the droids initially, but not on a thorough search of the station?

The room we had locked ourselves into was only large enough to hold a meeting table and chairs for about eight people. After having moved the table out and some heavy cabinets in, it was a squeeze, but we managed to sit ourselves semi-comfortably on the ground. Cables surrounded us: filling the cabinets, splayed on the walls, and covering our bodies. It occurred to me then that, because they were droids, maybe they avoided killing anything that resembled their own bodies. Maybe they had a blueprint of what a human looked like and hadn't expected innovations created by cyberdoctors. All three of us sat, studying the door.

The blood on my forehead had been wiped away, thanks to Joana's help, but the gash that was there would leave a permanent scar. My head still throbbed, and every now and again, when I moved too quickly, I lost my balance. But I had kept that to myself. There was no need to worry the others just yet. The nausea I experienced was the worst of my symptoms, though: I struggled to keep down the food and drink we had had earlier.

As we sat there all together, the quiet became almost blissful. The overwhelming fatigue from the shuffling of furniture crept up on me. I could close my eyes, but it would not be safe to do so. The droids could be here any minute. As could the rescue team. I perked up every so often, forcing my body awake.

"I think you have a concussion," said Joana.

"What do you mean?" I said. I had understood what she meant, but the idea of it didn't make sense.

"You bumped your head. Your movement is slowed, you seem confused at times. When we get out of here, you need to see a doctor immediately," she replied.

Nat turned to me and then back to the barricade. Any sign of movement, and he would pounce on it.

"I don't think it's that bad," I replied, my eyes closing once more.

"You literally walked into a wall earlier," whispered Joana.

"When?" I had no recollection of that ever happening.

"When we moved the table out." Joana's voice had the inkling of a smile on her lips, maybe trying to find the humour in the situation.

"You should get some rest the both of you. We could be here for a while," said Nat. "I'll keep an eye on you, Alex, just to be sure. I'll need to keep waking you up."

"I don't need you to look after me. I'm fine," I said rather abruptly. I couldn't figure out where this anger was coming from. I simply didn't want to be treated like a child.

"Yeah… Unexplained mood swings is also a symptom of a concussion. Get some rest," he repeated.

"Fine," I said, grumpy and tired. It didn't take long for me to fall into a deep slumber.

I awoke to a shake, gentle but pressing. Concerned, even. I straightened my back, my muscles sore from being thrown around the room only hours ago. No doubt I was actually covered in long-lasting purple bruises under that jumpsuit. Nat's hand remained propped up in the air—a sign for everyone to be quiet and listen.

My vision had somewhat returned to normal. Although still dazed. My head thumped loudly with every slight movement, and my wrist throbbed. Yet, I tried to focus my attention on what was happening past the door.

Outside, a slow click-clack sound moved past us and beyond. Turning in circles. Unsure where to go. They were looking for something. There was more than one; that much was clear. The nausea crept up my gut and into my throat. I couldn't throw up, not now. I moved my hand to my mouth, swallowing whatever vomit had made its way to my tongue. The burning, acidic sensation scraped my throat on the way back down. The click-clack outside the room continued.

I squirmed and sulked down onto the floor, holding my gut with my arms, my head pounding. I noticed Nat holding his gun pointed at the door. Just as the quiet started reassuring us, a metal coil broke through the wall, aimed at nothing in particular. It recoiled before another two crashed through the walls and lashed at the thin air, catching Nat on the shoulder. No one moved, not even Nat, who, teeth gritting through the pain, winced silently. I closed my eyes, hoping the pain in my head would disappear, wishing this moment would end sooner. Either leave us alone or kill us outright. I couldn't bear the thought of being in between life and death.

The droids attacked, but they didn't know what to aim for exactly. The cable theory was right; we were almost invisible to them; or at the very least, it confused them. We just had to keep quiet and still. No movement, no proof of life, in any way these creatures could detect. I opened my eyes again, as new coils flung at random into the small meeting room. Another and another came flying in at different angles and lengths, puncturing the air, snapping at nothing, trying to catch us. The cabinet behind the door fell over, propelled by another coil. It crashed to the ground with a deafening clatter. But we stayed quiet and still. A bead of sweat dripped from my forehead. I didn't dare move. My stomach churned. Another coil sprung out and smashed through the back wall above Joana's head, rupturing the panel. She jumped, clasping her mouth with her hand, and let out a small yelp. We had lost the fight with silence.

The puncture in the wall opened the room to the vacuum outside. The pressure dropped. The air syphoned out. More coils flung in as Joana leapt up from her place and ran to the other side of the room. Nat shot two rounds from where the coils had come from, the blast of the gun piercing the remaining air. Not sure when I had gotten up, I huddled in a corner with Joana. Defenceless and out of ideas. Confused and hopeless.

Everything stopped. No more coils. A moment of silence — like the droids' focus had changed. Something was happening on the other side of that door. The click-clacking of the metal droids, quiet below the sound of air escaping the room, continued but more frantic, almost stressed. Faster. Coils could be heard hitting objects. The clattering, smashing, and breaking of things in the room next door gave me the headache of a lifetime. I struggled for air. Joana and Nat stayed still, their faces showing utter uncertainty. But I approached the door, ready to face what was on the other side of it. Ready to find who, or what, had just saved us.

All noises from the Comms room had stopped. Had help finally arrived? Surely it was still too soon? Unless a nearby space station had sent someone? But none of those, especially BioTech, had any military-grade equipment—nothing to stop these droids.

My hands quaked, but I balled them into fists and took a deep breath, rescuing any leftover oxygen from the leak behind us. Nat and Joana had not said anything, but the expressions on their faces told me they were thinking the same thing. The quiet was threatening. What else had come to kill us?

I took a step closer. There were various holes in the wall, caused by the coils. Air slipped through them. Soon, there would be no oxygen in this area. We would need to move out of here. I peered through one and saw movement, but nothing more. The droids were dead, collapsed on the floor. There was nothing else to be done. I grabbed the door handle.

"Alex!" Nat's whisper called to me in the background, but the temptation to open it was too strong. I swung it open. And there it was. My breath caught in my throat as I stood, looking up in disbelief.

A living, breathing creature standing over two and a half metres tall. It was thin and balanced its weight on its rear hock joints: a digitigrade-type being. My eyes moved slowly up its frame. Its two arms extended long and blended in with its suit in a way that it was hard to tell which were its limbs and which were strands of fabric. Its chest protruded further out than its hollow gut, a crescent-shaped piece of armour spreading from its extended neck to its concave abdomen. Its dark grey suit, fitted to the creature's measurements, covered it from head to toe, other than its face, which was framed by a thin helmet and a purple visor. Behind the visor glared two wide, bright eyes peering back at me.

The nausea crawled its way back up my throat. My heart beat the fastest it could possibly go. Behind me, silence prevailed. Or were my new friends talking? I couldn't tell. Everything that had ever mattered stopped here. In this moment.

I noticed it breathing—its upper chest pumped up and down in quick succession. Was it tired? Or was that its normal breathing pattern? For the first time in a full minute, I blinked away and looked at the carnage surrounding the creature: the droids all lay on the floor, destroyed, broken, dead. It had killed them. But why?

I tried to speak, but my voice caught in my throat. What could I even possibly say? 'Thank you'? It wouldn't understand. 'Why?' was a more pressing question. But for this creature to understand the concept of 'Why?' within the first few minutes of our meeting would be impossible, let alone for me to understand its answer.

Movement behind the creature rattled me. More droids. I stumbled back, shaking, and bumped into the wall. Feeling Nat and Joana by my side, I was dragged back towards the open doorway, but not before I saw what happened next.

The creature swivelled and somehow readied itself, posed, like a tiger ready to pounce. A tangled mess of metal limbs approached, crawling over each other like a swarm of rats. They scrambled at full speed. The creature ran towards the pack, letting its arms mimic the strands of fabric alongside them. Camouflage. My lips quivered open in both shock and awe. We weren't just seeing an alien for the first time; we were watching it defend itself. Its speed was incredible. It stopped, the fabrics flailing forward in the rush of air, two thick coils flailing out in place of its arms and sweeping the droids off their feet. It danced around them, using more coils as extendible legs, walking over them, and escaping their attacks with elegance and beauty. It crushed the droids one by one, always with such precision that would have taken years to master. I watched its every movement. This creature may have saved them—twice—but it was still using the same tech the droids were. What was this creature? Whose side did it stand on? Was it an escapee? Or a dissident? Did it make these droids? Why would they unleash them, only to have one of their own save a few humans?

The creature swung itself into another sidestep, dancing with these metallic whips, directing them with exactness, silently stepping into place, and escaping every jab thrown at it. The thick coils it controlled lurched wide, piercing the cores of the last two droids. The lifeless carapaces fell to the ground as the coils retracted towards the alien and into a device attached to its back. It turned back to us. Nat and Joana were by my side now; I could feel them but had no idea how long they had been standing there.

"What the flying f..." Joana muttered under her breath.

I wasn't sure what to do... What was the procedure for this? Was there a protocol for *'alien saves humans'*? I stepped forward—the only thing I could do.

"Alex." Nat's caution was dust in the wind. Something drew me in. The creature closed the gap towards me.

"Alex, it's dangerous..." he continued.

It moved with caution, balancing its body weight perfectly on its hind legs, to the same degree a human ballet dancer would: with poise, elegance and full control. It edged around the droids devoid of life. Each step I took was a step closer to a connection no human had ever had. A connection worth unknown knowledge, unknown truths about the universe— dreams scientists had been yearning for, for centuries and millennia, ever since the first intelligent human being looked up at the night sky and wondered what else was out there. And like me, it seemed intent on meeting the new creature in front of it.

Soon, we were face-to-face. There was peace here. A moment of calm and recognition: there were no ill-intents, only a look of utter wonder and a hint of sadness in both our eyes. The creature lifted one gloved hand gently, and I noticed it only had three fingers and an opposable thumb. It placed the tips of its fingers on my chest and slid them wider, until its palm fully pressed onto my sternum. I felt an immediate surge of pain, a horrific pull from the depths of my chest, crushing all my ribs together, my heart suffocating in the middle. The hand left my body. I gasped and fell to my knees. Tears poured down my cheeks. The pain caught in my throat. Nat and Joana were shouting, but nothing made sense. The pain was... It felt like my chest and ribs were being ripped apart. An agony so deep, it paralysed me. As if this creature had pulled all the heartbreak and sorrow I had ever felt, to show me that it had seen it, that it knew. *'Here is your pain, your truth. I see it, and I see you'*. It lingered ever more. I held on, hoping it would disappear, but it didn't. The pain stayed. How much longer would this last? I gasped for air. What had it done?

The creature knelt down in front of me. It caught my eye and placed its own fingers on its chest and spread them wide. The pain renewed: a second flash of agony in my heart, but lighter than the first. The pain moved, swirled, evaporated somewhere else. Still felt, but not as strong. Veiled. I looked at the creature in front of me and saw the same affliction in its eyes. A shared pain. I understood now. This wasn't a new ailment or a new hurt. It was *my* pain, my heartbreak. The pain I had suffered, had stuffed into the depths of my person, had not wanted to confront all these years. All of it was here. Right now. On display, for this creature to see. No... to *feel*. It felt with me. It was sharing the load. I could see it now — a ghostly, purple tether, wispy in nature, connecting us both.

I dropped my head and stared at the ground. My mind spun, still pounding from the concussion. More tears came to my eyes. Nothing made sense. Why here? Why now? Why couldn't it have left me alone? It wasn't fair, to feel this much aching in one person. How could anyone survive this? Why would anyone *want* to survive this? This pain was a monster. It had lurked in the darkness, creeping up every so often to torment me. But I had pushed it down. Put it away. Left it to rot and succumb to its own horrific death. So I didn't have to deal with this. This...

This was my pain. I needed to accept it. I knew that. More tears formed as the discomfort remained and pulled at my heart. This was *my* pain. *My grief.* The weight of everything sank me into the ground, but I realised that this was normal. The hurt, and heartbreak, and grief... They were... normal. I was allowed to feel these things. Why had I not allowed myself to? Why had I pushed it all away? For work? For... my father? Had I been so scared to confront my true feelings?

The agony in my chest remained but subsided enough that I could focus on my surroundings once more. Where were we? Surely there could be more droids coming? I looked up. The purple tether floated between us, connecting me to this alien, a line tying our souls together.

Nat had the gun pointed at the creature's head. Joana was pleading with him. The creature's eyes were glued to mine.

"—the gun down! You don't know what it's done! Give it a chance!" shouted Joana. Her voice was shrill, each syllable a stab in my head.

"Do you see it?" I said finally, my eyes blurred from tears, focused on the creature, but I was talking to Nat and Joana. In my periphery, they hesitated, but I could see Nat's chest pumping up and down. Anger, through and through.

"See what?" said Joana.

I lifted my hand slowly, my fingers touching the tether between my chest and the creature's. I couldn't feel it. It seemed lighter in colour than it had been only a few seconds ago. Was it disappearing?

"Alex. What the fuck is going on? Are you okay?" asked Nat. The waiver in his voice gave away his fear.

"I'm okay," I replied, taking some deep breaths. "I think it… bonded with me in some way."

"What do you mean?"

The nausea still toyed with my gut, but, hidden underneath those immediate sensations, was something else. A feeling of empathy, alongside curiosity and sadness. And although I had plenty of those feelings myself, they were not mine.

"Emotionally. We're connected somehow. She feels my emotions, and I feel hers."

"Hers?" asked Joana.

"It's a she. I can feel it," I replied.

Nat lowered the gun finally, now aiming at the floor. Around us, the air from Comms was still being syphoned out through the holes in the meeting room. We only had limited time.

"This doesn't make any sense!" he belted out. "How does it have the same weapons as those droids?" He waved his unoccupied hand about in frustration. "Why did it save us? Why… Why is any of this happening?!" He knelt down, placing the gun on the floor, before rubbing his hands over his face. A patch of blood covered the top of his shoulder where he had been hit. Silence remained stagnant for a while as we all caught our breath.

The creature turned away, looking back at the mezzanine area of the room and back at me. Its— *Her* facial features were difficult to discern behind the visor she wore. But the tether reminded me I didn't need to read alien body language. She was scared. It was time to go.

"She wants us to follow her," I said.

"What do you mean? Follow her where?" asked Nat.

I felt her feelings deeply. A protected place. A place she could control. "To safety."

"Does that mean Earth?" he asked. "Because to me that means Earth. Home. *That's* our safety." His anger grew. "How does it know what is safe for us? It doesn't even know what air we breathe, or what atmospheric pressure we need."

"We all want to go home, Nat," added Joana, crossing her arms across her chest, tears in her eyes.

He sighed in frustration. Moving up to Nat, I grabbed one of his hands.

"I know this is confusing and scary, but I think she knows something we don't. She's trying to help. If she wanted to harm us, she would have done that already. If she was capturing us, we would be marching out of here by now. Trust me. We'll stop and get some suits before we go any further. But I *need* you to believe me." Our eyes met, and he nodded, reluctantly.

"Okay," he said. There was a lot more he wanted to say, I could tell.

OBSERVER DIGITAL ARCHIVE
Conduct, Safety and Security n. 4:

"Please do not use the docking bays unless authorised to do so."

Unauthorised docking is defined as follows: docking, the act of 'parking', 'landing', or 'anchoring' to the Observer, that has not been expressly agreed to, in writing only, by a senior member of staff authorised to do so.

Unauthorised docking will be punishable by law, as per Sections 32 to 34 of the United Nations Office for Outer Space (UNOOSA's) 'Convention on International Liability for Damage Caused by Space Objects' (amended 2042), and any perpetrators or alleged perpetrators will be brought to justice swiftly.

Negligent use of power, such as encouraging or allowing unauthorised vehicles to dock, by any member of staff or the public will result in severe legal consequences and possible incarceration.

Due to the possible environmental ramifications of unauthorised docking, the repercussions will not be light. These environmental ramifications could result in: damage to the external structure of the Observer, damage to the docking bays (destined for use by vital cargo ships), damage to the breathable atmosphere within the Observer, or possible disruption to the safe orbit of the Observer. Should the perpetrators be found guilty, any damages caused to the Observer will be repaid in full by the offending party.

The safety of our guests is our highest priority. Should you or anyone you know be involved in, suspect, or hear anything regarding unauthorised docking, please report to a senior member of staff immediately.

8

"I still don't think this is a good idea," said Nat.

All together, we had made our way back up the mezzanine, stepping over the corpses of droids, with their heads cracked and limbs flat on the ground, buzzing and whirring gently. Some of them contained bullet holes—Nat had clearly hit them, yet the bullets seemed to have only hit their surface, denting them rather than stopping them. I wasn't sure how many more of them were out there. But this alien, now marching with us, had managed to defeat them with relative ease. I couldn't be sure she'd be willing to do the same for us every time the droids showed up. What was in it for her?

With the power cut and the backup generators not connected, the computer screens at the top of the mezzanine sat dead. Lifeless screens that once told us where the damage was, that once shared footage of the few remaining lives left on the station.

"I know," I replied. He was right to be nervous; anyone would be. And the only reason I wasn't was based purely on the feelings emanating from this fading, purple tether, connecting me and her in a way that no human has ever felt.

Yet the thought saddened me: here we were, at the cusp of humanity's greatest moment, having just met, not one but two different forms of aliens, and we weren't sure we could fully trust the one that had just saved us. She was trying to whisk us away, to get us to safety. And Nat was right to ask the question. *What does safety look like to her?* Do they know what humans breathe, what atmospheric pressure they were used to, or if the suits would support the temperatures these aliens lived in?

But we had little choice. This station was crumbling under our very feet, and this creature, ambling behind us now, had offered us a lifeline. I knew we were safer with it, than alone.

We stopped at the Suit Station, the same one Nat and I had used earlier to repair the Comms link. It felt like a lifetime ago, but it had only been a few hours, and in that time, everything had changed.

"The suits give us a good ten hours of air. That gives *us* ten hours to tell them what humans need to survive," I said. My head was still drumming from the concussion, but luckily the nausea had alleviated.

Nat shook his head. There was more to it than that, but my heart pulled me to the creature standing there, staring at us as we changed into suits. I wasn't sure if my own curiosity did the pulling, or if it was this bond holding us together, an indistinguishable *need* to know, a need to be around her. There was a strong chance I would never know the difference.

The alien's lanky form stood still in the frame of the door; her head bowed so as not to bump into the ceiling. Her feet spread about a metre apart, like she was ready to start running if needed, even though there was no immediate sign of danger. Were their species particularly skittish, I wondered.

After helping each other fit our suits tightly, making sure there were no gaps, we all grabbed a helmet. Wristpads lay to the side, unused. I slipped one on, and it displayed the temperature, oxygen levels, and more numbers than I knew what to do with. I picked another two up and passed them to Nat and Joana.

Nat paused by one of the desks, and reluctantly placed the gun down, leaving it behind. We had recognised its futility in the face of the droids, and it would place more of a risk, if it were ever to go off and puncture a suit. It looked as though it saddened him to leave it, like he could have relied on it when in danger. Like he was now defenceless and putting his life in the hands of uncertainty.

Looking at him feel these things suddenly made me realise what was truly going on: we had no idea where we were going, or what would happen next. My stomach dropped as the fear settled in. The alien turned its head to me sharply, as if analysing my emotions. The peering purple helmet glared at me, inciting more nerves to course through my body. She stepped back. She didn't want to pose a threat.

"What's going on?" asked Joana.

I paused, inspecting her behaviour. "She doesn't want us to be scared of her."

"Good luck with that," muttered Nat. He turned away from the gun on the desk. "We ready?"

Joana and I nodded, and we turned towards the alien. She understood we were prepared and led us away from Comms and towards the concrete set of stairs by the elevator. She had not said anything; although I knew that if she did, we wouldn't understand anything anyway. She moved slowly, raising heavy legs down the stairs. Under the emergency lighting, the alien's slender and curved silhouette sent shivers down my spine.

We walked at a fast and steady pace, passing through doors in silence to not attract unwanted visitors. This was an area of the station I had not been acquainted with. We had descended further than Level 0, where the plaza and the shops were located, but not so far as to reach the hotel.

Above our heads, emergency lights flickered. The station

itself grew eerily quiet, continuing its powerless orbit distantly around the Earth.

A few signs on doors indicated we were in staff-only areas. On any other day, this place would have been bustling with staff and crew, monitoring the station's status and prepping for new guests arriving. Around us, the crew's ghosts chilled the air.

Pushing through a set of doors, we walked into another endless and unrecognisable corridor. And although this place was a maze, the alien took all turns with confidence and determination, as if pulled towards a clear direction.

But before I knew it, we had arrived at a large room, which I recognised immediately as the lobby of the station. Only a week ago or so had I entered this space for the first time. Had I been a different person back then? I felt different—all the things that had happened: the constant conflict with Hagen, meeting Nat and feeling a flicker of hope, of something special blooming, to watching David die a horrific death and being on the run ever since. And meeting an organic alien, full of life and energy and *feeling*. I sensed I was a different person, but I didn't know how, or whether the change was good.

In front of me, the displays of the Conduct, Safety and Security rules were still plastered across the walls, now useless to the empty halls and decaying station. The large reception desk remained intact, like nothing had ever happened. Somewhere beyond my sight, I heard a gentle rush, like air seeping from another breach in the hull of the Observer.

Our new alien friend turned, tapped my helmet, nestled under my arm, then placed her hand on my head. Her pressure was firm, yet not invasive or overly zealous. We followed the creature's suggestion, slipping the helmets on and fastening them to our suits, and waited further instruction.

Did it know *everything*? Where it was going, through the maze of staff tunnels on a space station it had never visited? When helmets would be life-saving to human beings? What else did it know?

For a fleeting moment, I wanted to know everything, to ask it questions I had only ever dreamed of asking. Did they understand some of the cataclysmic secrets of the universe? How did it all start, or where dark matter came from? Were there other species out there, and what was at the centre of a black hole?

But the rattling and scurrying of escaping air grew louder, and I was brought back to reality. We approached one of the tunnels leading to the docking bays. The thickness of my helmet could not cover the terrifying whooshing sound of air slipping through the cracks and disappearing into the emptiness outside.

I glanced around at my team, trying to gauge their feelings in this moment. Nat threw a passing smile at me, and his hand pressed in the small of my back, leading me forward with the rest of the group. Even through the thickness of the suit, the pressure was comforting. My heart fluttered for a second but was cut short when the creature stopped and turned to stare at me. Her helmet close to mine, she inspected me up and down. Her eyes flickered between Nat and me. Had it felt what I had felt? A rush of hot air crept up my neck now. There were never going to be secrets between me and this alien if that tether remained in place.

"What's wrong?" asked Joana. "Why did it stop?"

"I think it was worried," I replied.

"About what?"

"I don't know," I said, almost too fast.

We continued further down the docking tunnel, which stretched out before us, until we arrived at an airlock. The creature stopped in its tracks once more. This time, *I* felt a pang of fear. Adrenaline coursed through the tether, now almost invisible, before I had noticed the movement through the glass of the airlock. The metal coils slipped out from the contraption on the alien's back, imitating the strands of fabric hanging from her shoulders as it had done previously. The creature forced the doors open using the coils, pulling them apart with ease. The pressure dropped instantly.

"Hold on," shouted Nat through the helmet radio, as we felt the air slip through the widening crack of the airlock door. The docking tunnel wavered, holding on by loose brackets, and cracking under the pressure of a dozen or so droids tearing it apart. My weight lessened until my feet barely touched the ground. That all-too-familiar lurch in my gut brought me back to the moment. At the end of the shaft, in the few glimpses I could muster, I made out the form of a ship, or a shuttle perhaps. The alien threw herself forward using her coils, grabbing onto segments of the tunnel, and blocking attacks as she drew herself nearer to her enemies.

I stood by the top of the tunnel, watching the miracle it was to see an alien fight off a predator. But as my toes neared the edge, I noticed the tunnel give way, the last of the bolts and brackets cracking under the pressure. There were no loud thunks or snaps. Just a silent unravelling of metal off metal as it disconnected from the Observer.

"Watch out!" I shouted through the radio, hoping the creature could hear me. The three of us stood at the precipice — the void staring back at us, and the tunnel drifting away silently as the station continued its orbit. There, below us, was an unending emptiness, a direction leading to nowhere, a perpetual fall should one of us misplace our footing.

The alien shuttle shifted position, drifting away from the loose tunnel and closer to the Observer. The creature flung itself from the side of the new space debris. And, using a coil to grab hold of her ship, she manoeuvred herself, landing feet first by a large airlock door, leaving the droids behind. Throughout her actions, I felt her adrenaline pumping through my veins, felt the pull of her muscles as if they were my own.

The shuttle itself was of an unfamiliar design: oblong in shape and rounded edges all over, it seemed to have no up or down. It reminded me of old Zeppelins, a similar shape to the large ship I saw from the Comms room, although in a much, *much* smaller size. The same reflective metal coated the outside. Was this the standard for ships in their community? Towards the back, large engines sat idle. Small manoeuvring thrusters were dotted around its shell, which were used to close the gap between itself and our team.

Once close enough, the alien attached two of its coils to its own ship and two to the outside of the Observer. She was straining to keep the two that close without snapping the contraption on her back. The gap was still there though; the ship couldn't get any closer. Roughly ten metres of empty space—it wasn't much, but enough to give me a sense of vertigo I couldn't escape. I considered my friends: Joana looked terrified, but Nat nodded to me, false confidence in his gaze. I turned to the gap—the stars were waiting underneath. I jumped.

The propulsion had been enough to coast me slowly to my destination. Below, the emptiness sucked me in. I felt like I was falling—my heart dropped every second I watched the nothingness stretch out into infinity.

Being out here again was terrifying enough. The feeling of letting go, still there, still forcing me to choose if I wanted to live. But more than anything, after meeting the alien, after being *bonded* to her, I felt her pull was stronger. Is that what it took for me to save myself?

I landed with a thump close to the airlock, but before I knew it, two familiar arms had reached to grab me. The ship itself looked even sleeker up close: the metals covering it almost polished—a dark, captivating sheen that could engulf me in my entirety if I hadn't torn my gaze away. Was this a new element so completely impervious to space radiation that it would remain undamaged? Was this ship so new that it had never been scratched? The exterior was so bewitching, it was almost surreal.

"Do you want me to push you instead?" asked Nat to Joana. She nodded in response. "Let go, lift your feet." He placed the palms of his hands at the two weightiest points in her body and gave her a gentle shove.

"Ohmygod, ohmygod," she whimpered to herself as she crossed the gap. Joana's breathing had accelerated; it sounded as though she may be crying too.

"You're almost there," I said. "We've got you." Joana's face now in sight, I noticed the fresh tears on her cheeks, glistening under the light of her helmet. I caught her and held her tight.

Finally, Nat jumped and landed with a slight bounce. We huddled on a ledge, and before long, the dark mirrored façade of the airlock slid, and the creature ushered us inside.

This space was small, and the only light we could use came from the individual spotlights on each of our helmets. But the alien, coils retracted into her backpack device, tapped away at a small screen, too high for me to see. I felt her agitation, her stress, and, somewhere deeper, a feeling of guilt. Gravity pulled us down, enough that our feet were secure on the ground, but not enough that I felt my full weight. Was this the gravity on their home planet? The pressure changed, and my ears popped as we adjusted to it. I could hear the hum of the engine and the tapping and shuffling of Nat and Joana moving. The airlock cycled, and the doors into the ship opened.

The darkness enveloped us here too. Heart thumping loudly in my ears. My vision adjusted, and I spotted emergency-type lighting lining the apparent walkways. But before I got a real look at the interior of the ship, another alien blocked my view.

"Oh, shit," whispered Nat, more to himself than anyone else.

My breath caught in my throat once more. As tall and slender as the first, its helmet and visor were a different shade. The curvature in its spine, its hind legs—all those features were still there. They were the same species. But this one appeared a little bulkier, a little wider across the gut than the one that had saved us.

An abrupt sense of frustration enraged me, and it took me

a moment to realise it had come from the tether. As my eyes adapted further to the dark, I understood both aliens were moving, gesticulating, talking. They were having an argument.

"This was never supposed to happen," I said into my helmet, the sudden realisation dawning on me.

"What do you mean?" asked Joana.

"They're arguing. Like we weren't supposed to be picked up. Like we shouldn't be here."

"So, saving us was just an impromptu decision? Why us? Why didn't it find and save the people in the Hub Bunkers?" continued Nat, confusion rising in his voice.

The Hub Bunkers... I had been so distracted by this creature saving us and getting to safety, that I had completely forgotten... I stepped forward, trying to insert myself in the conversation. The only way this alien had spoken to me had been through hand gestures. So I placed a hand on my own chest, on Nat's, and then on Joana's, and pointed to the Observer, now hidden behind the airlock doors, as if to say, *"There's more of us in there."*

But my makeshift sign language didn't seem to do the trick. The alien I had bonded with touched my chest and gestured further into the alien ship. This caused another silent uproar from the second alien. But this one soon relented and disappeared round a corner, its long, gangly legs stepping away fast. We shuffled into the next room, and the airlock doors shut behind us.

Tall ceilings greeted us, along with dark metal walls. Alloy grating covered the floors, also serving as some kind of ventilation system. The hum of the engine was louder in here, and now, I could hear the air-circulation too.

The whole place felt hospitable—liveable even—for humans. I checked my wristpad for any data on the atmosphere we were in. The air pressure seemed about correct, the temperature acceptable. Did these aliens live in these same conditions, or did they know more about Earth than they could let on?

There were no windows to the outside—just a forgiving pull in the ship and a tender rumble beneath our feet as proof we were pushing forward at a gentle pace. It didn't take long for the full force of the ship to kick in: a violent tug that pulled us humans backwards. I stumbled and caught myself. Nat and Joana held each other as they found their feet once again.

The shuttle remained dark and sombre, a reflection of our sense of loss and uncertain future. But I could discern the edges of fixtures in the ship. The ceiling stood much higher here than it did on the Observer—a suitable room size for a species standing just below three metres tall. I felt petite for the first time in a long time. I had often associated feeling small with feeling protected; standing next to a vigilant, force of a man as a father will do that, I guess. But here, it felt oppressive to my senses. Here, I appeared almost insignificant.

As I glanced around the space encompassing me, I noticed Nat paying particular attention to the structure of the shuttle, bending down and inspecting gratings and panels up close. This particular room led to a corridor to the left and a bend leading to the right. Lights dotted the floor and ceiling in patterned colours, an organised yet still confusing mixture of blues and purples. The walls surrounding us were a dark metal, nothing I immediately recognised, but they sounded thick when we stepped further into the ship.

The corridor to the left slid into a compact area: a large seat nestled in the centre, and a series of screens semicircled the chair. The screens themselves were not like human-made ones, but they flickered and presented information and images about the shuttle just the same. The diagrams were understandable at least: a plotted trajectory from the Observer to an unknown, off-screen area. The alien that had argued with our saviour sat there, tapping away at something I couldn't quite see.

"I guess that's our pilot," I said. I had not used the radio— my voice had carried fine in this room.

Nat stood next to me, peering in the same direction. "You might be right," he replied, his voice muffled by the thickness of the suit and the helmet, yet the curiosity in his tone still present.

Round the corner to the right was a simple hole heading both up and down. A mystery for another time.

I turned to the alien I had bonded with. It was time to make things official. The sooner we could start communicating, the earlier I would be able to tell them about the other lost souls on the Observer. I picked up its hand and placed it on my own chest. Her arm, still gloved, was light and felt confidingly fragile. Looking her in the eye, I said, "Alex."

For a moment, I wondered if the creature would know the difference between a personal name and the name of a species. Humans had different names for distinct reasons, and each culture used names in a variety of ways. But I needed to start somewhere.

The creature tapped something on the side of its visor, and for the first time, I could hear it breathe. Its breathing was longer, smooth, almost imperceivable, but also drawn out, compared to the quick, short breaths she had given on the Observer. Had it been struggling in human living conditions?

"*A'ex,*" said the alien.

I flinched. Completely taken aback. My mouth dropped open—had she really just said my name? The first word this alien said was *my* name? Not its own?

"*A'ex,*" repeated the creature. Her voice was soft, smooth and delicate, much like the way she moved. At first impression, they were a cautious and gentle species. Minus the fighting.

The creature had struggled with the 'L' sound but not the 'X'. I wished in that moment that I had pen and paper, or a tablet or laptop, or something to write this all down on. The process would be difficult if I couldn't take notes.

The creature took my hand and placed it on her chest.

"⏐⊢ ⊓⊓╫," she said. For the first time, I heard this creature's language, but the individual sounds were completely indecipherable. They sounded almost guttural, from somewhere deeper inside her being, from an organ that humans maybe did not have. If I had tried to replicate them, they would sound nothing like the sounds this alien had made.

I opened my mouth but stopped myself. It was all too intricate, too… unattainable.

"⊩ ⊓⊤⧸," she said again. But even the second time around, the sounds were still incomprehensible to me. The alien dropped my hand and rushed over to her friend in the pilot's seat. Between them, sounds and voices and words were exchanged. The pilot used the same low speech, a slight shift in tone, but nothing I could make note of. Who knew if the tone difference was down to sex, dialect, culture, or emotional response, but I couldn't wait to figure it all out.

Our rescuer came back with a small, hand-held device between her wiry fingers. Similar to a tablet, it casted a large screen; but instead of a solid image, it more closely resembled a hologram: transparent in nature and viewable from different angles. Beneath the screen sat tiny projectors, all aimed up to cast the image above, and beside them, different buttons with unclear purposes.

The alien keyed in something, and the hologram projected a series of dots and strings. Nat and Joana stood beside us, peeking in at what this could be.

"Is that… A series of atoms?" said Nat. That made sense, but was this creature's name actually on the periodic table? "It's a series of atoms put together," he continued. "I don't know what it is though."

"⊩ ⊓⊤⧸," she repeated.

"Just when Google Translate would be most handy, it isn't here to use…" muttered Nat.

I shook my head, out of habit more than anything else. The alien shook her head too—a simple imitation, but she appeared to have caught on. She tapped some more on her tablet and up popped a hologram of a rock, green in colour, dull, but instantly recognisable.

"An emerald?" said Joana.

"⊢ ⊓⊤⊦," she said.

"Emerald?" I asked. The tether between us felt strong, a comforting tug mixed with a bit of excitement.

I pressed my hand on the creature's chest and repeated, "Emerald."

"⊢ ⊓⊤⊦," she agreed. But the sounds were still so completely foreign to me that I could never reproduce them.

Emerald placed her hand on me and said, "*A'ex.*"

The first introductions were complete. I repeated the process with Nat and Joana, although the actual pronunciation was closer to *''hat'* and *''oana'*. We then immediately moved towards the pilot.

"∟| ‖ ⊨," said Emerald.

Emerald brought up the hologram but stopped as the pilot spoke out.

"⊣ ⊢⊤⊦ ⊢⊤⊓⊦⊦ ∟| ⊢⊥⊦⊦⊓ ⊧," it said.

"⊔ ⊦⊓."

"⊤‖ ⊦⊦⊓ ⊥⊣⊦‖⊦⊓ ⊔⊦∟⊦⊓⊦⊦."

"⊤⊓ ⊦⊦⊤| ⊦."

The hologram popped up the image of something I recognised in shape: a thick trunk that spreads out at the top, a collection of branches permeating and leaves shaping off the ends. The tree became multiple trees and spread wide across the projected image, growing wider by the second. The trees themselves were of an unusual colour, reddish to me. The tree we had started out with was so small now amongst the many others, I couldn't even find it.

"A forest," I muttered to myself. I leant across to the pilot, mimicking the gesture Emerald had taught me, and pressed my hand against its chest for the first time, and said, "Forest." It hadn't flinched. Was touch a routine way of communicating?

"Interesting that they would pick natural elements in the world as their chosen names," said Nat.

"I do wonder if we've been given the equivalent to first, family or clan names or anything of the sort," I said, my mind buzzing with ideas and theories.

"Does it matter? As long as they're happy with the names, it should be respectful enough," he replied. "When you've hashed out the language, you can agree on what names to actually call them." He put his hand on my shoulder, a grin spreading across his face. "This is a ground-breaking moment; I hope you can see that."

I smiled and, in that moment, felt such a rush of pride and warmth that Emerald turned to face me once more. Her head lowered to catch my eye. Our helmets lingered close enough I could actually distinguish more features on her face. Those large round pupils stared right back at me; her eyes were surprisingly sharp, darting from one location to the next. And it dawned on me: these aliens could have evolved from a species that were nocturnal. It would explain the lack of light in the shuttle and the size and shape of their eyes. A working theory at least. Emerald's nose was petite, yet similar in shape to many felines on Earth. And I wondered if I could see fur across her skin.

I wished for a moment that the team of biologists on the Observer had survived the attack. They would have marvelled at the sight of this alien. They would have had so many more questions.

The attack itself still made no sense to me. The droids had intended to kill everyone on the station. But their true objective remained a mystery. Something didn't quite add up.

The shuttle continued at a decent pace, towards an unknown. The first thing I needed to know was where we were going. Looking at the hologram screens in front of our pilot, none of the text made sense to me, but the diagrams felt familiar in a way: scientifically accurate, even in a foreign language and culture.

"Nat, do you understand anything on any of these screens? Charts? Trajectory? ETA?"

He peered over Forest's shoulder. Pointing at one screen, he said, "This looks like a plotted course."

Forest removed Nat's gloved hand from the screen, tapped

the image a few times, showing their destination. An incredibly large ship—large enough to accommodate at least fifty shuttles the size of the one we were in, and more.

"That's a type of carrier ship," he said, pointing without touching. "It's fucking huge."

"What's going to happen to us there?" asked Joana. I peered at her—Joana's eyes were glassy, even in the reflection of the helmet. She hadn't been taking this well.

"I'll try to get that information soon; don't worry," I replied. Addressing Nat, I said, "I don't suppose you could figure out how fast we're moving towards that carrier? We'll need air, food, drink, toilets and sleep at some point."

"Give me a moment. I'm sure I can work something out."

"Em—" I started, but Emerald turned around so fast I didn't get to finish her full name. "Em," I said again, and she seemed to accept this shortened version of her name. "This isn't going to make any sense to you, so hopefully this does…" With a heavy sigh, I grabbed Emerald's hand and dragged her away from the screens and the pilot. Her skinny body followed me, taking half as many steps as I did.

I sat in the centre of the grated floor and tapped the floor opposite me. "Em," I repeated, my tired voice echoing back at me in the helmet. I hadn't realised how exhausted I already felt. My head still throbbing, my wrist still sending shooting pains up my arm and to my hand. Was I really going to be able to decipher a language with a concussion? I had to give it a go. Our survival depended on it.

Emerald sat, immediately catching on, sensing my curiosity through the tether, and matching my feeling. Her gangly legs folded neatly under her, and she waited for further instruction. The alien's spine curved in such a way that she naturally leaned forward, wavering under the sway of the shuttle. In the background, I could hear Nat and Joana talking, calculating how fast the ship had moved in the space of one minute and figuring out the distance left to traverse to our destination on the screen. It would be an approximation, but that's all we could hope for until I understood how they counted, their units of time and measurements, all relative to space.

I took a deep breath—hopefully this was going to work. "Alex," I said, placing my hand on my sternum. "Emerald." I placed my hand on Emerald's chest. I paused before placing one hand on the floor of the ship and one hand on the wall. I didn't want the word for *floor* or for *wall*. I needed the name of the shuttle, or the word *ship*. Em took a moment to reflect; her eyes darted to Forest, lingering on his hidden form behind the chair, and back to the floor, where my hand rested.

"⊓≼≽⊦," she said. Something had changed. The sounds Em had made were not the same. A different language? Had she switched because I had struggled with the sounds before? This collection of phonemes was odd, like sounds that were not supposed to mix. It featured a conglomeration of notes that shouldn't fit together but did.

I repeated the process, and Em replied with the word once more.

"⊓≼≽⊦," I repeated. I pointed to the hologram machine, and Em set to work, found a hologram of a ship, and displayed it.

I grinned. Excitement flowed through me, just as I'm sure it flowed through Emerald. One word down, an infinite number to go.

ALEXANDRA GAUTHIER'S DIGITAL ARCHIVE

From: Giovanni Costa

To: Alexandra Gauthier

Date: January, 21st 2048 11:45

<u>*Location*</u>*: Work Folder*

<u>*Subject*</u>*: Help?*

Good morning, Ms. Gauthier!

I realize it might be inappropriate to speak to you considering you're currenty on sabbatical (at least that's what the other students say!) but I really want you to know that it hasn't been the same since you went. The other students and me have agreed that the new lecturer isn't that great, and it would be super cool if you could come back again. The replacement lecturer doesn't really know us, like you do. I know it wasn't great how it went down last yer, with the whole bullying thing but like, that wasn't really our year group. It was the ones above us. And that was because they didn't really know your style of teaching. You're kinda strict and to me, that's cool. Anyway, I was hoping that, because you're no longer out lecturer that you would help with my assignment? I know spelling and gramma are not my "fortey". I've written most of it, but I'd want to see if it can be improved at all

Thanks,

Giovanni

9

We started by delineating some basic terms by pointing at various objects and parts of the ship and speaking the words out loud. Emerald and Forest also gave their names in this new language so I could repeat them fluidly. After the first fifteen words or so, the sounds slipped from my mind. I needed to find a way to write some of this stuff down. But, more than that, we needed to know whether we would be safe when we got to the carrier—whether we'd be limited by the oxygen of our suits running out.

I knew how to say *'spacesuit'* and mimicked the motion of taking off my helmet. Emerald stared at me with her large, wide eyes and understood, nodding, a gesture of agreement she had gained in the language learning process. It was impressive how fast she had picked up these mannerisms. Although, I regretted that feeling—the species with the superior tech was always going to be smarter.

With Nat and Joana by my side, I looked at my wristpad, where the collection of elements and their percentages were displayed.

"Nitrogen, Oxygen, Argon... They're all here, but I don't

know… I can't say for sure if that's the right amount," said Nat.

We had been on the ship for over an hour now, which meant we had only nine hours before our oxygen tanks would run out. Nat had managed to figure out the trip would take us over four hours to complete.

I mimicked releasing my helmet once more. Emerald nodded again, to emphasise her point.

"It's the right elements; how dangerous can it be?" I said.

"Well—" started Nat.

"Don't answer that," I replied with a smile.

I undid the latch on the helmet and let the air seep in. "I'll put it straight back on if something's wrong." What was there to lose? If we were dead in ten hours, then all this work would have been for nothing anyway. But I also had an inherent feeling that Emerald knew what she was doing. I sensed all of her feelings. Did that mean she couldn't lie to me? Maybe not. But why would she go through the trouble of saving us, only to suffocate us in her ship?

Nat watched me with caution; I could feel his eyes lingering on me. I lifted the helmet, and an overwhelming smell dug its way into my nose. I winced and scrunched my nose up, covering it with my hand.

"You okay?" he said, inching forward, ready to grab my helmet and slam it back on my head.

"It reeks, but I'm okay for now," I said with a laugh. "I don't know. It almost feels thicker, but it's breathable."

With some hesitation, Nat and Joana both took their helmets off.

"Oh my god, what *is* that?"

"It's like iron or something, but clearly not iron," said Nat.

Em sat up straight and analysed the way we had reacted. She grabbed each helmet and pushed them in our direction, begging us to put them back on. I shook my head, but Em insisted. I shook my head again, and Em repeated the head movement, relaxing back in her spot, but I could still feel the caution through the tether.

Emerald and Forest had kept their suits on the entire time. I had assumed it was down to the oxygen, pressure, and all the myriads of biological and atmospheric elements I didn't know well. But by now it had crossed my mind that there were other factors too: bacteria that could cause severe illness if passed from one living creature to another. The same way SARS, COVID or AIDS had jumped from animals to humans as the virus mutated. Or maybe it was only a matter of social etiquette.

I took off one of my gloves and picked up the hologram machine, inspecting it closer. It felt heavier than I had anticipated and cold to the touch. If I could make this work in some way, I could take notes…

Em took it from my hands, fiddled with some keys, and the size of the hologram screen grew in width, almost by a metre. It was blank and had a faint purple tint. Em scrawled with a finger, leaving a permanent mark on the screen, like a digital whiteboard. She was a smart one; she understood my obstacles.

I couldn't take my eyes off her—she was fascinating. She made correct assumptions and helped with things she knew I'd have trouble with. She understood me, even within the first few hours of us meeting. It was like finding a long-lost friend or sibling. Someone who knows you knows how you feel.

With the new whiteboard at my disposal, I made a variety of notes. The words I couldn't remember I scribbled down phonetically, inventing new phonemes to represent sounds that didn't exist in the International Phonetic Alphabet. I kept the process up, touching new things, asking for new words until soon enough, our immediate surroundings were covered. And through time, I soon realised that some of the sounds I had written down were similar to the ones David and I had picked out on the Observer. Those messages, although pronounced differently, used the same language. Our work had not been completely wasted.

I imagined David sitting here by my side. He'd have fallen in love with the process. He would have neglected sleep, food, and drink just to hear more words, to dissect their speech patterns, and their sentence structure. My heart ached at the thought of him. He never got to experience this. Soon, I'd have to ask Emerald what her connection to the droids was like. Were they from the same planet? Were they an invention? Were they allies or enemies? And what did any of this have to do with humans? But I couldn't leap too far.

I continued with simple concepts such as agreeing and disagreeing, thanks to the nodding and shaking of heads. Now, I needed to find a way to pose questions, something that would express requiring an answer. I started adding the word *'question'* at the beginning of any new word I asked for and forced myself, without much difficulty, to experience an intense feeling of curiosity—something Emerald would also feel through the tether.

"Question," I said in English. I placed a hand on myself, "Alex." A hand on Em, and in their language, *"Emerald."* And a hand on the object I needed the word for. In this instance on the hologram, "Screen."

In time, the word *'question'* would hopefully become the equivalent of *'I need an answer for this.'* Soon, we would be able to tell the difference between a statement and a question.

"A'ex," said Em. *"Writing, good,"* she continued in her own language, adding a nod for emphasis.

"Writing, good," I replied, with a nod and a smile.

We were making genuine progress. I was eager to ask the big questions—the ones we *really* needed the answers to. Time was fleeting. The shuttle continued its journey in an unknown direction, towards a destination that could be equally exciting and terrifying. But, thanks to the addition of *'good'* and *'bad'* in our dictionary, Emerald and I could express minimal opinions, feelings or fears. It would prove useful very soon.

"This is slow work, isn't it?" said Joana.

"It is, but the fewer errors I make now, the fewer will crop up when it's most important," I replied.

The two of us sat with our backs leaning against a wall of the ship—a break from the constant deciphering was much needed. We had stayed cooped up in this small area near the airlock since the beginning, and, although not unpleasant, my legs felt stiff and achy.

Emerald stood next to Forest, the two of them discussing something semi-important—the anxious feeling Em was sharing through the tether made me nervous in turn. Could they be talking about our arrival?

"I can see you're enjoying it though," replied Joana with the hint of a smile.

"Yeah, it's my job." It felt dry to describe it like that, but it was true. This was my livelihood. Not *this* exactly, but the deciphering and the understanding of language. I could never imagine not enjoying it. "Although, to be honest, I've done enough talking to last a lifetime. I could use some water." My mouth had been dry for a while now, and I knew from previous long presentations I had given in the past, that soon my voice would begin to croak and crack.

"I wouldn't mind a nap either," added Joana.

"I know what you mean." I smiled and glanced further down the room, where Nat had decided to take a quick nap. Unable to help with the translation, he'd expressed feeling exhausted and useless. And since only Joana and I had been able to sleep, barricaded in that tiny meeting room, he had decided a twenty-minute kip wouldn't go amiss.

"What do you think they're talking about?" she asked, looking at our saviours further down the hallway.

"I'm not sure," I said, leaning my head against the wall in tiredness. "I imagine it has something to do with the fact that Emerald was never supposed to pick us up. Maybe how we're going to be received when we arrive at the carrier."

"Hm," mumbled Joana. "It's a complete shitshow…"

"It is," I added. "But we'll make it." Even though I had

said it, I wasn't sure I believed it fully myself.

"I don't know about that," she replied. "I'm not cut out for this stuff." She lowered her eyes to the ground, looking defeated.

"You've survived this far, haven't you?"

"No thanks to me," said Joana. "It was Nat and you that went outside and fixed the Comms link. It was you that figured out how to stay hidden from those creatures. It was Nat that threw me onto this ship. I wouldn't have had the courage to make the jump."

I listened to her attentively. She wasn't wrong; we had helped. But that didn't mean she hadn't contributed. "It was you that gained us access to Comms, that set it up. I wouldn't be so quick to devalue your help."

She shrugged. "It's like Nat said. There's nothing he and I can do right now. We both kinda feel pointless. Like, what am I even doing here?" A grimace across her features, she stared at me as if I had the answer.

"What are any of us doing here?" I replied. "None of this was planned or thought through. Life just sort of happens sometimes. It throws curveballs your way, and you need to ride it out."

Since when had I ever been so optimistic or encouraging? I had always been the one that needed cheering up. At least for the past few years that had been the case.

But things had been different since the moment Em had found us. The tether that linked us together had changed everything. The hurt I had been holding so close to my heart since even before my father had died; it hadn't gone, but it had diminished. I had accepted it, but I had also taken the pain it had caused and grown from it—I was ready to try harder, and for the right reasons this time. This was only the beginning of something remarkable, even though the chaos and destruction that had occurred now coated this beautiful moment in a sticky layer of ash.

Joana was quiet for a while, taking in what I had just said.

But then she added, "Life back on Earth will never be the same. I don't know if that's a good thing or not. I don't know if *we'll* be alright. But things certainly have changed." Joana's hand pushed past the stiffness of the suit to touch a delicate necklace hanging by her clavicle. A graceful cross on a thin chain.

"I mean, we know alien life exists now, that we're not alone in the universe. That must be a significant human advancement. It must put things in perspective. Maybe even give people hope," I added.

"For some, I'm sure." She paused. "I keep thinking back to Hagen. To the way he ran the Observer. People like him will never change. I'm surprised another billionaire didn't meet us on the Observer just to be *the first* to talk to an alien. The greedy will always be hungry. We're stuck in a perpetual loop of capitalist and consumerist bullshit. The big guys want to keep winning. And why wouldn't they?"

I thought back to the man I had stood up to in the boardroom. Hagen had been a piece of work—even before his rise to fame, he had had a reputation of pushing people down the ladder of success if it meant he could climb higher faster. If he had lived, would he be any different? No, even in the minutes prior to his death, what he wanted was to be the first: the first person to set up a hotel in space; the first to install a colony on Mars (and had yet to succeed); the first human to speak to aliens. That was his goal—when he had sent those messages with David and Frederickson's voices. If he had been alive, he'd have wanted to be the first human to negotiate a trade deal; the first person on an alien planet; the first person to shake 'hands' with a big tech corporation on another world. The list could go on. No, he would never have been a better human, nor would humanity be better off with him around.

"If the change goes well, if we live past this, we both know things will only change for the rich and the upper-class," continued Joana. "Everyone else will be left to stew on that dying planet." Her fingers twiddled the cross around her neck.

"And sure—I took the job working for the rich man. So, I'm no better."

"Well, why did you?" I asked, simply interested in her story. I didn't think Joana would be able to torture and slam herself continuously. Surely, there was something about herself that she liked.

"Because you *have* to, to survive. Values and morals don't get you the good jobs, the money to pay the bills. Self-respect goes out the window if you want to live." She crossed her arms across her chest, or as much as she could in the bulky suit.

I stared ahead of me, trying to find a way to spin the conversation to something positive, something that would give her some value. "Did you enjoy working on the Observer?"

"I did, and I didn't," replied Joana. "I hated everything about the job—some of the company morals—"

"Like what?"

"Like… Spying on what our guests were accessing on the internet, or looking into their wallets, compiling how much money they had, so we knew how to get them to spend more. Or, giving special digital privileges to special guests. I mean, my main job was cyber-security, protecting the digital well-being of the company, keeping hackers out of the system. Sometimes that meant breaking the system to know how to protect it."

"Don't you think there'd be some use for you here? Maybe learning their systems?" I say, indicating towards Emerald and Forest.

I watched as Forest tapped away at his screen, Emerald keeping a close eye on him. Between them, they passed incomprehensible phrases.

"I'm sure that when things have settled, when this has been sorted, that you could be the first to look into *their* cyber-security," I said, but as I uttered the words, I realised maybe that wasn't what she wanted to hear.

She stayed quiet before muttering a low, "Maybe."

"Do you believe?" I asked, nodding to the cross hanging

from her neck.

Joana immediately let it fall back, not realising she had been holding it.

"I do," she replied. "I was raised in a Catholic household. I rebelled against it at first—it doesn't really fit the modern world, or at least that's what I thought, but my mother introduced me to God in a different light. She told me that it isn't about the traditions, modern or not. It's not about the services, or mass, or Sunday school. It's not Christmas, and it's not even praying. And yes, all those things matter. But not as much as simply believing in *good*. Not even having faith that evil people will have their comeuppance and that the good people will be rewarded for their deeds. It's about truly believing that everyone can be kind, preaching forgiveness and understanding. And when people are unkind, that you can show *them* kindness, they will see a better way.

"This," continued Joana, her hand pointing at our surroundings and bringing us back to the original subject, "This could radicalise people. And I'm not just talking about religion. Not even politically. Socially." Joana hugged her knees to her chest.

From the year I had been born in, 2016, the world had never been more divided, my father used to tell me. It was everyday life for me: this idea that people belonged either in one camp or the other. There was no middle ground to agreeing on political or social issues. You either agreed or you didn't. 2016, my father had told me, was the year people truly showed their division. Presidents had been elected, votes had been held, tax havens discovered, and the breach between beliefs had grown larger. And years later, we had discovered that big tech companies had elaborately and, maybe even knowingly, caused the mass divide. I had read a paper on technofeudalism, and the subject had interested me intensely.

I wondered then what kind of society we would be met with on the carrier. Had they evolved past capitalism and democracies? Or does nature always overtake, with the survival of the strongest always leading the charge? Does their culture enable a monarchy to strive, or, like my country of birth, had they overthrown their leaders in favour of their people? Was there another way to run a country that we, as humans, had not thought of yet?

But Joana was still stuck on another thought, still ruminating over the potential for disaster in the here and now, the *us*.

"*This* is *too* much. Some people will look at Emerald, face-to-face, and still claim this whole situation is a hoax. And the wealthy will use this as an opportunity to get ahead. There's always someone out there that wants to enslave or conquer, or God knows what else." She paused for a moment before continuing, "Change like this is scary. We've always mused with the idea that aliens are out there. That they could contact us. But we didn't imagine what the real repercussions were. What does it mean for *us*? Us as *humans*? The way I see it, we're not ready for this shit." Her voice shook with that last sentence.

I remembered the same words being spoken to me by the friendly face I missed. *'I'd tell them to come back later. We're not ready for this.'* David. The words had seemed unbelievable to me when he had said them. But after witnessing Hagen's demise, almost being killed myself, and seeing an alien for the first time, they never sounded truer. So many questions still remained: why had all this happened? Why had we been saved? What would happen now? And what the hell was this tether between Emerald and me?

"You might be right," I said finally. "But it has started, and there isn't any way we can stop it. All we can do is keep looking for answers and try making the right decisions along the way."

"I'm not sure that's going to be enough," replied Joana, silent sadness in her eyes.

In the time it took to close in, Em and I had managed to cover a few more words, a few more topics, now written down on the hologram whiteboard in a never-ending stream of thoughts and sounds. We had peered over Forest's shoulder and pointed at various things on the screen to find out what those translated as, or as close a translation I could come to. On top of that, the whiteboard had also served its purpose as a canvas—anything that couldn't be pointed at was drawn, in a pretty mediocre fashion usually. Covering a variety of verbs as well, I had mastered a—very—primitive form of speech. For each sentence Em or Forest had uttered, I needed to look up the sounds produced on the board before understanding the full meaning of the phrase. But the more I practised, the easier it got.

Once that had been completed, I decided it was time to ask where they were from.

"Alex. *Planet. Earth,*" I said. "*Question. Em. Planet.*"

"⪝⊒≰╟├⊥ᴗ," she replied.

I wrote down the phonetic version of the word.

"*Xoeesco,*" I repeated back to Em, who nodded back immediately. I continued, "Alex. *Human. Question. Em.*"

"⊓≱," said Em.

"*Verax,*" I repeated. The sounds felt heavy and clumsy in my mouth. I promised myself I would practise when we would have a quiet moment. I also noted the prolific use of the letter 'x' in their language—something I would delve into when I had more time.

"*Verax,*" I said again, getting used to the word. I felt like I was going to be saying it a lot in the near future. "Thank you, Em." Forcing myself to feel an exaggerated version of appreciation, I hope she would get the meaning.

"Thirty minutes," said Nat, coming back from the cockpit.

"Thanks," I replied. Looking to Em, I continued, "Okay, the difficult ones now..." I cleared my throat. In Em's language, I said, "*Question. Carrier. Arrive. Us.*" I pointed to myself, Nat, and Joana. We hadn't covered tenses, or the future, or the concept of linear time. But I had started to understand Em's thinking. Emerald was rational and intelligent, even prepared for the difficulties we would face.

I didn't have to wait for a solid answer to that question—I felt the change through the tether: this overwhelming sadness and minor frustration. The feelings dug into me and reminded me of a time when, as a child, I had felt so completely misunderstood, it had enraged me. An argument or a fight. I had tried to express myself but to no avail; my father wouldn't listen to my reasoning. I couldn't remember the context of the disagreement, but the feeling lingered in the back of my consciousness. Yet I didn't understand why Em felt this way. Were those emotions in relation to humans interacting with the Verax species? Or was this Em herself? Had she not left on good terms?

I decided to push this further. "*Question. Carrier. Em. Good.*" The question itself was clunky, but there was no better way for me to put it.

I watched with caution, and Emerald's sadness deepened. Something wasn't right. "*Carrier* ⊑⊣ⱥ⚹ *no good Em,*" she replied in simple terms.

"*No understand* ⊑⊣ⱥ⚹," I said, the repeated foreign word and their thick syllables sticking to my tongue.

Em stepped towards the hologram machine, where she input some terms. She showed me an image of a hierarchical breakdown of people. Was this an individual family, royalty, or the crew of the ship? Yet the idea was clear: *leaders.* Whoever ruled on the carrier was not happy with Em.

"*Question,*" said Alex. *Why*? Would Em understand my meaning?

Em shook her head, the sadness ever-present. She either didn't want to share the information, or maybe she didn't have it. It could even be a cultural difference. Out of respect, I left it there.

"*Question. Station. Humans. Breathing. Em.*" I pointed at Nat, Joana, and me. *Why had Em saved us?*

She shook her head once more. Around us, the hum of the

ship had quietened as it continued its deceleration towards the carrier. Frustration coursed through the tether once more, but different this time. I related this feeling to not being able to find the right words. A language barrier. Em walked away before I could push the issue further. She descended into the hole in the floor, using the coils to guide herself down.

"Did you get anything from that?" asked Joana, with Nat at her side.

"Not much. Something doesn't seem right, though. I don't think we'll get a warm reception when we get there. She walked away without even trying to answer why she saved us. I have a feeling it's connected to the lack of enthusiasm from the carrier. If I was to guess, I think she went against orders to come and get us. But I don't understand why. What could she gain from that?"

"I checked the oxygen tanks as you were talking to her," said Nat. "You have about six hours to convince them we're worth saving. You've made a lot of progress; I'm sure we'll be fine." But his tone betrayed him.

VERAX DIGITAL ARCHIVE [TRANSLATED BY GAUTHIER]

FIRST TRANSLATED WORDS (as recorded by GAUTHIER)

Emerald - or potentially rock, gem, gemstone, geode

Forest - trees, wood, thicket, woodland

Ship - possibly the specific name of this ship, or vessel, craft, spacecraft

Carrier - possibly the specific name of the ship, or another descriptor that indicates its size

Pilot - noun, but possibly the verb, maybe commander

Earth - possibly planet, human planet, rather than

specifically what we call Earth

Spacesuit - or environment suit

Helmet - no other possibilities

Action: nodding - yes, or agreement in general

Action: shaking of head - no, or disagreement in general

Hologram - possibly screen, computer, internet (or cultural nickname), data processor or information processing system

Wall - possibly panel, divider, enclosure, or metal

Floor - possibly ground, deck, or grating

Seat - chair, seating

Sit - first attempt at verb, might have been misunderstood as posture

Walk - might have been misunderstood as move

Agree/Yes - the same word, but understood thanks to nodding

Disagree/No - the same word, but understood thanks to shaking

Good - maybe like, acceptable, enjoyable, or even wonderful

Bad - maybe unpleasant, unlikable, dislike, or not enjoyable

Writing - might have been misunderstood as communicating

Question - started in English, but soon translated; this might be how they pose questions, or could be simplified for us, could be use as what or why, but doesn't quite work for when, who and how many

---

10

The slow and steady approach to the carrier was the most hauntingly stressful moment of my life up until that point. The structure on Forest's screen stretched much wider than the Observer, expected for a carrier, yet still the largest made object I had ever seen out in space. I managed to convince Emerald to get a better look at the layout and design of the ship, which is when I noticed it didn't look the same as the ship standing outside the Observer, the one I had seen through the window.

"How many ships *are* there?" asked Joana.

I shrugged—far too many, and yet none had been picked up on the Observer's radar. How was that possible? Unfortunately, we weren't at a stage where I could ask Em that question.

As soon as we docked, the hum of the engines died down, and both Forest and Em collected some things from their ship. The flurry of stress leaping around the tether, coming from both Em and me, became infinite, and even though the temperature in the shuttle had cooled, I had begun to sweat.

Helmet back on, I looked around to my new-found friends:

Joana stood apprehensively fiddling with a strap on her suit, and Nat caught my eye—silent fear visible across his features, which escaped in the odd quickened breath.

We waited quite a while, standing impatiently and nervously at the door. Emerald and Forest were quiet too. They had spent a portion of the voyage disagreeing on things—the frustration I had felt from Em almost made me believe that Forest was not exactly an ally.

The airlock doors opened to a large tunnel made of a similar alloy to the shuttle. The pressure dropped once more, but the gravity remained intact. In front of us stood a small cluster of Verax, all a similar build and dress to Em and Forest, wearing suits of different shades and patterns. I wondered if the coloured suits meant anything to the species. If they were the equivalent to army uniforms. If they represented rank, class, status, or gender. Or if they were only aesthetic choices. The Verax, now surrounding us, had a multitude of tints across their suits and visors: different hues of blues and purples. Their size and body shapes varied too, another trait our species had in common. On each of their backs, they also had the device which allowed them to use coils. Another mystery I had not gotten to yet.

Pushed forward, we made our way through the corridor, the ceiling so tall it made me feel that much smaller again. Metal bars hung from the ceiling like a horizontal ladder, and only a moment later did I realise why those were there.

As we arrived at an intersection, the chaos of life on a large carrier became apparent. There were Verax walking, running, swinging, and hanging from a variety of directions, all busy with their individual jobs and lives, doing what needed to be done to maintain this monstrosity of a ship. My breath bounced back in my helmet as I watched them elegantly manoeuvring to their destinations.

"Holy…" I heard Nat mutter through the helmet radio.

The metallic sounds of the clamping and shifting from coils to ceiling to floor, and opening of doors screeched at the front of my head. The concussion still caused me issues, but I hoped it would soon disappear. I *needed* it to.

I noticed a large gap in the floor and realised that some of their corridors travelled upwards and downwards too. For a species using long metal coils that clamp into place, it made sense to create a ship that would utilise their technology in the best way possible. Em and Forest used their coils to bring us humans across the gap without incident, hugging us tightly and swinging across. For the brief moment I hung above the void, I felt dizzy, much like I had felt standing at the edge of the Observer, a deep precipice below my toes.

The group of Verax accompanying us swung effortlessly across, the same way a human child might make a jump across a puddle.

We marched forward still, passing large doors and signs and other corridors, enough to feel immediately lost and confused. Even if I could speak the language, the place was so large it left me feeling out-of-control and disoriented. Dotted along the walls, screens displayed some kind of information in a text that I hadn't even begun to decode yet. Getting the verbal elements of the language was hard enough; writing would have to wait.

My heart pumped hard and fast as the walk continued, a seemingly endless traipse. I saw Em glance over to me occasionally, and the only thing I wanted to do right now was explain to her how humans felt. The way stress affected a human body, the way fear could spread, raising every little hair on end, the way adrenaline triggered blood vessels to contract, pushing the blood to vital muscles. I wanted to tell her that I was scared, that I was fearing for my life and my future. But none of those emotions could be expressed in any way right now, so I contented myself with a deep gaze, and I hoped the tether would do the rest of the work.

Our pace was brisk and so much faster than a human's. With their height, they each took long gliding steps to their destination, whilst the rest of us were stuck somewhere between a fast-paced walk and a light jog. Analysing her body movements, I realised how much more effortless Emerald's walk was now, compared to when she had boarded the Observer. Had she been strained by the pull of gravity? By the increased atmospheric pressure? Had she suffered or put herself in danger, just to get us out?

All together and surrounded by strangers, we approached a large set of doors, a good metre taller than the Verax themselves. One from the guarding group stepped up and punched a code of some kind into a small screen by the doors, which slid open.

In front of us stood a semicircle of Verax. These ones were dressed differently: although they used the same suits as the rest of their population — or the ones that I had seen so far — they also wore longer garbs on top, in a cape-like shape, trailing to the ground. Their colours were not as vibrant as the others either. Edging closer to whites and opalescent shades, their radiance brightened the already shiny metallic room behind them. Atop their heads were possible displays of their status: a circlet, raised maybe ten centimetres above their helmets, in the shape of crescent moons and garnished with decorative silver-like white metals. One Verax stood at the centre of the semi-circle in a stunning silver suit and cape and a pale blue helmet.

"*Leaders,*" muttered Em to me as we stood side by side, awaiting our fate.

My mind was spinning. The glory of the sight before me, tarnished by the idea that we could be held captive, that Emerald and Forest could be punished for bringing us aboard.

Behind the semi-circle, a small crowd mimicked the same shape, a crescent moon, all wearing similar shades of suits to the rest of the Verax, akin to Emerald and Forest.

From the presentation of the room and its individuals, I guessed they were a democratic council of some kind, supported by a small senate representing the people. But would the leaders of an entire species be aboard one large carrier? Or would each ship have their own council of leaders?

The silver Verax stepped forward and began speaking. The language it used was the one I had not understood, had not been able to replicate. Was it safe to assume this was the Verax's native language?

The silver one spoke fast. I could not make a single word out, not even Emerald's name, if it had even been spoken. I waited, glancing around, but the Verax were a difficult species to read.

A pang of pain spread from the tether to my core, enough that I clutched my chest and stumbled back, catching myself from falling.

"You okay?" asked Nat, his arm around me.

But before I could answer, the room erupted into short mutters and whispers. The semicircle of Verax stood still, but I noticed the silver one glance towards the others, before continuing to speak its undecipherable language.

The tether still exuded pain, first sharpened by the whispers, but then muffled with feelings of injustice and misunderstanding. And even further below that, a quieted passion, ready to burst from Em's chest.

When Emerald finally had a chance to speak, it was with ardour and urgency, and in the language I had become acquainted with. It almost felt like an invitation to speak, to be a part of the conversation. Em spoke swiftly; the only words I had picked up were *'shuttle'*, *'station'*, *'humans'*, even without the whiteboard to help me translate. *'Tether'* had been mentioned too; another round of murmurs had followed. When I heard *'planet'*, I perked up again. This was my home world they were discussing, and so, surely, I needed to be a part of this conversation.

"They seem so angry," said Joana behind me.

But I knew anger couldn't be read into the body language of a different culture, let alone a different species. Joana's fears had seeped into how she read the room.

I stepped up, forcing their eyes on me and interrupting their conversation. "Alex," I said as I positioned my hand on my own chest, just as Emerald had shown me. "*Speak. Human. Planet,*" I finished. My voice had bounced back in my helmet, and I was left with the echo of words that hadn't meant anything to these leaders. My nerves rattled inside me. All I had done was spout random words that sounded so primitive, they—

They ignored me. The silver one turned and continued speaking to Em in their native language. I thought back to my time on the Observer in that meeting room, being ignored by Hagen on more than one occasion. Was there any point to this? Would they ever understand how significant of a moment this was for humanity? Had *they* not also experienced their First Contact moment? I shrunk further into myself, almost embarrassed.

Before long, I realised we were being escorted out of this room. I felt cheated, like I hadn't been able to say everything I wanted to say. I needed to make my case. As far as Earth knew, we were still on the Observer, still under attack. They would be putting themselves in danger. Earth should also know *where* we were. Not that I had an accurate answer for them.

"*Emerald,*" I started, then remembered our construction for inquiries. "*Question. Emerald.*" But I received no reply. She was walking behind me, and my helmet didn't allow me to turn that far around.

We trudged on for a long time once again. I didn't know how far or how long we had been walking. The hallways all looked the same. My mind caught on one thing: how could I tell them how pressing the situation was? How could I make them listen? I ran scenarios in my head, but each of them failed and ended with me being silenced or dismissed, my concerns negated, and my feelings left void. But Em had spoken to this Leader. She must have answers.

A chamber door opened in front of us. Em and Forest

removed their backpack-coil-contraptions and handed them to the Verax guards. They were being… disarmed? Was this a cell? The guards stepped out, and the door closed behind us.

The enclosure was large enough to accommodate four or five Verax without issue. A smooth, cushioned room, soft under my feet, maybe even comfortable to sleep on. The walls too were made of the same material. A cell, a confined space, but not an inhumane prison by a long shot. Towards the back was a separate room, which, as a human, I imagined could be a bathroom of some kind, probably unusable to us.

By the side of the door, a control panel sat perched on the wall, which Em immediately approached, tapping away at it. She waited a while, everyone watching her next move.

"Helmet. Off," said Em, once turned around. She had cycled the air. It was one less battle to fight.

Em bent down, and, out of a side pocket of her suit, she pulled out the hologram machine. This was going to make things easier. We had so much to explain to each other.

Behind me, Joana pulled off her helmet. "I still don't understand how they know what we breathe. Have they been spying on us this whole time?" Sudden realisation crossed her face. "Are they the UFOs people have been witnessing?"

"I doubt that," replied Nat, his tone dismissive and quiet. "Their ships look completely different. All you need is a good telescope and a scientist to figure out the chemical composition of a planet."

Joana nodded in agreement. "So, what's the plan?" she asked, looking to me.

"We have air, and, right now, we have time. I think Em has some explaining to do," I replied. I had so many questions I wasn't even sure where to start.

Em and I sat opposite each other once again, hologram machine in the centre. On one side of the hologram was the whiteboard I had made notes on, and on the other Em searched for something, tapping away at the screen before I had even asked a question.

She must have been as desperate as me to communicate. Through the tether, I felt a sensational feeling of excitement. If I had to compare it to anything, it would be close to adrenaline, yet not quite that energy-inducing. Em soon found what she was looking for and opened it up: a list of words written as a collection of symbols.

And so, the work began. Em would say the word out loud, and I would write it down phonetically as close as I could. Em would search the word and find a suitable hologram image to represent it. Sometimes, this initiated a discussion in which we needed to find words to correlate the original to. I would then write down the meaning. There were bound to be mistakes, bound to be misinterpretations, but if I could at least get close to the meaning of what Em was preparing to tell me, it would make everything so much easier.

The words were random in places, but we also discussed pronouns: 'I', 'you', and plurals, without touching upon gendered pronouns. More verbs and numbers were also added to the list. In the background, Nat and Joana murmured at times, but they also kept an interested ear to the language deciphering, while Forest sat in his own corner. I wondered if he was mulling over the mistake of accepting us on his ship.

Em closed the search screen but left the whiteboard as it was. An hour or so had drifted by, and, as I turned around, I realised my companions had fallen asleep. Nat, head back, mouth slightly ajar, was unmoving; and Joana, head tilted towards Nat, had a strand of hair pressed against her cheek.

My back grew stiff from sitting on the floor so long. I stretched out my legs and felt the muscles tense and then relax again. My head felt heavy; waves of sleep had threatened me many times already, but I had to push through the tiredness. The scratchiness of my throat had intensified, and my tongue felt dry. How long had it been since we had last had a sip of water?

Em spoke, articulating and enunciating the syllables for

me to catch them. I wrote them down immediately—I would still need to look up each of the words individually until I knew them off by heart.

I turned the words around in the sentence, trying to find how they each connected, until the sentence structure became a formula. A simple sentence in the English language followed the structure 'subject-verb-object' but here, in the Verax language they used, the structure was 'verb-subject-object'. I knew a few languages on Earth that followed that structure: Classical Arabic, Filipino, and Māori, to name but a few.

I looked at the words again and reorganised them in my head. Some terms were missing: conjunctions, tenses, prepositions, and so on. I would need to fill the gaps where I could.

"You are no[t] allow[ed] [to] be here," I repeated. First sentence down.

Em continued, and I searched my list for the words, with her fingers pointing towards some of the same phonemes.

"You are no[t] allow[ed] [to] be tether[ed]."

Repetition of the same structure and same words made everything a little bit easier. So, tethering was the act of bonding the way Em had with me. I held onto my own questions until Em was finished.

"I am [a] prisoner."

'Prisoner' may not have been the right word when we had initially translated it. It could have been 'convict', or 'restrained', or anything to indicate that loss of freedom. But I was not sure if that related to a crime being committed.

"Question. Because of [the] tether?" I asked. My voice cracked as I spoke.

"Yes," replied Em with a human-like nod. *"Because you are [on] carrier [as well]."*

'Because' was one of those words that had taken a while to grasp. How does one indicate the causality of something in a foreign language? But that made sense: Em had rescued us without authorisation from her Leaders.

"Question. Why are we [on] carrier?"

Adding 'question' at the beginning seemed redundant now that I knew how to say 'why', but it had become a habit of sorts.

"Because of [the] tether."

I paused a while. The tether had been created by her, so she knew what she was doing when she did it. But that didn't explain why she came to us in the first place. Or how she knew where to find us. It certainly didn't make sense that the tether could bring us together, *before* it was even created.

"Question. Why?" I asked.

I couldn't tell if their words for 'why' and 'how' were the same. My father had taught me, throughout my childhood, that asking 'why' was always going to get you answers in some shape or form. So, I had asked it anyway.

Em paused before saying, *"Feeling."*

A feeling of attachment before the tether took place? Is that what she was saying? Or more of a gut-feeling? If they even had such a thing. Maybe I had misunderstood the word 'feeling' altogether. Maybe what they called 'feeling' also included things like beliefs, sensitivities, reactions, or ideas. Maybe even faith or fate.

"From [the] tether," I concluded.

"Yes."

So, according to what Emerald was saying, if I had understood it correctly in the first place, the tether existed *before* Em had created it. Like we had been fated to find each other.

I wasn't much of a believer in these sorts of things. Destiny was what you made of it, for the most part. Of course, the situation that one is born into could be a setback or filled with privilege, but after that, life is what one could make of it.

Was it fate that had brought me to the Observer and not my hard-working career? My father had been the one to push me to succeed; if he hadn't, I wouldn't have worked as hard, and I wouldn't have been here.

No, not for one second did I believe that all those things had happened to lead me to this one moment. This could only ever be a chance meeting.

I nodded, agreeing for now, but someday I would bring this subject back up. At the very least, I had understood the concept.

"Leaders [do] no[t] understand A'ex." Maybe it was "unsure" instead. *"[But] Leaders trust Feeling."*

Their society believed in fate and destiny and whatever feelings it conveyed to them. Whatever the tether was, it was their guiding light. Em had tethered herself to me, and that meant something to their species. I had a mountain more questions, but there was one I was dying to know the answer to.

"[The] fight [on] [the] station. Question. Why?"

The whole reason we were here, on this carrier, was because of the droid attack on the Observer. Before Em could answer, she opened up another search window on the hologram. We compiled new words, albeit with great difficulty, and over a considerable amount of time. I was parched and exhausted, but none of it would get any better unless we learnt more of each other.

Em started again, *"Group of leaders."* Maybe a council? *"They are [the] rules."* They are the law. *"Droids are unhappy [with] Leader law."* Em shook her head. She was getting herself muddled, or maybe, she lacked the words. *"They are happy with* ⩽⊩⊒⩾ *law."*

The unidentified sound stood out. It had force and depth, using a vowel for Em that emanated from the base of her throat. Yet I recognised it somehow... I thought back to my previous conversations with Emerald, with Forest, with the Leaders, and none of them had uttered these sounds in this specific way.

Then, it clicked. The message we had received on the Observer. Still, that did not explain its meaning.

"No understand ⩽⊩⊒⩾," I repeated.

As Em searched for the relevant words to explain this new one, I looked to my friends once again. Joana's head had fallen further towards Nat, but he was now awake. Sleep still lay across his eyelids, but he delivered a smile when our eyes met. My heart warmed at this hint of affection. I smiled back, although I wasn't sure there was much to look pleased about. The information Em had provided did not sound positive in any way. All five of us were in a predicament that I didn't fully understand, and, roaming in the background, remained the idea that our home was still under attack. Hundreds of people had already died on the Observer, and none of us had yet spoken to the UN or any other major organisation capable of dealing with this plight. *Could* we cope with this situation?

Em had finished her search—she showed me a collection of images. The hologram images weren't of a specific species but a *depiction* of one—the same way cavemen from Earth had drawn mammoths on the walls of their homes, but present-day humans had never truly seen a mammoth. Whatever species this was, they were large and dark and terrifying. The drawings and sculptures expanded over large sections of the walls, each a different shape and form. It was no use in trying to find this creature's face or define its body. There was nothing to discern. Nothing to see but a large, shadowy form.

Was this finally confirmation that there was *another* species out there? Another organic one, as opposed to the droids? Another planet that was habitable to life, another way life had survived out in the universe?

Em went back to searching and soon came up with a compilation of images from her own species. But before she could explain what she had come up with, she noticed my confusion through the tether.

"⧖⊩⊒⧐ *not droid.*"

So, the droids followed this new species's laws and rules. I still couldn't fathom the idea that there were now, potentially, *three* alien species out there, playing politics and getting into wars.

"*Verax, droids, and* ⩽‖⊢⊒⩾," I said out loud, counting on my fingers, the same way Em had done earlier when we had briefly discussed numbers. Although I wasn't sure the droids could be included, with them probably not being organic life.

"*No. No, thirty-six,*" corrected Em.

I double-checked the number and stared at her. "Thirty-six?!" I shouted in English.

Joana stirred from her slumber. My head spun with possibilities—how could there be that many, out there, in a universe that was not kind to life? And Earth hadn't found a single one on its own.

"Thirty-six what?" asked Nat.

"Species. Out there."

"Aliens? Alien species?" he asked. And before I could answer, he said, "That's fucking insane. How did we miss them that long?" He paused but a second, his face frozen from the realisation, and repeated, "That's *fucking* insane."

"Hm?" muttered Joana, waking from the depths of her sleep.

"⩽‖⊢⊒⩾," Em said again, bringing me back to the conversation. "*Word mean[s]…*"

Pointing at the picture of the Verax on the hologram, Em directed my attention to specific traits. Frail, struggling to get up, slowed. Old, perhaps. So, this new word could mean anything related to age, or how long the species had been around. 'Senior', 'Ancient', or 'Elder' came to mind. 'Elder' worked well; it allowed for both possibilities and didn't have the negative human connotations that 'ancient' would. I wrote down the word.

"*Droids happy with Elder law,*" repeated Em. "*Elder law is different feeling.*" Different *beliefs* from the Verax and their council? "*Want be Leaders of galaxy.*"

This started to make more sense: an Elder species wanting to assert some kind of dominance or control over a galaxy; younger species evolving and discovering space and territories already under Elder control. It was a familiar story. The idea of colonisation, of being an unbeatable empire, to enslave 'lower' species or races. It felt like this pattern would happen no matter where life began. There was always someone vying for control somewhere.

"Droid fight station. Question. Why no destroy Earth?"

"Elder and droid want humans be happy with Elder law. Want humans happy with different feeling."

So, it *was* colonisation, but not for slavery or planetary resources. It was indoctrination. To force humans under their law, their beliefs, rather than belong to this Council the Verax were involved in. The politics of it started playing with my head. I *needed* sleep soon.

"Question, why?"

"Control. Domination. Fight."

Those were the words that had made me nervous earlier. I had waited for them to appear in the conversation but had dreaded the moment. That was one piece of the puzzle solved.

But only a second later did I realise it was an insensitive thought to have. I had been so focused on problem-solving, on piecing the puzzle together, that I had forgotten the lives that had been affected. Lives had been lost, and lives would be lost again.

"Question," I started, *"Earth and droid fight?"* I wanted to add 'now', but didn't know the word.

"No. Verax fight also." Em asserted herself further—was that pride I felt in the tether?

I paused. My stomach rumbled somewhere beneath the environment suit.

"Question?" was all I could manage, wiping my brow, forcing myself awake.

"I take you [off] station. Droids see. Droids feeling we [want] [to] fight them."

"Oh," I replied. That wasn't good.

"We fight. Because [of] me."

Sadness spread through the tether, but alongside it whisped a feeling of righteousness, of having done the correct thing. So, not only did Em break her orders and bring humans aboard a carrier illegally, she also, somehow, started a war, for the benefit of humans?

"Jesus," I muttered.

"No understand," replied Em.

"No[t] important."

Now was not the time to explain the concept of religion and their figures, or why it had become a common colloquialism to say their names when things were going terribly wrong.

Nat and Joana had been listening for a while now. I turned to my friends and explained everything Em had told me.

"Thirty-six?!" said Joana, her mouth hanging agape.

"I still don't understand how a tether can point Em in the right direction to find us, when it doesn't exist yet?" said Nat.

Our stomachs were rumbling from hunger and thirst. Very soon, we would need to talk about natural survival for human beings: food, water, sleep.

"There will be minute details to things that we can't figure out yet; those will have to wait for later," I replied. It had puzzled me too, but in the back of my mind I had explored the possibility that some species were simply able to connect on different spiritual levels. The same way a twin seems to always know what is going on with the other. Or how an elderly couple may die only days apart from one another. A deeper connection than can be explained — the way one soul is tied to another.

It was something I was struggling to wrap my head around: how a stranger, a different species, could do that. Understandable for people who have known each other their whole lives or spent fifty years together. But, as Nat had said, Emerald found *us* on the Observer. She *knew* where to look.

"So, what happens now?" asked Joana, still waking from her sleepy daze, her hair disordered.

"As far as I'm aware, there's a war going on out there.

Earth is involved, but we have a bunch of information they don't have. And the leaders of this carrier don't know what to make of us, so we're kind of in limbo at the moment." I turned to Em and said, "*Alex,*" hand on my chest, as I had done so many times before, "*speak to Earth.*"

Em nodded, "*Yes. We try.*"

I nodded too. Maybe convincing the Leaders would be the most challenging part.

Em hesitated. A pang of pain stung me to my core. She had been holding onto something.

"*Also,*" started Em, the fear spreading through the tether, "*Station fall.*"

"Question?" That couldn't be right.

"*Station destroy[ed]. Droids push. Station fall to Earth.*"

The Observer? How could it… It would take a lot of force to do that. Would the droids doom a planet this way?

"That can't be…" I said, more to myself than anyone specific. If it fell, the consequences would be catastrophic. "No…"

"*Station fall.*" Overwhelming sadness and empathy flowed towards me, but I didn't want to hear it. I stumbled back, losing my sense of self, lost in the fear. I tried my best to accept it before turning around and facing Nat and Joana.

But the lights went out, the ground shaking below our feet.

OBSERVER DIGITAL ARCHIVE [RETRIEVED]

Conduct, Safety and Security n. 5:

"Have fun!"

Although the Observer requires guests to be cautious and attentive of their surroundings, first and foremost, we ask you to please have fun!

Even though the Observer was constructed to be a research station, its current primary objective is to allow people, such as yourselves, to experience the breath-taking and ground-breaking sights from the station proper.

Discover Earth from another angle with our new shuttle stop, taking you into outer space —

—should you wish to stay longe —

—4D cinema is in Se —

—restau —

—variety of fo —

—wond —

—experience should be shared with the f —

—playpen for k —

—courtesy of Hage —

11

"What the hell was that?" asked Nat, leaning further into the wall to maintain his balance. "Is everyone okay?"

Our cell had clouded in darkness; the steady, blue emergency lighting lining the floors and ceiling our only source of illumination. Below our feet, the engines still rumbled. The power wasn't out completely—only syphoned to the more important parts of the ship.

I stood up; the shake had thrown me to the floor, but the padded ground had protected me. "I'm alright. Joana?"

"Yeah, I'm good," she replied in the darkness, not too far from where Nat's voice had come from.

My eyes adjusted to the light, and I saw Emerald and Forest not too far, bringing themselves back up. A shadow covered the panel by the exit, and I realised Em was tapping away at the screen.

The ground shook once more—less violent this time, but enough to frighten me. What the hell was going on out there? The Observer had been knocked from its orbit by those droids. Was this the final confirmation I needed to know they were not on the Verax's side? Confirmation that they were malicious, not just against the Observer, but against the human race? We were in danger here, but more pressingly, the entire planet could suffer a worse fate.

"Alex *speak with Earth!*" I said, possibly louder than I should have. Fear seeped further into me; I knew Em could feel it too. I could already imagine the Observer sluggishly penetrating the atmosphere, picking up speed, and turning into an inescapable ball of fire. And no matter what Earth threw at it, missiles or nukes, the damage it would cause when it fell would be irreparable. The twisting and pulling in my gut made me feel sick. I *needed* to know what was going on.

Em paused her tapping, turning to me, analysing my emotions; then, she turned to Forest.

"*Leaders?*" suggested Forest. It was the first time he had spoken the language I understood, involving me in the debate. I was thankful he was trying; maybe I had finally proven that I cared about people, someone other than myself.

"*Yes,*" replied Em.

This response spurred Forest into immediate action. Though my sight was reduced by the lack of light, I noticed the shuffling in front of the door panel. Em had been pushed to one side, while Forest had taken centre stage.

"What's happening?" asked Joana.

"I'm not sure. I think Forest might be trying to break out of the cell," I said, though my certainty at what was happening solidified in the next few seconds when he pulled the panel off the wall and fiddled with the wiring behind.

"Those doors could open at any second," said Nat. "Helmets on."

We each slipped the helmets on as suggested and secured them.

The bubble around my head muffled any sounds, and for a moment I felt the most isolated I had been in a long time. Nothing was right. Cocooned loneliness suffocated me. Everything was disguised and coated in a sheen; the outside world wasn't real, wasn't tangible unless I could feel the air on my skin. The helmet protected me from the elements but also made me impervious to the reality of the world. Strands of hair had matted to the sweat on my forehead, and I regretted not having pulled it back better before the helmet had been locked into place. The throbbing of my head worsened, exaggerated by the lack of water and sleep. Even if we managed to get out, would we survive this next part? Would we die of dehydration eventually? With all the dangers we could potentially find ourselves in, would thirst be a less painful death?

"*Question. Carrier happy with fight?*" I asked.

"*No happy. But* ⊋⊥≢¢," replied Em.

"*No understand* ⊋⊥≢¢."

Forest continued his search for wires whilst also looking at the screen he had pulled out, as if a new 'open door' button would show up if he messed it around enough. Joana stepped up to him, peaking at the screen and wires herself. She was a good hacker; she'd proved that much on the Observer. Maybe she was trying to use those skills to provide some help.

I admired the two of them—they knew the stakes; we all did. Earth could have already been attacked. Now, the Observer was falling. Its length longer than a kilometre—an asteroid that size could wipe out most of humanity. The devastating plunge would poke a hole in the atmosphere and, depending on where it would land, would cause mass geological and climate issues. I knew that scientists and military organisations had preventative measures in place for a situation like this, but that all depended on the speed and the angle at which it was travelling. Was it already too late, I wondered. Had it breached the atmosphere? Had they shot it down, so it collided with Earth into thousands of smaller pieces, ultimately sacrificing the few people still alive on the station?

I felt stuck here, unable to communicate with a human being on the ground, unable to warn them, unable to tell them why this was happening in the first place, even though some of that information still eluded me.

Em searched on the hologram machine once more and brought up a variety of creatures. They looked like animals, but not animals I had seen before. They were of unrelated species, so they must have had something in common. My eyes flicked between the different pictures before realising the common trait. They looked strong or tough in some way: a thick carapace, tough skin, and a creature resembling an ant carrying something twice its size. The carrier was strong; that was good to hear.

"*Question. Droids strong?*" I asked, using the new word.

"*Yes. But carrier strong.*" It felt like Em had repeated herself, but maybe this one was a comparative or superlative: 'stronger' or 'strongest'. I hoped for our sake that it was 'strongest'.

"*Question. Carrier strong. Why droids fight?*" Would they sacrifice themselves for the beliefs of the Elders? Would they start a war they could never win?

"*They feeling [that] they are right. [That] rules are right.*" Em held herself from saying much more; I could feel the frustration of the language barrier through the tether. There was so much more I wanted to ask, and so much more she wanted to answer.

These droids were certain their way was righteous; they would stand against a large carrier like this. It reminded me of the divide back home—the right or wrong beliefs of people radicalised—they would never back down or admit they were wrong. They truly believed they knew better. Even when facts were given to them, their beliefs held firm. Facts had been misrepresented and labelled fake news for so long, no one knew the difference between reality and fiction anymore. Had the same thing happened here? Had misinformation spread like wildfire? Had the droids been told what to believe, or had they been programmed into it?

"*Question. New word,*" I started. I tried my best to explain the difference between organic and robot, before even thinking of introducing the idea of A.I.. Were they sentient, was the question I wanted to ask.

"*Droids are robot,*" confirmed Em, but I wasn't sure she had understood the question. I would have to leave it for now, until our vocabulary had developed further. But I thought back to the moment Nat, Joana, and myself had hidden from the droids, using cables to confuse their sensors.

But before I could ask a question, Forest interrupted, talking to Joana. "*Stay.*" He pointed at a button on the panel.

She turned to me confused.

"I think he wants you to wait. To push the button when he's ready," I explained.

She nodded towards me first, then to Forest, whom she eyed with caution. It would take us all a while longer to fully trust one another.

Forest pulled up a cushioned area of the floor aggressively, discarding it to one side. He broke into another panel and started messing with some wires.

"*Yes*", he said, looking to Joana.

"Go for it," I explained to her.

She hit the button as Forest held two wires together. The airlock doors opened.

Joana and Forest had actually coordinated the trip-wiring of the cell. All together, we were starting to make a strong team.

"Hey, look at you go," smirked Nat.

"Forest did the hard work," replied Joana, lowering her gaze and averting attention.

There was a noticeable lack of guards behind the door. But before I could cross the threshold, Forest stepped up to me, snatching the hologram machine from Em's hands. He tapped the image a few times and opened up a virtual map of the carrier. The purple image flickered and caused reflections in our helmets.

I followed his other hand from where we stood to where we were headed: the room where we had met with the Leaders. The route wouldn't be straight forward: a number of downward shafts would need to be hopped over, without the help of coils and no weapons to fight possible intruders.

"*Question. Droids?*" I asked, pointing at different areas on the carrier.

"*Yes. No,*" replied Forest. *Maybe*, then.

It had been the first time he had addressed me personally. Perhaps he was getting used to the idea that humans were not so bad. Maybe they were worth a chance. If Forest could change his mind about us, maybe the Leaders could too. I hid my smile and focused on the task at hand. I traced the journey with my finger in an effort to memorise the path ahead.

"*No, no,*" said Forest. With his own hand, he pointed to one room and said, "*Leaders,*" and then to another, further away, "*Speak to Earth.*" Comms. A longer journey than expected, but still manageable.

The emptiness of my stomach caused deep-seated pains in my gut. I wasn't sure how long we could keep this up.

"*Question. Fight?*" I asked, pointing at the map once more.

Em changed the map to an image that showed the carrier out in space, rather than its insides.

"*Fight* ⊤≽⊂," she said.

"*No understand* ⊤≽⊂," I repeated.

She tried her best to explain, but I couldn't focus on her words. We had limited time. We *needed* to get going. My best guess was that it meant 'here', as in the fighting was happening mostly on the outside of the carrier. But it didn't stop the possibility of droids having made their way inside.

I eyed the open airlock. Silence echoed from the hallway outside, yet below, in the depths of the belly of the carrier, low rumbles continued to resonate. Even my feet felt the distant shakes. I wondered if I would ever feel solid ground again.

"*Follow,*" said Forest.

The turnings into each of the corners of this long corridor were endless and confusing. Each one confounded me a little more as the labyrinthine twists and turns kept coming. Darkness enveloped us, with the few emergency lights guiding us in the right direction. The lights themselves were dull and void of any life, yet bright enough to cause a sharp pain in the back of my head any time I looked straight at one.

I felt the pressure weighing heavily on me. The sooner I could talk to someone, the sooner I could tell them what was going on, the better chance we would have of stopping a tragedy.

We had had to take detours. Airlock doors had refused to budge, although it was unclear why. Had the damage to the carrier been that significant? Or had certain areas been locked down? The journey felt a lot longer this time. Em and Forest helped us across the large gaps in the floor, which slowed our pace.

Much deeper beneath my surface exhaustion and confused state, I kept a steady sense of anxiety. I had no idea what I would say to the Leaders when we would find them. Earth would look for diplomacy and charismatic charm, neither of which I was particularly good at. My father had taught me the value of being polite, but I had been a strong-willed and opinionated child back then, and little had changed. He had taught me right from wrong. There were no grey areas for me when it came to diplomacy. But now, in a situation that could echo down the rest of humanity's existence, would I find the strength to be diplomatic, the way it was expected of me? To work in favour of humanity? It couldn't be that hard.

However, a lingering anger had bled into my thoughts. They had been so dismissive, almost arrogant about humans being there, not involving us in the discussion, ignoring us completely. Our species was in danger. And although I kept telling myself that one couldn't assume, the lack of help for our species had given me enough of an idea of where the Verax's values rested. A tactful approach may not be what lay ahead of us.

Previously, I had studied and worked on dead and extinct languages—tongues that would not speak back to me, that would not have arguments, disagreements, or diplomatic issues. Hagen had been right all along. Maybe I was not the best placed to deal with this situation. Would he have done a better job? No, if I was sure of one thing, it was that he would have failed here as well.

The pace had begun to tire me. Em and Forest's long legs were serving them well, but for the rest of us, running in large space suits remained a little out of our league. Pumping through the tether, adrenaline flooded me. This was my own, I recognised, and I wondered for a moment how Emerald would be taking it. Was an adrenaline rush something they experienced, or was this a new feeling for her?

Joana tripped and fell, smacking her elbows on the ground and letting out an "Oomph." I spun around to make sure she was okay.

"I got you," said Nat. He helped her up, but Joana brushed him off.

"I'm fine."

Nat knelt down, extending an arm.

"I'm fine," she snapped, a quiver in her voice.

He let her be, and she brought herself up with a limp.

"Are you hurt?" I asked.

"I said, I'm fine." She glared at me, but I couldn't decide if I could see fear or anger in her gaze. We were at our wits' end, confused, weary and beat.

A little further along, Forest stopped in his tracks. The doors were sealed shut. He poked at the screen by the side of the entrance.

"*No,*" he said.

"*Leaders,*" I said, half a question, half a statement. This was supposed to be our first stop.

"*No,*" he repeated.

Through the tether, I shared Em's worry. This was where we had seen the council. Had they evacuated, or simply moved to Comms to take control of the fight? Had they been attacked the way we had been in that boardroom? Shattered glass, cracking under the force of the droids, crying for help, bleeding out, bodies sucked out into the vacuum outside... I shook the images from my mind. Not everything was going to end that way. Life couldn't repeat itself eternally.

"Follow," he said again. *"Speak with Earth."*

Forest started down the hallway we had just come from. Along the walls, holographic images jolted awake as the energy in the ship rebooted. Text lined the walls, an emergency alert of some kind. I vowed to get Em to translate it when we had a second to breathe, after we had established some kind of communication with Earth.

As I stepped forward, trying to match Forest's pace, my mind went back to the Leaders. If they had died, I'd have no clue how to approach getting in contact with humans. Would the leaders be replaced immediately, or would the process of finding new ones take a long time? Would new leaders make the same choices as the old ones? So many conflicting ideas, but none of them relied on any form of certainty. Yet they were all linked with this intricate loss of hope. Somehow, in the depths of my heart, I knew I would not see Earth again. At least not the way I had left it.

A dark and wide shaft waited above us. Along it stood a rusty alloy ladder—the steps protruded out of the wall in three-foot increments. An efficient ladder for a species three metres tall.

I began my climb immediately behind Forest, who could have easily swung his way to the top if he had his coils. Each step demanded effort. Even in lower gravity, the space suit still pulled me down. My lack of energy became quite apparent halfway up. Beads of sweat slipped down the back of my neck, and that one strand of hair had curled and bounced in an irritating way. The smell of sweat in the suit permeated throughout, stinging my nostrils.

The route to the bridge of the carrier grew more and more convoluted. Forest had led us one way but had arrived at a dead end, crumbled ship debris blocking the path. We had turned around and gone a different way to find that had been obstructed too. Had Forest and Emerald both had their coils, they would have swung over it in no time. Unfortunately, they were almost as useless as humans were on this ship.

Another ten minutes or so had passed before the ladder ended, leading us into another larger hallway. The lights had flickered back on, in full force, which, for the Verax, was not bright at all. Yet shadows were cast as we approached our destination, and further shadows appeared ahead of us.

As we drew closer to the bridge, the amount of Verax increased—each of them swinging, running, and pacing in various directions, each with a job to do and little time to do it in. A Verax hung from the ceiling, their coils holding them close while their hands patched a hole in the roof. Another paced, coils helping them move faster along to another room while their hands typed tirelessly on a hologram.

As we turned the corner, we found ourselves in the height of the excitement. I had never seen so many Verax in one place. Yes, this felt like the bridge of a ship in the middle of a crisis.

With scarcely enough space to move, let alone for humans to see past the shoulders of the Verax, we shuffled along in this compact space. Stares from above lingered on us as we passed them by.

I felt the pressure mount—the claustrophobia crept up to me and lingered on my shoulders, and my breath accelerated, bouncing back into my face in waves of inescapable hot air. I felt jostled and pushed, but I could not tell where from. Above me, the ceiling could only just be seen through the crowd of tall heads and heaps of bodies flying past. And for a brief moment, I thought I might be drowning. Yet my legs pulled me forward a step at a time, and before long we walked beside a wall, further away from the streaming crowd of Verax.

As the mob abated, we picked up the pace once more, darting between people going the opposite way. I found myself running, my dissociation and vertigo now blending as one. I ran but had no idea if I was running to or from something. My ears rang; a high-pitched sound echoed in my head yet felt so far away.

A Verax collided with me, and I fell to the floor.

"S-sorry," I said in English, too tired and dizzy to think straight.

I tried to pull myself back up, but my arms felt weak. Before I knew it, Em picked me up, arm under arm, and pulled me forward to the bridge.

A wave of concern flooded the tether. I felt it, yet my eyes kept closing, and I kept tripping over my feet enough that I couldn't make sense of much anymore.

After a minute or so, I found my feet once more. The dizziness hadn't left, but I felt strong enough to run by myself again. My skin tingled as I flushed from hot to cold in seconds. We stopped quite unexpectedly, and I looked up to find we were standing in front of large double doors. The metallic sheen here gleamed similar to how it had appeared across the ship, yet its colouration was closer to sand: dull yet mesmerising. The airlock doors opened.

The scene before us resembled a painting. The bridge sprawled into a large, open, and curved room with a domed ceiling. A wide glass panel arched from the left to the right at the far end, leaving an open sight of the stars outside. Before the stars, the remainder of the ship extended in full view. Some of the side ports were damaged, and small chunks of debris were left behind, and the carrier, so large in size that I couldn't see the end of it, advanced towards another large ship. The one I had seen from Comms on the Observer. Its reflective metallic material still shone and mirrored the stars, fusing with the space surrounding it. Yet smaller ships poured out of the enemy carrier in vast quantities, spilling like fluid out of a tipped cup. It looked otherworldly.

I pulled myself back into the room. A large and splendid semi-circle work surface stood in front of the glass pane. Its white sheen reflected the light above it. At the centre, a wide hologram of the carrier fluttered in place. Only there could I see the smaller ships dotted around. They engaged in tactical combat, evading attacks and disabling enemy ships. I couldn't tell what kind of weaponry they used, but I imagined the military team on the Observer would have been fascinated by it. In times like these, I wished they had survived. Although the team had been dysfunctional, and Hagen had been drunk on power, their expertise would forever have been invaluable.

I had done it again: focused so much on work and what information I could garner that I had forgotten. There was life in those ships. There was life on this carrier. People had died, and people would continue to die until this fight ended. It occurred to me that I had never asked why the Verax had followed the droids in the first place. Had they known in advance what the droids had intended, and had they come to stop them? Or was this all a chance encounter?

I tore my eyes away from the hologram. Verax crowded smaller screens around the semi-circle of desks, each speaking in their native language, presumably providing key information about the fight. Dotted around the room stood some of the Leaders, their capes and circlets giving their status and location away immediately. The silver Leader stood close to the large central hologram. So, they *had* survived.

Silence fell as we entered the room. A flutter of muttering erupted once more as the crisis continued. The silver one spun and intercepted us before we advanced further.

The Leader spoke their native language to Emerald and Forest. Through the tether, I noticed a strong sense of resilience, of pride. Em held up an emotional barrier, and she would not be stopped until her beliefs concerning human lives had been shared. That fortitude gave me a similar energy. For a moment, we felt unstoppable.

Words were exchanged that we humans could not understand. And as the feelings in the tether shifted, I felt that familiar threat of not being able to help crawl into the back of my mind. However, when Emerald finally answered, she spoke in their common tongue again, giving me a chance to understand, to participate once more.

The ground shook again as an enemy ship impacted the side of the carrier. The central hologram fizzled, then regained composure. The minuscule impact peppered its side. Small particles faded away from the hologram. I wasn't certain if the hologram represented the effects of the fight accurately, or if the strike had been so small, it had seemed insignificant. The heated conversation continued between Emerald and the silver Leader.

Another shake of the floor sent me to the ground. My dizziness had not stopped. Still on my knees, I checked my wristpad. 18% oxygen left. We would need to find somewhere to remove our helmets soon.

Nat and Joana didn't seem to be doing great either. Joana wheezed; I heard the short gasps of air through the radio. And Nat looked pale, even through the reflection of his visor.

I lifted myself off the ground, one hand on the nearby wall. The conversation between Em and the Leader continued; the tension through the tether rose in waves. I focused my mind. If only I could catch specific words.

I couldn't understand why Emerald, a relative stranger to me and a complete stranger to humans, would be so strong-willed and defensive of our species. Even if there was such a thing as destiny in their belief system, would it be so strong as to compel an outsider to protect a foreign planet?

The anger between them escalated. The silver Leader turned around and punched a few keys below the hologram. The image shifted, and the feelings through the tether changed once more. Despair seeped in, a painful kind of fear that ached the heart.

Earth stood before us—its form flickered in place as it spun slowly. Ever since I had left, I had had this secret feeling that I had only taken this job to get away, to run from my emotions—reminders of a past I wanted no association with. But I *did* want to go back. Not only was it my home, but it was also my safety, my memories, my father's grave. Those impressions—those parts of me—remained real and were a keepsake of who I was. Yet I forever felt torn between leaving them behind and cherishing them.

In the shadow of the large blue planet, I recognised a familiar speck immediately as the Observer. So small in comparison, yet large enough to cause catastrophic damage. The hologram showed the plotted trajectory in a thin white line—so innocent and delicate for something so devastating. I followed the trail around the planet until it finished in the Atlantic Ocean, just off the coast of Morocco. Stepping forward, I saw more detail now. It was close. The trajectory repeated, the thin line landing once again so near to the land. I saw my home, France, where I had grown up. I visualised my friend's house, where I had done my homework after school. I saw my dad's pharmacy, his life so centred around that little shop. I saw my neighbour, in that shoddy apartment complex, walking her small papillon, a fluffy little dog with a big attitude. Could I live with myself if I couldn't speak to someone on that planet, one more time, to tell them that there was so much more going on? To say that there was an alien here trying so hard to look after them? Trying to convince her entire species that humans were worth saving.

"*Speak with Earth,*" I said, but my eyes still watched the hologram, the thin line circling the planet once more.

"*No,*" replied the silver one.

The word stabbed at me. The first time a Leader had spoken to me directly, and it had refused to help. I glared at the silver Verax. It stood so much taller than me. My anger grew at this creature's indifference.

"*Why?*" I asked.

The Leader replied in the language I had started to understand, but they spoke fast and with no regard to my limited vocabulary. I stood confused and clueless and helpless.

Em must have felt my emotions. "*Leader unhappy with Earth,*" she said.

"*Why?*" I asked again, more disdainful this time. Even

though my father had said it was a good idea, I was starting to grow tired of always asking 'why'.

"*No Council,*" replied Em. That would have been 'not in the Council'. So, this was it—we were not part of their intimate group, so humans were left to rot. The anger rose, and any remnants of diplomatic tact had all but gone. I glared at the Leader.

"How fucking dare you?! You show up out of the blue, with these fucking droids; you have your little war in our solar system, and you're so fucking uptight about your Council, you can't even take responsibility for your actions?! You can't save a planet that had nothing to do with this war in the first place?" This was too much. The anger, the fury spread, and I choked on my words as I spat them out. Em took a step back, but I continued, "Are you just going to sit there and let this happen? How can you live with yourselves?!"

I remembered all those deaths, all the bodies lying on the decks of the Observer. That boy sitting in that one Hub Bunker, the tear going down his cheek, his leg bouncing up and down in anxiety. He would be crying now. Holding on to dear life. Utter terror.

"Em. *Help.*" I turned to my new friend, tears in my eyes. The idea that the planet I and all humanity called home could dissolve under our very eyes, on this stupid fucking hologram, while the Verax played high-class snobs in their carrier... I crumbled, the tears free-flowed down my cheeks.

"Alex... What's going on?" asked Nat, his voice distant in my helmet.

"*Speak with Earth,*" I repeated through tears. Nothing of my outburst would have made any sense to them. Except maybe Em, who had felt the sadness and rage flow through her too.

Silence as the room stared at me. They had witnessed their first human breakdown. Of course they were shocked. Nat and Joana had witnessed my outburst; they must have been full of questions too.

"Please, let me speak to them," I said. Out of ideas and

depleted from energy, I had no idea what else to add. The suit on my shoulders felt heavier than ever before. The moisture in the helmet, both from sweat and tears, congested my nose.

I only wanted to talk to someone over there. To know if they could handle it. Could they destroy it? Could they save the lives of millions, or were they scrambling on the ground like lost ants? I needed to know if I was to blame. Somewhere along the way I had made a mistake. I had not stopped Hagen fast enough. I could have. If I had tried harder. Surely, I could have tried harder.

"Speak with Earth," I repeated once more.

Why had my fear shown itself this way? I could have saved myself the emotional outburst, the fear and discomfort I had caused in the room. I could have remained diplomatic and serene and patient and understanding. But there was no time for that. No time for understanding. The Observer inched closer and closer to its final destination. And it had all happened because I hadn't put my foot down. Hadn't stood up to Hagen one last time. This was my fault, and I had failed to stop it. More than once.

"No."

ALEXANDRA GAUTHIER'S DIGITAL ARCHIVE

From: Dementia Support Line

To: Alexandra Gauthier

Date: January, 19th 2045 15:03

Location: Bin Folder

Subject: [Re:] Advice to cope

Good Afternoon, Alexandra,

Thank you for your email to the Dementia Support Line. We are glad you decided to email us rather than continue to push through your struggles.

Caring for a parent with dementia can be very challenging. Your initial email talks of your struggles with taking time for yourself, caring for your own feelings and protecting yourself from abuse.

We have extensive experience helping both patients with dementia and their carers, which is why we have an online course, available to all for only £240 per module (concession charges apply for people on benefits). You can take a look at our course, which features interviews with medical staff and highly trained carers, via this link. We've also attached a booklet with preparatory information about the course, including a taster of the advice we have to offer.

We're sorry you are experiencing difficulties as a carer and can only imagine the hardships you must be facing.

Please note: Our organisation is no longer supported by the government, and although we are doing everything in our power to help people in need, we have had to make drastic cuts to our personnel. This is why we ask anyone who visits our website to please donate. Every penny goes to our organisation and helps vulnerable people get the care they deserve.

Thank you for contacting Dementia Support Line, and we hope you have received all the advice you required today. If there is anything more we can do, please don't hesitate to contact us.

Yours sincerely,
Louise
Administrator
Dementia Support Line

12

I checked my wristpad once more. 12% oxygen. An hour or so left. Would that be enough to see it through? As we sat, shoulder to shoulder, slumped onto the floor, I watched a smaller hologram of Earth and the Observer conducting their final dance, next to the hologram of the carrier and its damage. As the Observer advanced towards its resting place, it seemed to be taking longer to fall than I had anticipated. No, an hour wouldn't be enough. But it was enough to rest a moment.

After the heated argument, I had given up. I had stood at the centre of that room in complete disbelief, and slowly, we had shuffled to the sidelines, where we had watched the rest of the battle develop and come to a steady resolution. Smaller ships had been destroyed, and it was clear the Verax had lost a number of people. Currently, both carriers sat in the darkness of space, side by side. It had been a quick fight. It had reminded me of seeing Em for the first time, fighting them off with ease in the Comms room. They knew the droids' weaknesses, it seemed. If not suspiciously so. After taking down some of their smaller ships, the Verax had disabled their carrier. What happened after that, after the Verax boarded the droids' carrier, was a mystery to me. Although, I did wonder if the droids had actually come prepared for a fight. Maybe their sole intention was to come to Earth—without knowing the Verax would shadow them.

Yet, even after this, the Verax had refused to step up and help Earth.

I tilted my head back, the rear of my helmet colliding with the wall behind. The scratchiness of my throat had been painful for a while now, but I saw no point in trying to ask for water. We would all be dead soon. And if we weren't, there would be not much left of home to go to.

If the Observer followed its projected trajectory, it would land in water, causing a tsunami off the coasts of Morocco, Western Sahara, Portugal, and Spain, inundating, if not demolishing, the Azores and the Canaries. The ramifications would also be felt elsewhere, continuing to spread over many countries and peoples. The break in atmosphere would cause debris to fall from the sky and get carried by the winds across the African continent. The air blast alone would be experienced halfway across Africa. The ecological and geological impacts from the resulting dust cloud would affect the rest of the world: famine, droughts, and the sun would disappear for a few decades. Global warming would seem like child's play.

I watched as the Leaders danced around the bridge, guiding their staff and directing operations. The silver one fluttered around the room in much the same way, yet they were clearly in charge of this ship.

Once the fighting had finished, Emerald had also approached the Leader to demand help for Earth, but she had been dismissed almost immediately. Since then, Emerald had wandered between Forest and me, attempting to talk, attempting to bring hope.

I felt her through the tether: her anxiety, her concerns, her protective nature. I wondered if all Verax could care as much as Em did, or if this was specific to her beliefs and personality.

The things we could have talked about... We could have

shared so much: a new type of friendship, the kind of close bond found in siblings. We could have discovered each other's species from fresh: how we each evolved from a single organism, how we first started to discover and build things, how society evolved and in what way, and what terrible political and social mistakes were made and how that affected life on our respective planets. How we had first reached for the stars... Why we had first believed there was other life out there. How that made us feel. What made us laugh and cry. What our hopes and dreams were. What inspired us and why we were the way we were. But all those things felt out of reach now.

"You know," said Joana, "my family is still over there." She hadn't spoken since we had first seen the trajectory of the Observer's collision. "My mum and dad."

"I'm sorry," said Nat, sitting on my other side.

There wasn't much more to be said to a woman about to watch her family die from hundreds of thousands of kilometres away, with no way of saving them. We would have to sit and wait. Earth could still have a plan. They had ways of predicting when asteroids would swing close to the planet; surely, they *must* know.

I considered myself lucky in that sense. My parents had died, and I had no immediate family to speak of. But Joana's wouldn't be far from the blast zone. There was no way they would make it out alive.

"What was one of the happiest moments of your life, Joana?" asked Nat. His gaze lay straight ahead.

"I don't think I really want to—"

"Come on. Life isn't going to get better from here on out. You may as well indulge me." He had lost that cheeky smile I had grown to like, but I still saw right through him. He had a way of making us get through the tough moments.

Joana took a moment to think. "My family took us on vacation once. Nothing too crazy, but it was one of the first family holidays they could afford, when I was about twelve.

We rented this little apartment on the outskirts of Rome. And one morning, I opened the window wide, and there were these balcony railings, and I just leant there. Sunshine on my face. Smell of fresh bread coming from somewhere down the street and that morning hunger when you wake up. It was the first time we had gotten up, and there was nothing out there that *needed* doing. No chores, no homework, no stress about money, just nothing. That kind of childlike bliss of being truly on holiday." She continued to stare at something on the floor, lost in the memory.

"What about you, Alex?" asked Nat.

I couldn't think of a happy time. I had been so focused on the bad moments recently, on the grief and the pain, that it felt like there had never been any good memories. Surely, I must have been happy at some point?

"I remember my dad taking me to football practice a lot. When I was a kid. He'd come and cheer me on at every session, every match." The cheer of the small, local crowd rang in my ears once more. Only the parents and families of the kids involved, but it was all we had needed to hear to keep us going. My dad had shouted my name and clapped and encouraged me. He had been proud of me then. Yet, somehow, the memory of stopping football at age thirteen had trumped all the good times. We couldn't afford to pay the club membership, and the coach wouldn't take us on unless we paid. The year before, my father had scrounged up what we needed, but that year had been different. The pharmaceutical business had suffered, with rising wholesale prices and customers unable to pay. My dad had always had a kind heart—forgiving debts for the sake of a stranger's health. Ultimately, he had to remortgage the house to cover the business debts. It seemed like such a long time ago.

"When I joined the army," said Nat, "I struggled to fit in, to make friends with the lads I was bunking with. I felt too… young, too inexperienced. I was quite self-conscious back then. I thought they didn't like me, and I felt like quitting and going home. But I had made a promise to myself to take this path. And one night, one of the guys, Tone, said a few more words than he had the previous day. The following day, I said a few more to him. And each day, it grew until, by the end of the week, I became one of them. That feeling of fitting in, when all you had was that anxiety, and it suddenly lifted. That was a happy moment." He smiled to himself this time. A personal victory. These intimate, small moments mattered most. There was a short pause before he asked, "First love?" Nat eyed Joana.

The hologram flickered in the centre of the room, and the image changed from the damage of the carrier to Earth once more. The silver one stood by the panels at the base of the hologram. The image flicked back to the carrier. Whatever they had just thought of, it had disappeared within a second.

"There was this girl I really liked," Joana said, her voice dry through the radio. "We were acquaintances, nothing more. I was about sixteen. It started out as a crush, but soon I had these really deep feelings. It was like a boulder crashing down onto my stomach. It made me want to throw up." She chuckled lightly to herself. "It lasted for almost a year. I'd get stressed and anxious when I used to see her in the corridors. I'd avoid her, but I also didn't want to be rude, so when she did speak to me, I agreed with everything she said and nodded along like an idiot, but I was dying inside." She laughed again but stopped herself. "Her name was Camila."

"I was in a long-term relationship in my early twenties," began Nat. "We'd been dating since I was about nineteen. I had started my studies, just after the army. That's how we met, actually. We stayed together until I was twenty-four. Then we drifted apart. Or something like that anyway. I don't remember why things changed, but they did. We agreed we were going in different directions. It was... amicable but sad. We still keep in touch, every now and again."

It was my turn, but I had nothing to say once again.

"I don't think I've ever been in love," I said. "I've had

crushes. When I was in school. I dated a guy for a couple of months in my late teens. And a woman in my early twenties. But it just... wasn't my focus." I thought back to those times with indifference. How had those moments slipped by and not mattered? Love was a powerful thing, but to me it had been a useless distraction. Work had been my objective, and both those short-term relationships had taken too much time, too much attention away from my studies, away from what was important. I had had clear goals, and love had not been a part of them.

"Any regrets?" asked Nat to Joana.

"Not really. You can always wish that things were different, but they never will be. We need to be thankful for the life that we were given; otherwise, what's the point, you know?" She paused. "But... I always thought there would be more. I don't know, maybe... I guess I didn't know what I wanted to do with my life. I went into cybersecurity because I had the grades, because there was a lot of demand, not because I found it interesting. I feel like life threw me a rope, and I've been dangling halfway down it ever since. I'm not sure if I want to climb to the top, and I'm not sure if I want to let go and find my own way."

My thoughts travelled back to the rope I had found myself at the end of, hanging from the Observer. Inches away from letting go. If I had, I wouldn't have met Emerald. I would never have seen an alien face-to-face. But I also wouldn't be sitting here, witnessing the destruction of a planet.

"Alex? Regrets?" asked Nat.

Everything, I thought to myself. Everything in my life had felt so wrong, so incomplete, so damaging. I stared ahead of me, my eyes fazing out the hologram. I wanted to redo everything. I wanted everything to change. How could anyone not agree with that?

"Everything," I muttered, a tear rolling down my cheek, finally saying the dreaded truth aloud.

"Why?" asked Nat after a short time. I had obviously

paused too long because he added, "You've got nothing to lose. I have," he checked his wristpad, "11% oxygen left. After this, they'll shut us in a room with more oxygen. If we're lucky, they'll send us to a planet in a catastrophic state, although I doubt anyone will come save us if the atmosphere is a massive dust cloud. I doubt these guys want to keep us alive for any reason. My point is we're not going anywhere, and we're hardly in a position to judge. Let it out."

I paused. Maybe this was the liberation I had been waiting for.

"Everything... is a mess. I—" I felt that familiar lump in my throat threatening to make me cry again. "It feels like it wasn't supposed to happen this way, but that it was always going to." I mused on this supposed *'fate'* Em had talked about—the tether that brought us together; it was always meant to be. Why had things happened this way? Was I meant to suffer to be here, right now? Had there been no other way?

"I wish my mum hadn't died when I was so young," I continued. "I wish my father had raised me differently. I wish my father hadn't been diagnosed with Alzheimer's. I wish he had received the care he deserved. I wish I'd had more courage to help him. To care for him. I wish I had tried harder to— I wish he'd—" There was that lump again. "I wish he—" Tears fell. I clasped my chest and forced myself to take staggered breaths. "I wish he hadn't killed himself."

I could see it all again. I could smell it and feel it. The familiar scent of his kitchen, the stuffiness of the room in the middle of summer. The putrid smell of death, in an apartment that already needed the window cracking open. I had seen his body, lifeless and unmoving, dead, head tilted to the left—just the same as David, peace in the chaos, stillness in the upset. I had felt the weight of his body in my arms as I had tried to lift him from his legs—a weight I couldn't carry. It had been too late. Far too late.

After the police had taken him away, I had stood on the same kitchen chair, my head next to the noose, and I had taken a knife to the rope. Each individual fibre snapping, one by one. When it had fallen loose in my hand, I had stood there a while longer and imagined the last thing my father had seen. The kitchen, from this particular angle, at this specific height.

There was nothing I could do with these memories now other than accept them. They were a part of me. Yet they burned and choked me all the same. But what did they mean in the face of all these people dying? All the children of the world, if they survived, would have similar memories of pain and grief about their families.

I cried some more. The pain in my chest became monumental, yet it had been a relief to say the words out loud. Em sat by my side, but I remained stuck in my bubble, in that helmet that wouldn't allow me to connect with people, wouldn't allow me to touch, or hug, or feel anything real until it was off. The tether never lied, and so it became a comfort, knowing that Em would always be there, to feel my pain with me.

We all sat together in silence amongst the sobbing. Nat's hand on my knee. Joana's own tears fell too. Em, with Forest at her side, attempted to understand what we were feeling.

But, all I wanted to do was ask Nat if he had any regrets, to pass the burden of attention onto him. The pain stuck to my throat, and I felt unable to utter a word. By the time the tears had passed, the moment had moved on.

A short time had elapsed before Em had dragged us away from the bridge. My legs felt stiff and sore as we shuffled into a nearby room.

This entrance was smaller—not grandiose and imposing like the one to the bridge. The door was made of a similar material to glass—see-through and lightly tinted. Anyone could look in or out of this area.

Inside, silence reigned. This space had a softness about it: curved edges to the walls and flooring and even fainter lighting. Opposite the door were some smaller glass panes looking out the side of the carrier. The ship itself was nowhere to be seen, so I presumed we were towards the back of the carrier. Only the stars stretched out before us, a calming presence much needed in a time like this.

Forest tapped the panel by the door, and I monitored the oxygen change on my wristpad once again.

With my helmet off, I took a deep breath. Although I had been hot in the suit, the air chilled my skin. The temperature was comfortable at around twenty-one degrees Celsius. Everything felt real again. Life was palpable, touchable. The suffocation from that suit caused me to feel like my existence was always on the line. Like time was my enemy, but now the three of us stood in a void, with no purpose, no future, and time seemed not to matter anymore.

I pondered whether the Verax would have a need for three humans aboard their carrier. With everything I knew about them—very little, that is—the one aspect I could rely on was that they functioned with accuracy and with meaning. Em and Forest had proven themselves kind and compassionate, caring of our surroundings and our comfort. If she was capable of feeling those things, then surely all Verax could.

A decision needed to be made soon with regards to us being here. I knew the time was approaching, but I couldn't decide if I wanted to hear the verdict or not. If they refused to let me speak to anyone on Earth, why would they bother sending us back? What would they do with us?

Forest locked the door behind us, stopping any other Verax from disturbing the human-friendly atmosphere he had just created. But both he and Em had been quiet since we had entered this special room, its tranquillity undisturbed.

"Question. What is room?" I enquired.

"New word," started Em. She pulled out the hologram machine, and together we found a word that was close enough. *"Room is calm."*

The possibilities for this word were endless: it could be a place of meditation, or religious significance, or maybe even a place for the Verax to rest or sleep, although there were no beds, nor any seats like the one I had seen in the little shuttle.

"*Why?*" I asked. My heart was not in it. Of course, I wanted to know everything about this species, but I couldn't see the point in anything right now.

"*Room for feeling.*"

It tied in with their beliefs, their idea of fate and emotion. A meditation room, I assumed. My legs ached enough that I soon sat down on the cushioned floor. I had a million more questions but no spirit to ask them. Yet, I needed to ask them one more.

"*Question.* Alex, Nat, Joana. *We go to Earth?*" I should have felt scared and anxious about the answer, yet I felt nothing. My heart had despaired so much it had grown empty. Devoid of any sentiment. Ready for its own annihilation.

"*I don't know,*" replied Em.

I wished I could feel what Em felt through the tether, but for some reason my own emotions clouded everything. An empty nothingness hung in the air, like a thick fog, and no light at the end of the tunnel. Em seemed to be weighed down by my emotions; she slumped to the floor, mirroring my hopelessness.

"*Yes, you say,*" said Forest. "*Say to A'ex.*"

It still surprised me when I heard one of them speak my name. This was Forest, who hours earlier had been so dismissive. I couldn't understand his change of heart. Nat and Joana had also perked up at the sound of my name.

"What's going on?" asked Nat.

"She's not telling me something," I explained, turning my head towards Em, my eyes scratchy and my head heavy.

Em shuffled herself in front of me. "*New word.*" She tapped at the hologram, compiling another list of symbols I couldn't yet understand. It took us a long time, but we worked each of the words out individually, and I noted them down. I was sure I had made mistakes, and when I found one, I erased it from the whiteboard and began again. My head felt so cloudy, my eyes couldn't even see straight. A persistent ache in my arm, both from the sprain and the writing, made itself known.

"Leaders no trust humans. Humans no ready for Council."

Through the tiredness, I became captivated with figuring out this puzzle once more, enough for my brow to furrow and for my attention to focus. I could understand humans not being ready for the Council. This Council had probably been around for millennia, so of course humans would seem too primitive, too early in their space age. Nat and Joana sat either side of me, forming a circle around the hologram.

"But why no help Earth?" I asked. Being involved in a Council had nothing to do with helping.

"Verax help. Human and Verax have relationship. Humans no ready..." Em blanked.

We drew up a new list of words. An odd collection, yet I could tell where this was going.

"Biology, feeling, physiology, politic issues. Humans no ready."

I couldn't disagree with that. I had no idea what waited for us out there, in the rest of the galaxy. I scratched my temple; the sweat had made my skin rough and tacky.

"She says that we're not equipped, that we haven't progressed far enough, to be a part of the Council," I explained in English. Nat nodded as Joana stared at the ground.

"Humans no ready," I agreed. *"Droid attack is Verax issue. Council issue. Humans in danger. No human issue."* It was hard to have an argument in a foreign language.

"Understand." Em nodded in her non-human way. *"But rules are no... New word."* We looked it up, and I added it to the hologram whiteboard. The list stretched so far now that it took a minute or so to look up a word I didn't recognise.

"No interfere."

"Why?"

We searched another word, and Em confirmed my initial thoughts.

"Human too primitive."

"Too primitive..." I repeated in English.

Of course, it all came down to this. There was no arguing that point. The Verax had ships to travel through space, as did the droids. They *were* more advanced. I wondered if their rules allowed them to watch from the sidelines, until a species looked impressive enough to allow on the Council. Until they could be approached with a document to sign, proof they were not going to be a liability to whatever rules this Council followed.

My sleepiness turned to frustration. I shook my head. The human species would go extinct because someone else brought a war over here, and Earth had been too primitive to defend itself. A solid argument lay somewhere in there for fiscal-military states. Had Earth focused on military and tech advancements, we could have defended ourselves without a problem. But chances were, whichever human would have been in charge wouldn't have thought twice about attacking the Verax as well as the droids out of 'self-defence'. I shook my head a second time; what-ifs were useless now.

"Question. We go to Earth?" I asked. Em hadn't answered the question the first time I asked it.

"Yes, but I don't know... in shuttle?"

"So, they just don't know *how* to send us back," I said to Nat and Joana.

Nat shrugged in response—no, neither did we. Would they send us down now, or would they shuttle us down into the cloud of dust that could blot out the sun for decades?

But something still didn't make sense to me.

"What is tether?" I asked. The question had been burning inside me since the moment we had bonded.

"New word."

It didn't take too long for us to proceed—I was picking them up faster and faster, a sign I understood how Em thought, her way of explaining things.

"Tether is trust symbol. Give to family, partners, or close people. Create trust. No break. Emotion connection. Forever."

The only thing I could equate it to was a marriage, or

another cultural or civil union, but only in that there was an emotional bond between the two. There was nothing legal about it, unless...

"Question. Tether is politic or... culture?"

"Tether is emotion. Feeling. Tether has rules..." Her mood dipped, a sudden shift from comfortable to uneasy, or maybe embarrassed.

"What rules?"

"Tether is connection forever. Em say 'yes'. A'ex say 'yes'. You no say 'yes'."

So, the tether was a consensual and loving act, yet Emerald had tethered to me without my consent or my knowledge of what it meant. That must have been why Em was in trouble with her Leaders. I had no way of knowing how much of an issue this was within their culture, nor if this affected Em's legal rights or her status in their society. All those things would come later, if ever. This also meant that I, whether I liked it or not, would be forever bound to Emerald in this way. It created an unsettling feeling in me, something like betrayal, but dirtier, like our impromptu friendship had been sullied. I was sure she could feel my discomfort, but I saved that conversation for another time.

"Okay," I nodded. *"More tether rules?"*

"Culture, yes, and more. Tether is ceremony. Tether to four or five people. Maybe live all five people together. Tether is no one group. Tether maybe connect with different group. Maybe all people connected."

This sparked my curiosity. I remembered doing a project for school once that posed the question: can trees talk to each other? I had read into the underground fungal networks beneath tree roots that connected them all.

"Hm. If you tether to Forest, and Forest tether to other people, and you feel sad, other people feel sad?"

"Yes," replied Em. She paused to look for a word. It didn't quite translate, but I understood it all the same. *"Emotion pandemic. All connected sad."* If depression or anxiety could be

caught and spread like a disease, this would be one way that could happen.

Only now had I realised how emotional I had been throughout all this. I had met Emerald when my life was in danger; we had connected when I had been grieving. I had felt hope, friendship, attraction, but also fear, despair, and emptiness. I had been an emotional wreck, and Em had suffered through those emotions just as much.

"Question. Verax have big... feeling and emotion?" I couldn't phrase it any other way, but I wanted to understand if we felt feelings to the same extent.

"Verax have big..." She looked up another word. *"Big range of emotion. But not strong. Human have strong emotion."*

Em had said that with the utmost honesty, yet I could see the pain in her eyes, behind that visor. Had I caused her to suffer? Had Emerald doomed herself by tethering to an emotional species?

"Question. Em, number of tether?" I asked.

"One," she replied, with a nod.

"Good. *Good.*" I took a deep breath. I did not want to be the cause of the next emotional pandemic among the Verax.

"Anything of use?" asked Nat.

I shrugged. "Just information about the tether, that... bond, between me and her. Sounds like it might be more trouble than it's worth."

Nat looked at me dubiously—maybe he didn't believe in this kind of stuff.

Rubbing my hands across my face, I thought up my next query. *"Question. Tether is fate?"*

"Culture, yes. Feeling of tether is here before tether," replied Em, factual and honest.

Like the tether had been invisible, like the connection had been so strong, so meant-to-be, that it had already existed. But this was where my own scepticism played a part. I couldn't deny it was there, couldn't deny it had happened in an odd way, with Em finding us on the station the way she did. But how could something that hasn't happened yet already be in the works?

"No understand."

"Culture. We believe feeling." Em pushed her long, gangly hands to her chest.

"You believe feeling more than... rules?" I had wanted to say 'anything' but didn't know the word. Yet 'rules' was a good example. Could one believe their faith in this tether more than their own laws, both social and legal?

"Feeling is... New word." A quick search and we had it. *"Most important."*

That... made sense. And in some way, that helped our case.

"Alex speak with Leaders."

Em looked surprised but agreed almost immediately, sensing my heart rate quicken.

"And," I added, *"new word."*

Searching for the right terms had been harder without knowing how to use the hologram machine. But we had managed to find a compromise, and I found the ones I needed to make my case.

The silver Leader stood behind the pane of glass at the door, obvious disinterest in being there. I wondered if I *could* actually read the Verax's body language better each moment, or maybe my own subconscious played tricks on me.

"What's this about?" asked Joana. She had stood up and followed me to the airtight door.

"I think I can convince them..." I replied, my heart beating fast at the prospect. I was certain of nothing, but I had a strong feeling. I felt I was learning from the Verax way: trusting my gut and following my emotions. Hopefully, Em could sense the same conviction through the tether.

"Why ⊣≷ ⊢Ⓦ human ⊋⊦≲∪ ⊐∉ speak ⊔≱≳⊔ me?" said the silver one. The unknown words threw me off, but I wasn't going to back down now.

"Tether is connection," I started. *"Tether is forever. Tether is destiny. Em tether to me, because of destiny. You know destiny is most important. Respect destiny and tether. Help save Earth from station fall."*

"You want us ⊐¢ help you save ⊥⊁⊄ ⊋∪⊏⊐⊆ planet ∪≼ you ≽⊏ ⊊⊥⊐≺ ⊤⊥≼≳≲⊅ ⋔≼⊐∩⊢≲⊀. ⊥⊁⊄ species ⊐⊁⊄≺≻ no ≽⊏ ⊓∩⊢⊅ station ∪≼ they ⊢⊨≳⊒ no save ≲∪≲⊐∩∪⊆ from. ⊥⊁ ⊅⊊∪ ⊐¢ me ⊏⊐ you ≽⊏ ⊤ ⊄≲⊏ ⊢≲⊅⊊∪≼," replied the silver one. Their tone and pitch differed from the others I had talked to. I wondered if they spoke with the equivalence of an accent, or maybe it was a social status indicator. But my vocabulary had not developed enough to understand all the arguments the Leader was making. So, I persisted.

"If tether is destiny, Alex, *me, stays alive. If tether is destiny, if tether is more important than rules, maybe destiny is for Leaders to save Earth."*

The silver one paused. I couldn't tell if it was working.

"This, here, always happen. Earth future is yours. You, Leaders, speak with me, Alex, *now and here, because of destiny."* I wasn't even sure I believed this myself, but I hoped it would be enough to show that I had some basic understanding of what the tether was, that I knew about their rules, that I cared enough about the Verax to learn about them. *"Help save Earth. Because this is future."*

A pause. The silver one opened their helmet on the other side of the glass. They peeled back the visor from their face. Dark, wide eyes stared back at me, pupils so large, I could only scarcely discern them from the irises. A light coating of silver fur covered their skin, except for the tip of their nose, which stood out in a darker shade of grey.

"Yes. Speak with Earth." The silver one's mouth moved in astonishing fashion: thin lips curled, and a large, odd-shaped tongue articulated the words.

They turned to Em and spoke in their native language. The discussion continued for a while, but I was too preoccupied by the Verax's face, analysing their movements and facial features. Immense relief flooded me, yet I felt an underlying sense of worry from whatever the two Verax were discussing.

The silver one left, holding on to their mask with one hand, and walked back along the corridor they had come from.

"What Leader say?" I asked, full of excitement, joy, and a side of nerves.

"Leader want you to speak to Earth, explain that station fall. We help. Leader say that Earth will have debt. Earth work to be in Council. Not easy. Leader angry with me for tether."

"Okay," I said with a nod. *"How we help Earth?"*

"I have idea," replied Forest, who had been listening from the sidelines, with a mimic of a human smile.

VERAX DIGITAL ARCHIVE [TRANSLATED BY GAUTHIER]

CARRIER NEWS BULLETIN:

VERAX WIN WAR

Losses: Five ships, twenty-eight lives

Enemy losses: Twelve ships, thirty-two lives

Enemy commander brought aboard. Surrendered. To be brought before Council for final judgement. Will answer for endangering sub-species.

Three humans aboard. Human planet in danger. Space station collision inbound. Leaders have decided to help. Unsure where this places humans in hierarchy. Humans still considered sub-species.

13

"Earth, come in. My name is Alex."

The vast expanse stretched out in front of me. The carrier faced the wrong way to see Earth. By my side stood a makeshift desk, and atop it, another hologram serving as some kind of radio. The radio signals were directed towards Earth so that any satellite dish even remotely pointed in our direction would pick up the communication.

My hands shook, not from excitement or nervousness but from lack of energy. My eyelids felt heavy, and the hunger pangs had subsided and given way to a permanent ache.

Nat stood not far; his face directed towards the stars. His body language gave him away, because although he stood straight, his head hung low—an after-effect from the thirst and light-headedness we all suffered from.

Less than twenty or so minutes ago, I had described water to Emerald. I had given her the elemental structure and crossed my fingers they would bring something filtered enough to not cause us any harm.

However, in the meantime, with our helmets back on, we had helped move some equipment into this new room. The

Leader had given us access to all that we required to communicate from a far-off distance. A bold move from someone who, not long ago, wanted nothing to do with humans. I still wondered, even now, waiting for a reply from our planet, if I had not doomed Earth in a different way by asking for the Verax's help. *Earth will have debt*, Em had said. I couldn't possibly imagine what that could look like.

"Earth, come in. This is Alex," I repeated.

It had taken us a while to agree on how to send this message. After a short debate, we had concurred that a simple communication, sent out to anyone who was listening, would be the best option. So, there was my voice, flying through the vacuum of space and landing on a number of satellites and devices across the planet, possibly to all of them, possibly to none. Yet no one had answered. The Observer hadn't approached Earth enough to have affected the satellites around the planet, so, at least using my current knowledge, there should be nothing stopping them from replying.

"Joana, how does the Observer communicate with Earth?" I asked, my words raspy in my throat.

"Umm…" she replied, raising her head from the floor she had been resting on. "Radio frequencies, because that's how we sent our SOS." She paused a moment, waking herself up. "Oh. But it would help if they knew where we were to reply. With the Observer, we had a plotted trajectory, so if messages were sent, Earth would send them to the location we would be in a few minutes later. Does… that make sense?"

"So they need to know where we are to answer?"

"That's my guess. I assume the Verax don't use radio frequencies, but that's *our* only space communication method," replied Joana.

"I would have thought that the tech the Verax had was strong enough to pick up any replies," I said.

"That may be somewhat true, but if Earth sent something in a Northeast-like direction using radio waves, and we're Southwest, we're not going to get it."

"So," interjected Nat, "we need to know where we are, and we need to convey that to Earth."

I turned back to the hologram and, on a blank piece of the whiteboard, drew a rough representation of our solar system and placed the carrier ship somewhere not far from Earth.

"When Em gets back, I'll get the location from her." I wiped my hands over my face. "I hope she brings something to drink, to be honest."

"Until then," said Nat, "why don't you get some rest?"

"I just feel like I could be doing something else…" I straightened my back, in an effort to give myself some vitality, but my bones cracked, and my muscles ached. If we survived this, it would take me weeks of rest to recover from all that had happened.

With the hologram machine in hand, I began rearranging my notes. A quick tidy-up to keep wide awake.

Nat sat back down, his head against the alloy walls. I knew he worried about me. But there was no time for worry. I needed to get this communication through to Earth. I needed to know what was happening down there.

Em and Forest entered the room a short while later, carrying a container between them. A translucent liquid jostled around in the tub, filled to the brim. They dropped the container on the floor, not far from us.

"*Water*," said Em.

I approached the tub and sniffed at it with caution. Unfiltered water was one of the most dangerous things to ingest, yet nothing seemed off about this.

"Did you know," started Joana, "that humans have ways of determining the potability of water with only our senses? Just one of those natural instincts we have for survival." She closed in on the tub as well, dipped a finger in, and promptly put it in her mouth. "Tastes fine to me."

I scooped the water with my hands and brought it to my face. The slush of the liquid down my throat felt revitalising and blissful. An odd aftertaste lingered on my tongue, like when water has been left in an old bottle for too long, like the plastic had started to decompose around it. But it was water, and it was all I ever needed right here and now. I took a second handful and drank that immediately.

"Take it easy. You don't want to make yourself sick," said Nat. He was right. I felt like my stomach had shrunk and could only take in small amounts at a time.

"Water stay here," I insisted, my hand on the side of the tub. Em nodded in return.

"Question. Carrier. Location in space," I said. Although I had directed the query at Em, my eyes glided over to Forest, who perked up.

How does one relate the position of an object in space? It needed to be relative to something. On my whiteboard, I drew a line between Earth, the Moon, and the Observer, and led them all to the carrier. Triangulation. In all my years, I had never imagined needing to use Pythagoras's theorem outside of graduating high school, but here I was. To manage this, we would need to discuss units of measurement and how to convert those without a tape measure or ruler.

"Nat, do you have any way of explaining measurements and helping convert those into their units?" I asked.

He took a step towards the hologram whiteboard and drew a line and broke it up into approximate one-centimetre chunks until he reached ten centimetres. Then he copied the ten centimetres ten times, until he reached a metre.

"The carrier is a big ship. If Earth misses by even a kilometre or two, it should still reach us. Hell, maybe they've even got powerful receivers here. But Earth has no clue where we are, so if we can get a rough direction, that will help." He paused and looked at his makeshift ruler. "You need to explain that a thousand metres is a kilometre and get Forest to figure out what he wants to convert it to. Then it'll be fairly easy."

Forest had understood the concept and worked on a separate portion of the whiteboard. Soon enough, he had managed to come up with a series of numbers, already converted to the metric system. The Verax worked damn fast.

"Thank you," I said.

So, we were 532,500 kilometres from Earth. It would be surprising if we could get a clear message from the planet at this range. Using the units of distance from three different locations, someone should be able to pin-point our approximate position. Forest provided those without issue.

Opening up the radio, I spoke clearly and slowly, "Earth, come in. This is Alex again. We are 532,500 kilometres from Earth. We are 165,300 kilometres from the Moon, and 517,200 kilometres from the current position of the Observer. Please reply urgently." I waited a moment before repeating the message once more, making sure to slow down when giving the numbers.

"Comms have gotten a little faster over the years, but you might still need to wait a while before you get anything back," said Joana. "On the Observer, it could take a good three minutes to get anything from the ground."

We waited about fifteen before a voice crackled through the radio.

"Alex? Alex, come in. This is Deputy Administrator Harper Carlson from the National Aeronautics and Space Administration. First questions first: where the hell are you? This is an open channel; all of NASA can hear you. The UN have been informed and are present too."

The woman's voice was stiff and firm. Yet it was such a relief to hear another human being, one on solid ground, speak. Em must have felt the solace through the tether as she placed a hand on my shoulder, something she had seen us humans do between each other and merely copied.

I didn't know where to start or what to say. I had so many questions.

"Hi, Harper. This is Alex again. We're..." Was I going to be believed this time? "We're on an alien vessel, like a carrier ship. We *were* on the Observer. There's three of us here. It's a long story." A nervous laugh escaped me, but the shake in my voice put me back in my place. There was nothing to laugh about. Yet this remained a small victory all the same. "I'll happily tell it to you. But I need to say this first: the Observer, it's falling. And the ship I'm on, they want to help. I think they have a plan."

Should I have added anything to that? The last time I had told a stranger what had happened, they hadn't believed me. They must have known by now that something had happened up here. When I had spoken to the small BioTech station, they said they had passed the message along. They knew the Observer was falling. This couldn't have happened without outside interference. So, why would they doubt me?

"What do you think they'll say?" asked Joana, after taking another sip of water.

"I doubt they would refuse the help," said Nat.

The voice crackled through the radio minutes later.

"Jesus Christ. I… I don't know whether to believe you, except why else would this signal reach you. The carrier you've mentioned isn't showing up on our equipment. If you can change that, that would help us confirm your position. If you think these extraterrestrials have a plan, I take it you've established a line of communication with them?"

"How do we get the carrier to show up on Earth's equipment?" I asked.

"Why *isn't* it on their radar to begin with?" said Nat.

It didn't make sense. How does an object this size not appear on radar? Did the Verax and the droids use the same stealth technology? Was that even a thing that existed? I thought to myself for a moment—there was no real way of asking the question. I'd need to explain how radar worked and what stealth tech was, and I didn't have the vocabulary for either of those.

"*What is ship?*" I asked.

"*Ship is… ship,*" replied Em, uncertainty coursing through the tether.

"Umm, not quite what I was after," I replied in English. And to Nat and Joana, "We need to find a way to make it seen."

"I mean, we don't know what they can or can't do; it's not easy…" said Nat.

"*Question?*" intervened Emerald.

I felt flustered, unable to say what I wanted to, but full of excitement and pressure to get everything on track. To save the planet from devastation. "*Earth want… sign. Carrier is here.*"

"*Use carrier engine light?*" asked Em.

"That could work…" I muttered. Thoughts and possibilities flew around my mind like chattering birds. I turned back to the radio. "I have managed to understand the basics of their language so far. Once I know what your plans are for the Observer, I might be able to communicate that to them and see if we can adjust or help in any way. As for proof, watch the sky." Looking at Em once more, I said, "*Use light.*" And to Nat and Joana, "Do either of you know Morse code or something?"

A pause before I observed them shake their heads.

"Oh, but I know enough about binary to work something out," replied Joana, one finger up and excitement on her face.

Once the word had been translated to binary, thanks to Joana, I passed it to Em and explained they needed to flash the rear engines in a specific pattern to send a message to Earth. Emerald agreed and left the room with Forest once more.

I couldn't stop smiling. We were finally doing this, doing something worthwhile.

While we waited, I wondered if, on their way to the bridge, Em and Forest ever talked amongst themselves about all of this. Like a couple of schoolgirls between classes, gossiping about a teacher's grades. Did they speak of humans and how primitive they were? Or did they share a sense of excitement about meeting a new species?

The light sequence was set to loop for over twenty or so

minutes. I hoped that with a good enough telescope, the flashes of light could be visible.

The radio crackled up once more as Harper's voice rose through.

"Thanks Alex. You can stop lighting the skies with your name now. I also want you to know that you are currently still broadcasting to the world. Anyone with a half-decent radio can hear you. They're following your every movement." She took a deep breath before continuing, "So, here's the deal: we have a plan, but it's not a good one. The estimated impact is in about six hours, but the sooner we change its course, the better. The UN has missiles ready to launch, but that would only change *how* the Observer crashes, not *if* it crashes. I'd like to hear what your new allies have thought of. If it's better, if their tech is more advanced, which I'm assuming it is, their plan might just save millions of lives. And the sooner, the better." Another breath. "And at some point, an explanation of what the fuck is going on would be great too."

"She sounds pissed off," said Nat.

"Understandable. Anyone who's in charge and has no control over a crisis is going to be tense." I needed to place more trust in the woman. She was no doubt doing her best. But it was now or never. *"Question, Em. Plan to help Earth?"*

"Yes," replied Emerald. *"Plan. Forest, explain plan."*

"We ran the numbers." Harper's voice sputtered through the radio once more. "And they are right. If they can do what they say they can do, then this is the better outcome. At the expense of whoever is left on the Observer." A pause and a sigh. "We'd be reducing the immediate casualties from the millions down to the thousands. But I'm going to need the specifics. Trajectories and times, as accurate as they can make them. The UN needs this to be concrete and foolproof. We can't risk any errors." A brief silence stretched out before Harper continued. "I take it you trust these extraterrestrials?"

The communication ended, and I was left with the

lingering question. Did I trust this species? I wasn't sure. But I trusted Em. I could feel her emotions, so unless Emerald could fake her feelings and conceal a betrayal, there was no reason to have any doubts. Em had never given me any suspicions since the tether had bound us. And even if I *felt* betrayed by the tethering, if the tether was always 'meant-to-be', then you could say that neither of us had a choice in the matter.

"I'll get the numbers to you immediately. As for trust, I have no reason to believe they could mean us any harm. We have one or two here that have personally saved our lives more than once. I'd vouch for them, if that meant anything to you." I eyed Em and Forest with something similar to admiration. Yet, in the back of my mind, my thoughts loitered again on what Em had said earlier. *Earth will have debt.* Could that be a betrayal to come?

I turned from the radio and towards Nat, "How could we get the plans over to the UN? Could we send them—"

"You could see if these guys have something like a VoIP system?" interjected Joana.

"A VoIP system?"

"Voice over Internet Protocol. It's like… the basics of the internet. A bit old-fashioned now, but reliable. Astronauts use it to speak to their families back home. The Observer worked off it too."

"Okay. You alright explaining that to the Verax?" I asked with a smirk.

Joana laughed. "I thought you were in charge of communicating. Tell you what, I'll draw a sketch of it, you can explain. It's not too complicated, and they must have something similar in place anyhow, what with the hologram machine being able to pull information from thin air. We need to make them compatible, that's all."

Placing herself in front of the whiteboard, Joana drew a series of gadgets, from Wi-Fi routers to servers to telephone networks. This must have seemed like a caveman drawing to the Verax, a basic and rudimentary schematic to send audio and video footage from one location to another.

But within minutes they had attached a hologram screen with a built-in camera. Indecipherable text hung on the hologram, ready for someone to tap buttons and give it orders. Em explained each one so I could operate it on a basic level.

With the help of the Leaders and Forest, we figured out the trajectory of the frigate-type ship we would use to launch this plan into action. The details and projected courses were sent as video communication back to NASA's headquarters. Still unsure if they could open the file, I sent my own communication alongside it.

"Hey, this is Alex again," I said. A clear 2D image appeared before me. The first time I had looked at my face since all this had happened, and I couldn't recognise the figure looking back at me. Still in my bulky spacesuit, minus the helmet, I looked tired. My eyes sunk further into my head; the large bags under both eyelids doing me no favours. My hair was greasy and pulled back in an unflattering way. My complexion missed that glow I had often had on a sunny day, and the skin around my lips had cracked from dehydration. Across my forehead were the remnants of the thump that had knocked me out, the gash itself covered by dried blood.

I looked away. This wasn't how I wanted to be known or to be remembered or to be seen. "I've sent you the file with all the info. As you can see, we have video footage now. This is Em." I pointed to Emerald, who was only just in the frame. Still in a full suit, Em's size and shape were a clear indicator that she was not human. "Em. *Copy* Alex," I said, and I waved my hand at the camera. Em copied me, forcing her long, awkward hand into the video footage. I would have broken a smile if I hadn't been so tired, so hateful of the way I looked in the video. "That's not her full name, but we can talk about that later. Our ship is changing position, so I've also included our projected trajectory so we can keep communicating. Let me know if you have any questions. Em. *Close call, please.*"

Emerald shut down the video call, as I took a deep breath.

My head felt so heavy. Turning to Forest, I said, *"Okay. Explain ship cores again."*

"We study black holes. We understand. We understand how create black hole. But we... change direction. Black hole pull everything in. White holes pull things in but never reach centre, and releases object back out. Black hole gravity is strong, pull light in. White hole release energy, create eternal fuel. No eternal, but close," replied Forest. *"We study. We create..."* He hesitated.

"New word," said Em. And she explained the concept of a mimic, or an imitation of something.

"We create mimic of white hole," continued Forest. *"Control environment around mimic. Use this metal..."* He brought up the atomic breakdown on the hologram.

Nat shifted. He hadn't understood any of the conversation, but when the plan had first been explained, he had shown some concern. "I don't know what that is, but as far as I'm aware, there is nothing, and I mean *nothing*, that should be able to contain a black hole or a white hole. It doesn't make sense. It's impossible."

"Where is metal?" I asked, pointing at the atomic breakdown. *"Which planet?"*

"Elders," confirmed Em.

"Elders create white hole mimic?"

"Yes."

"And Elders create metal?" I asked.

"Yes."

"How?"

"We don't know. We recreate white hole mimic. But metal is... New word." She searched once more, and it took a while to convey, but it made sense. *"Limited. No made by Verax."*

"And ships made of this metal?" I asked.

"Yes."

This explained their dark mirror sheen—a metal so soul-sucking, so unique in look, and possibly, so expensive to create. *"So there are no extra supply of ships?"*

"We," started Em. *"New word."* A quick search. *"We re-*

purpose metal. It shape easy, but no destroy easy."

These Elders held onto some of the oldest secrets of the universe. I toyed with the idea of meeting them, speaking with them, and finding out this incredible knowledge they must have. But this metal now became the biggest mystery of all.

"Question. Humans speak with Elders?" I said. It didn't hurt to ask.

Em shook her head almost immediately. *"No. No speak with Elders. They protect."*

An odd phrase. Had she meant the Elders were protected, or that they protected themselves? And why would they seal themselves off from communicating with a new species? Maybe their opposing beliefs stopped the Verax from even speaking to them.

"Why?" I asked.

Em hesitated, but Forest cut her off.

"Long explain. We talk about plan for Earth." He was right; we would have plenty of time to talk about the Elders after this—after the Earth was saved.

I nodded, "Sorry, Forest. *Explain plan."*

"White hole mimic in ship and carrier and shuttles. Connect to engine. Infinite energy. No need fuel. No limit to power," he continued, his hands and arms extremely active during his description.

"So," I continued, *"to help Earth: take out ship core, remove metal, release mimic white hole next to station. Gravity and energy pull station away from Earth. Put metal back on white hole. Earth is safe."*

"That is plan," concluded Forest. He brought up a hologram display of their proposal.

There, I saw the small frigate ship advance towards the Observer, which was still making its descent towards Earth. The frigate paused and released a small box. The box opened once the frigate was at a safe distance. The white hole sucked all objects towards it, and the box sealed remotely after the Observer changed its course, but before it affected Earth. The frigate collected the box, and the Observer headed further into space.

It still didn't make sense that the Verax ships would be immune to black or white holes. How could one metal defy the laws of physics this way? The whole plan seemed unlikely and marginally crazy. However, it might actually work.

Nat stood close by. He scratched the back of his head whilst looking at the diagram.

"And plan B is to shoot a shit ton of nukes at it, right?" he said, then shrugged. "I prefer plan A."

"This ship," I said, as I pointed at the frigate dropping the white hole. *"In danger of station."* If anything were to go wrong, that frigate would take a large hit from the Observer. I also knew that Earth had space debris and satellites floating in its orbit. All that material would also be flung in their direction.

"Ship is made of metal," replied Forest. *The* metal, the fantastic one that doesn't seem affected by anything. *"Ship is strong."*

"And satellites?"

Forest zoomed in on the virtual plan, where hundreds if not thousands of tiny dots appeared. Watching the hologram, I witnessed some satellites get pulled away from Earth; some fell, and others changed their orbit. It would take years for any of Earth's scientists to put them back as they were. But as I looked closer, yes, some would head straight towards the frigate at an intense speed due to its lighter structure. Whoever was on that ship could be sacrificing themselves for this planet.

"Yes, some satellite fall to Earth, some go towards ship," said Forest, confirming my thoughts.

"It's still a better plan than whatever the UN came up with," said Nat.

A moment later, the radio crackled, and Harper's voice spoke out once more. Her tone became more and more drained as her messages came through.

"Yes, well, I have lots of questions about *"Em"*, but I don't think this is an appropriate time to ask them.

"We've received the plans, and the UN has reviewed them. They've agreed that this is the best course of action. You may proceed with any preparations, as will we. We'd like to keep in constant communication with you. Once you are closer, the time delay between messages will be shorter. Please let us know when this plan will go ahead. We need to be aware of every movement you make. Needless to say, again, the sooner the better.

"And I have one final request from you. We will need someone, someone that can speak a human language, to be present on that ship. This is the future of the planet we're talking about; we need an extra layer of security for this operation."

That ship. The frigate dropping the white hole. Nat, Joana, and I looked at each other, eyes hopping from one person to the next. Harper was asking us to not only split up, for the first time since this had all happened, but to potentially sacrifice one of our own. How could she ask us to make that decision? One of us might die. And I did not feel ready to deal with that. Not today. Not after everything we had been through.

My eyes fell to the ground. I already knew what would happen. Everything had already played out in my head. Maybe destiny and fate were real. Maybe everything had happened, here, in this specific way, with these specific people, for it to end in this manner. I shook my head before tapping the radio button once more.

"Copy that. We're moving closer to you now. I'll give you notice when the frigate leaves the carrier. Someone will be aboard. We'll get them to install an open channel so everyone can hear each other. You might want to look at the satellites around the Observer." My low voice rang listlessly in my ears. Someone should be aboard that frigate, but it shouldn't have to be one of us. Had we not sacrificed enough already? Had we not seen enough death?

I turned from the hologram machine and caught Nat's eye. We both knew it would be him. Because I could speak to the

Leaders from here. Because Joana did not feel confident or comfortable going. Because Nat was the only other option. Because Nat would jump at the opportunity to help. Because he was selfless and caring and thoughtful and everything someone should be.

ALEXANDRA GAUTHIER'S DIGITAL ARCHIVE

From: Claude Gauthier

To: Alexandra Gauthier

Date: August, 2nd 2047 23:52

Location: Favourites Folder

Subject: Funeral

Hey couz,

Long time no speak. The family are flying over soon. Well, some are anyway. Look, I don't want to make this awkward. You know where we come from. You know our family. They don't deal well with these mental health issues. And even though the laws changed in whatever year, suicide is still one of those things that a lot of the older generations don't accept.

Grandma is not coming. I guess that's what I wanted to say. I'll be there though and my mam will be there too. But forget about Uncle Aimable and Auntie Jeanne. They had a row over the phone with my mam. Went on for ages. I swear, I feel embarrassed for them. Grandma is the one I can't get over. Why would anyone not attend their son's funeral? Well, I guess it's one of those things.

We don't talk about your dad anymore, like he never existed. It's really sad. Whenever he and you come up in conversation, Grandma gets up and walks away. I know she's still grieving but... well, anyway.

I'll text you when we land. Can we crash at your place? Or, wait, are you still living at your dad's? Maybe we can find a hotel.

Let me know.

Claude

14

"Oxygen," I said, pointing to the chemical composition of the element.

Em nodded, taking the notes with her this time, and left the room in search of oxygen to refill the tanks on our spacesuits. Without this, there would be no way a human being could board that frigate. But I knew they would manage to find some. If they could get water for us to drink and change the atmosphere of a room, they could find oxygen for the tanks.

We had a short period of time ahead of us—two hours or so—to take a break from everything until the carrier arrived at its destination, next to Earth. With rumbling stomachs, we decided to take another sip of water and lie down to catch some shut eye.

Em came back as I was getting settled, and so I tried my best to explain the concept of sleep. Did the Verax sleep at all, I wondered? If they didn't, some of the animals on their planet would do something similar, even if compared to hibernation. The idea of closing one's eyes and not being disturbed by noise didn't seem unfamiliar to them. As a species that was emotionally attuned, Em respected our time and quiet. Although, presumably she had other things to do as she slipped out of the room, leaving us humans to our slumber.

Sleep came easy to me. Although the concept of sleeping on an alien ship made me uneasy, the tiredness weighed me down. I drifted off without much resistance but found myself back on the Observer, in the park by the fountain. I felt so small—a tiny creature with this large dome of a ceiling ahead of me. And when I looked down at my hands, I was eleven again, my fingernails painted in a peach varnish, my hair tied back. I wore a sweater I loved, a woven jumper knitted in a multitude of colours ranging from burgundy to cream, with sprinkles of glitter threaded throughout. I tugged at my jumper, which felt tight across my shoulders now. I remembered my father had insisted I should give it up, but I had refused; stubborn as I was. But he wasn't here, on the Observer. So I wondered, a lost eleven-year-old on this space station I knew but didn't know. That I recognised but was different. I walked slowly and with caution, but silence rang in my ears, other than the hint of my trainers tapping against the floor. I stumbled into the boardroom. The large glass window looking out into the nothingness around it. I tiptoed closer to the window and saw my reflection in the glass—so petite for my age. So fragile. Not yet hardened by life. Not yet bitter. Eyes wide, I stared out and spotted the brightest stars. My father should be here, surely? I was only eleven. Maybe he had strayed to the reception area, or maybe he had gone to security to tell them he had lost me. I turned around and followed my way back out. I held onto a toy now. A bright yellow rabbit I used to sleep with. He kept me safe. He made sure I wasn't lonely. And so, together, we went looking for my father. I traversed the plaza once more, searching for the security desk, but everything had changed. Nothing was as it should be. Where could he be? He would never leave me alone like this. Had I grown up enough and not realised it? Did he think me capable of being by myself? Was this a test? Tears threatened my eyes, but… If I was being tested, then crying would be seen as a failure. I held my rabbit a little harder. I didn't need my father to get by. I would sit here, on this bench, like a grown-up and…

A loud crash from above me… The domed ceiling had collapsed, and I ran, dropping my rabbit behind. There were those droids. So many of them. They chased me, and I ran and kept running and got to a door, but the door wouldn't open, and I…

I jumped out of my sleep. My muscles ached from lying on the unusual floor. My heart still thumped in my chest, panic seeping from my body. Opening my eyes, I remained still in this quiet, relaxing Verax space. I peered around and spotted Nat. He sat, with his back against the wall. He looked tired, like sleep hadn't come to him at all. Not far away, Joana took deep, sluggish breaths.

I crept up to Nat as quietly as I could, and we sat together in silence for a second.

"Couldn't sleep?" I asked him.

"No. Nightmares?" he asked back.

"Yeah."

He nodded, and silence returned. But only for a moment.

"You know, I think I should—" he started.

"I know what you're going to say, and I don't want you to say it," I interrupted.

"What *do* you want me to say?" His eyes were on mine.

"That you want to stay. That you won't go," I said.

"And then?"

"And then, I'll get back to Harper and tell her it isn't possible. I'll say that we don't have enough oxygen to spare."

"You think she'll believe that?"

Would the Deputy Administrator of NASA believe an alien ship, one capable of mastering the understanding of a white hole to fuel all their ships, capable of finding water for humans to drink, to not be able to find enough oxygen for one tank? I doubted it. I lowered my gaze.

Nat shifted in his suit. "Why... Why did you want me to stay anyway?"

My heart skipped a beat. I had never felt so captivated by someone. With his umber eyes and his cheeky smile. Why was it that Nat made me feel like the teenager I had never been? I thought back to the answer I had given about my first love. Was this it, or was this some silly crush or some desperate attempt to connect to someone while the world had crumbled around us? Was it his constant need to protect me that I found alluring? Was that something I had missed somehow, after my father had become ill?

I cleared my throat. "I care about you," I said, looking at him.

He grabbed my hand. His skin felt rough and tacky against mine. "I care about you too."

I felt relief—it was nice to hear, even if I didn't know what I felt exactly—that it was somewhat reciprocated.

Somewhere, at some point in my life, I *had* missed this. This feeling of being cared for, of being wanted. Although my previous partners, serious or not, had been a part of my life, none of them had been so honest with their feelings. Nat had shown me true honesty, humility and courage, and shared parts of himself, his personality, without fearing for... For the first time in a long time, I opened myself up to the possibility that having a partner could actually be a lovely feeling, not a box that needed to be ticked. Family had asked me if I had had boyfriends, when I would get married, when I would have kids. But the truth was, my answers remained indecisive and often forced me to realise I wasn't ready for those kinds of things with that particular person. So, I would break it off.

"Actually," I began, "that's not the truth. It's more than that."

And in that moment, I regretted everything I had just said. What if I *had* misread his body language? What if I had ruined a sweet moment between friends?

"I'm kinda glad you said that," he chuckled and rubbed

his forehead with the back of his hand.

"I'm sorry, I'm not good at this talking stuff." I looked back to Joana to see if she had stirred. But her chest rose steadily. "The talking usually happens after all the other stuff." It felt awkward to admit, but it had been true. If I had felt a physical connection with someone, that's what usually started my relationships. But I saw for the first time, maybe, that that might not be the best way to approach relationships.

"That's okay. We each have our own ways of doing things. I find the talking helps. You get to know someone better that way. You figure out what makes them smile, what they believe about themselves and others, what their fears and flaws are. Not to shame them, but to respect them. That way you can be kind to each other."

"You know," I said, "I've never met someone like you." My brow furrowed. "You are honestly so kind and caring. I look at myself, and don't think of myself as a kind person. Who made you, and are there more to be found?" I smiled, and he snickered.

"I'm the one and only, baby," he said with that familiar cheek. Nat had been so innocent and fun when we had first met. I wished we could return to a time before this had happened, when things seemed simpler and the world had, only slightly, less dread.

"So… What happens now?" I asked.

"What happens now is… we get this done, and we go home. I seem to recall owing you a sandwich," he replied with a grin.

"And, some Vietnamese food," I added.

"Yes," he said with a nod. "That's right. But to be fair, I would kill for a coffee right now."

"Oh, God, don't mention coffee," I said. I collapsed back, dropping my head against the wall. "I don't think I've ever been this tired in my life."

"Alright. Coffee first, sandwich second," he said with a fatigued wink.

I nudged him playfully and dropped my head on his shoulder.

"You didn't get *any* sleep, did you?" I asked him.

"No. I feel like I'm in an observation room or something with the glass looking out into the corridor. Do these guys not enjoy privacy?"

The idea of privacy right now enticed me more than I wanted to admit. And although I was tempted to tease Nat, maybe now was not the time to do so. I dropped the thought.

"I guess they want to keep an eye on us," I replied instead.

"Makes sense."

Nat interlaced his fingers with mine. I stared at him, unsure where this unexpected movement had come from. But I leaned back into him. Nat had been a constant comfort recently. I felt envious that some people experienced this level of care from someone else on a daily basis. How had I missed this my whole life? He was sweet and considerate.

Thinking back to my previous relationship with Clara, things had been so different. There had been moments when I hadn't even liked her—when she had been disrespectful, rude or ignorant of my feelings. And we had argued *so* much. It hadn't been that different from the guy I had dated in my late teens either. But Clara had caused a lot of issues. I had gone from someone who struggled to open up, to someone who actively rejected everyone. I knew that now. The lies and disregard for how I had felt had ruined me. When we had broken up, I pushed myself even further into work. Until my dad had become sick.

All this was too much to think about.

"Thank you for being you," I said. And before he could reply, I turned to face Nat and kissed him. He relaxed into me, and I felt the touch of his fingers by my jawline. My heart leapt from my chest, and when I pulled away, I couldn't help but crack a smile to myself.

A bang on the glass interrupted us. I glanced up and saw Em glaring at me. Her eyes darted between Nat and me, and for a moment I thought I had seen Nat blush.

"A'ex, *good?*" asked Em.

"*Yes,* Alex *good,*" I replied. I couldn't get away with anything anymore.

Nat laughed to himself and whispered, "At least I know where you stand. I'll be worried when Emerald doesn't show up."

I laughed at the thought too; the slight embarrassment washed over us. Not far, Joana stirred in her sleep, and our only moment of privacy disappeared.

"Alright," said Harper on the radio. We now had a visual for the NASA Administrator: her short, dark hair, speckled with greys, bounced around her face with energy, and her stature held her firm in place. A woman of great dominance in the room. Behind her, a man hovered in place; his balding head and shaggy, oversized suit almost made him seem out of place. "We're as ready as we'll ever be. We'll be following your every movement, and we'll give you updates from the ground when we can. I need clear and concise information from whoever will be aboard that frigate."

Since we had advanced towards Earth, the replies had been coming in faster. Now, perched at the edge of Earth's high orbit zone, the communications were only delayed by a few seconds, making it feasible to have live conversations.

"Thanks for letting us know. Nat Hoang will be the one on the ship. He'll be updating you with the immediate progress. Joana and I will be staying here, with an open channel so we can communicate any major issues from the carrier."

I closed the call and let out a long sigh. It felt like I hadn't been given a choice. A lingering certainty hung in the room that, even this far from Earth, far from the people giving us orders, we could not break the rules or make our own decisions. Both NASA and the UN were involved—those were some high-up organisations to deceive.

"I feel kind of useless here," said Joana, fiddling with the straps on her suit.

"Me too," I replied. "But at least we're doing something to help. In some way." And although I said those words, I wasn't sure I was being entirely honest with myself.

"Are you scared?" Joana faced Nat.

"What's there to be scared about? Being on an alien ship, where I don't know the language, can't ask for help when I need it, and releasing a mimic of a white hole near Earth? This is a normal Sunday for me." He laughed, but his eyes didn't.

"Alright, Mister humour-as-a-defence-mechanism. I get it. Laugh all you want; I'd be shitting myself if I were you," replied Joana.

"If I had eaten anything decent in the last couple of days, maybe I would," he said with a chuckle.

"Do you have everything you need?" I asked, bringing us back to seriousness.

"I think so," he started. "Oxygen was the biggest issue. A tank of that will keep me busy enough for the mission, with some extra in case I panic. And Em said that comms were set up on the frigate, right?"

"That's right. And they've managed to link your internal headset too, so you don't even need to push a button. Although be careful what you say, Harper will hear everything," I said.

"And when we're done and we get back to Earth, I'm taking you all out to dinner. A little celebration of our exploits out in space, yeah?" he said with a smile.

"I'm down with that, if you are, Alex?" Joana smiled, but a hidden anxiety resided on her lips.

"Of course. Dinner sounds good."

"Before we start, Alex, I'd like some questions answered. I need to know why this is happening. And I want you to get as detailed as you possibly can. Once Nat is on his way to the frigate, I'd like to get your version of events." Harper had mentioned this previously, but there was only so long I could keep pushing this off. On one hand, it meant finally telling a human being on the ground everything we had been through; on the other, it meant revisiting the trauma that was now plaguing my nightmares.

Nat stood by the airlock as he attached his helmet to the rest of his suit. I put my thoughts about Harper's message to one side. I checked the seals on his helmet. Joana stood nearby, the sadness on her face visible from miles away. The quiet stung the air. No one wanted him to leave. We had been together almost from the start. With one of us gone, it felt like I couldn't breathe. Like I would only be whole, only be comfortable and reassured if we all stayed together.

I slipped the headset from my helmet on. "Can you hear me?" I said, watching every movement of his eyes.

"Loud and clear, ma'am." His smile shone through the reflection of the helmet, yet his voice quivered. Nat patted himself down one more time. "I guess I'm good to go."

I nodded. "Keep safe," was all I could manage to say. But he immediately pulled me in for a prolonged hug. We clung to each other's space suits as tight as we could and stayed in the embrace only a little bit longer than we should have. When we released each other, Nat pulled Joana in too. She looked so petite next to him.

"Don't forget about that dinner," said Joana.

"I was thinking, if I made dinner a Vietnamese sandwich, I could kill three birds with one stone," he chuckled through the radio.

"You can't do that; it's cheating," muttered Joana.

"Don't make promises you can't keep," I added, intending it to be humorous, but the serious undertone crept through.

"Alright, alright, two meals it is," he replied.

We escorted him to the door, placing our own helmets on until the oxygen and pressure in the room balanced out to the rest of the ship's. He slipped through the airlock and gave us both one last smile, accompanied by a tired salute, before turning around and being escorted away to the other ship. My gaze followed him down the hallway. A pang across my chest jolted me.

"Can you still hear me?" I asked through the radio once he was out of sight, jittery at the idea of no longer being in the same room as him.

"No problem so far," he said with a heavy breath. His tone had shifted—maybe reality had settled in. Maybe his terror had grown in ways I would never understand.

"I'm sorry," I whispered.

"It's okay," he replied, but we both knew that wasn't true.

I held onto that feeling of loss for a little longer. For some reason, I found I never wanted to be separated from that man ever again. He had been so kind and thoughtful. He had been a rock, keeping me steady throughout all this. He had grounded me when I had most needed it.

Joana rested against a wall not too far, and I wondered if she felt the same way. Would I have reacted the same if Joana had been the one to leave? For a split second, I wished it had been Joana to go. But I cursed myself for the selfish thought and walked up to the Verax computer hologram once more.

"Nat has just left for the ship. He should be updating you from there shortly." I focused my thoughts before honing in on Harper's question. "There are thirty-six other species out there. Some, although I believe it is most, are part of a Council. This Council have their own way of doing things, their own rules and policies. There seem to be strict terms to enter the Council, and humans don't currently meet that requirement. Why? I'm not sure yet. It seems to be down to being *too* primitive, but I can get the details later.

"There is a war, or, at the very least, a disagreement, going on, and we just happened to be in the middle of it. This is down to one of the other species, which, for now, we called the Elders. Named that way because they are the oldest species in the galaxy, according to Emerald. They created the white hole mimics and the metals surrounding the ships that are immune to... Well, to physics."

It sounded so silly to explain it that way, but it was the only way I could put it. The metal was such an impossibility that it needed to be mentioned.

"The Elders live by a different set of rules, which the droids support. The ones that attacked the Observer. So, there are two factions, each vying for a different type of power, each trying to bring the other one to justice. And it seems the Elders and the droids were trying to recruit us—or colonise, I should say. It appeared to me that their reasoning lied in *gaining* people, not in gaining our resources or our planet. My belief, from what I know so far, is that they attacked the Observer to gain control of it, to threaten us with it, in case we didn't comply. That's the working hypothesis, at least. And that if they had any difficulty in 'recruiting' us, then they would destroy us instead. So that the Council didn't gain us as allies.

"I don't know why *us* and not another planet, another species," I continued. "In terms of what happened on the Observer, I can give you a full report of everything I saw and experienced when I get back. But the important thing I want to say is that..." I hesitated, remembering the incident that started it all. Would they blame me for not stopping Hagen? Who *was* to blame for all the deaths in that meeting room? And those across the Observer? I knew the answer, but it would be my word against a dead man's. "Hagen pushed the team in a direction most of us were uncomfortable with. He grew defensive of the station, but it came across as aggression. I still don't fully know if the droids understood our messages. I thought they might have. I'm not sure why they didn't attempt to help us understand their language. But, umm, Hagen replied in a forceful manner. It was General Frederikson—the President of Security at the UN—it was his voice in the message, but they were Hagen's words. When he sent that message off, the attack happened minutes later." I took a pause.

"It seemed, at the time, that they wanted to kill anything

aboard the station and gain control of it. Like I said... Something about using it as a threat, but I'm making up theories here, so don't..." I shook my head. Less rambling, fewer theories, more facts.

"Things changed again when Nat, Joana, and myself were saved from the Observer. Like the intervention of another species, one the droids knew, was—" I was doing it again, hypothesising, but I couldn't help it.

"I think... I think the resistance and the calls for help that we sent out... Our lack of receptivity to the droid's plans—to their words—those were the reasons the Observer was nudged towards Earth. By then, they knew that the Verax were involved. They knew we had help, that we were, maybe, already 'corrupted' by the Verax. So, they wanted to eliminate us instead." Could it have been the messages I had sent to BioTech? Or had Em's arrival dictated the shift from attack to annihilation?

"I guess what I'm trying to say is that there are larger things at play right now, things we don't understand, myself included. The politics of the system—of this Council and these Elders—we don't know what they are. What they stand for. We got caught in it all, and human greed made things so much worse." I glanced ahead of me, at the endless stars, at the nothingness—an emptiness so vast, so full of mystery, that all of this felt superficial, so unimportant yet life-changing. "That's what I know so far. Those are my thoughts."

I ended the communication and closed my eyes. It was all too much: too much to think about, to explain, to relinquish to another person in power who might abuse the situation again.

I realise now that I left out crucial information when I sent that message. The tether, the debt we would owe the Verax. I was scared. Of what it could mean, of how Harper, someone in power, could either use it to her benefit, or share it with someone who would. I didn't want to risk it all, when we had the chance at a pact, an alliance that could unify us against another faction willing us harm. No, I wouldn't make that mistake again.

Joana had sat down as I had spoken to Harper. Her eyes were focused on something straight ahead, like she was lost in her own thoughts. Minutes passed by, and I wondered if Nat had reached the frigate yet.

"Nat, are you there?" I asked through the radio.

No answer. He needed to be in range of the comms set up on the frigate for the signal to bounce. All I could do was wait.

The silence from Harper extended much longer than I would have wanted. But with all the information I had provided them with, it wasn't surprising. It was a lot to take in; I knew that. Yet my nerves grew more unsteady and intense as I remembered the firm stance I had taken against Hagen.

Oskar Hagen had been liked enough to become successful. He had made a name for himself, made trade deals with the other rich and powerful entities on the planet. Some of those could include NASA or the UN. It was believed by some that there were rules for a possible First Contact moment, yet Hagen had only ever done whatever he wanted. So, how many world leaders, billionaires, ruling class people did he have in his pocket, to be able to have kept this hidden for two weeks? I wondered if he had doomed my new friends, my colleagues in that boardroom. And, if this got out, if people knew what Hagen had done, would we, as humans, see billionaires, the top one percent, as faulty or susceptible to power grabs? Would we finally admit the truth, put our foot down, and say no to them controlling our lives?

Even dead, Hagen still held sway over the world. His death and how it was portrayed in the media could dictate the future of the planet somehow. His successor, of the company or of his family, could surely take his place, fill his shoes, and keep up the secret trades and blackmailing businesses to keep the power attributed to the Hagen name. They would have no need for this kind of advertising and might already be working on saving his so-called prestige. No one had a need for the people stuck on an alien ship who wanted to go home and ruin the reputation of one man holding the world in his palm.

The radio crackled, and a voice came through.

"Hello team, this is Nat Hoang. I'm safely aboard the frigate now. We're getting ready to depart soon."

A flush of relief flooded me to my core. He still felt far away, so distant even through the headset balanced so close to my ear. I wanted to talk to him, to explain what I had just told Harper. To tell him I was scared. Scared of this plan. Of the power behind Harper's voice. Of everything that might happen in the next few hours. But I pushed all that down.

"Hi, Nat. We're receiving you on the carrier," I said.

"Good to know," he replied, and, in his voice, I could hear the hint of a smile.

Harper's voice crackled through next. "Received loud and clear, Nat, thank you in advance for your contribution to this mission."

I waited for Harper's voice to rise up again, the nerves begging for a quick and easy reply. A simple 'thank you for letting us know' would suffice. But it took another minute or two to come through.

"Thanks for the run-down, Alex. I've passed it to the UN, and we've had a brief chat. We're going to need a lot more answers, a lot more details. So, when this mission is over, we'll need a full report, in detail, from the three of you." A pause. "You said something about 'when you come back', and so I will nip this in the bud—you won't be coming back. Not yet anyway. We've decided the best course of action is to keep you on that carrier until we tell you otherwise."

My jaw dropped. My eyes moved back and forth across the screen, watching as the woman on the video told me I would not see my home, not feel solid ground under my feet, not even after everything I had sacrificed. I couldn't utter a sound, even if I wanted to. The video ended. When the shock faded and the anger settled in, I tapped the screen to begin a message.

"What the hell do you mean?! You can't just drop that and not give any context. Are you leaving us up here to rot?" That had been angrier than I had intended, but I sent it anyway. Deep down, I held the belief that my position on Hagen had compromised us. "Shit…"

Joana got up and stood by me, her focus on the hologram.

"What? Why won't they let us go home?" asked Joana, her eyes misting over.

"I… I don't know…" I said, trying to calm my breathing.

We waited. In silence and fear, we waited.

"I understand you're upset," replied Harper a moment later, a tad angry herself. "But this is in humanity's best interest. Think of yourself as an anchor. You're the only thing keeping this new species, the Verax, as you call them, and this Council *anywhere* near us. If you get off that carrier, we lose whatever communication we have with them. I'm sorry, Alex. You're staying put." She let go of a sigh. "The UN made some enquiries into you, Alex. You don't exactly have a lot holding you back here. No close family to speak of. A few friends back in your home country. A flat in London. And a couple of jobs coming up that, quite frankly, seem a lot less interesting than this one. Maybe, it's for the best."

VERAX DIGITAL ARCHIVE [TRANSLATED BY GAUTHIER]

CARRIER NEWS BULLETIN:

FINAL PREPARATIONS TO HELP HUMANS

Ship depart with one human aboard. Mimic to release to redirect space station. Leaders of Earth in contact with humans on carrier, despite regulations.

Two humans still aboard carrier. Verax, Emerald, tethered with one human. Emerald to face justice for unlawful tethering with a sub-species. Uncertain if human will remain aboard carrier, due to tether.

Uncertain if physical or psychological conditions have transferred to Emerald. Doctor reviews pending.

15

The first and only person I wanted to speak to was Nat. Deep inside, I felt this burning rage and betrayal at what Harper had suggested. I couldn't for the life of me understand why someone would force me to stay aboard this carrier. Couldn't Earth send someone else up and swap us out? Someone more qualified to be diplomatic? But even I knew it wouldn't be the same. The Verax had a rapport with me now—they knew I spoke some of the language, understood some basics about their species, and that I respected the tether enough to side with it. Some new attaché would never understand what I understood. Hell, I hadn't told Harper about the tether—an aspect of the Verax that another human being would have to work to understand.

But Nat sat on another ship now, inching closer to Earth as I ruminated on these thoughts, and so I couldn't express my fears to him unless I found a way to create a private channel. Yet the system in front of me displayed a language I hadn't mastered. Emerald had left a short while ago, and there was no way to open a private channel without her.

We had some time in front of us until the frigate would be

in place to launch the mimic. Until then, I waited. I waited for Em to come back, waited for Nat to say they were in place, and waited for Harper to change her mind.

I wasn't sure if Joana or Nat were meant to stay behind too. Harper had made that part of the message so personal to me, so blunt, slighting even. I wondered if the UN had done a background check on Nat and Joana too. Had they found more solid roots for my friends? Had they only found pressure points in my life to force my hand? Or did they consider them less *needed*?

Forest hadn't been around in a while now. I knew he and Emerald both had jobs of their own. This had provided some confusion initially. I assumed that any jailed person would have lost their privileges and, or, positions on the carrier. But, maybe, because I used the tether as leverage in my argument, it had been assumed that I had waived some right to press charges against a non-consensual tethering. And in doing so, maybe I had allowed them to continue performing their duties aboard this carrier. Or perhaps, the situation was so dire, so demanding, that they required all hands to be on deck.

Various tech equipment had since been installed in this meditation room, including a sizeable hologram machine illustrating the fall of the Observer. As I stood nearby, I witnessed its slow approach, the thin line circling the planet until it stopped, still close to the Moroccan border. But, nearby, wavered the image of the carrier, and, in between both, a series of smaller ships, one of which was Nat's. I could see its plotted course; its final destination stopped close to the station. The perfect proximity to redirect the Observer, somewhere in mid-Earth orbit.

The radio crackled.

"Hey, Alex," said Nat. "I think I've managed to rig this, so it should only come through to you. But I'm not sure it worked, and I'm guessing you can't reply without Harper hearing you, so I might never know. And if this *is* actually broadcasting to everyone, well, then... Hi, Harper. I guess you'll have to sit through this like everyone else. But if this is functioning as intended, I'm guessing Jo is there and can hear me also."

"He's smart, that one," muttered Joana. She got up and stood by the radio to hear him better.

"In the last couple of hours, I've had enough time on my own to do some thinking," he continued.

Joana and I now stood shoulder-to-shoulder, waiting on his every word.

"It has crossed my mind that I've not been great to be around. Well, most of the time, I have, let's be honest." He chuckled to himself. "But there are things I need to apologise for. I feel like I've... I've been angry. I snapped at times I shouldn't have. And there were decisions that you both made that I disagreed with. And had you listened to me in those moments, maybe the Observer would have fallen. So, I'm sorry. For the anger, the stress, but mostly for those instances when you wanted to make a decision, and I doubted you. Like when I resisted following Emerald when we first met her. And it turned out to be the best decision we've ever made. *You* ever made, Alex. Without them, we wouldn't be here, saving Earth, or trying to anyway. So, I wanted to say I'm sorry. I don't want you to doubt your capabilities. Sometimes, fear will make you want to run the opposite way. But anyway... I'm not sure how to end this. But I'm sure I'll hear your voices on the open channel soon enough."

With that, his voice disappeared. There was so much I wished to say, and for a brief moment I thought about using the open channel, disregarding any confusion it might cause Harper, and just to reply to him. But Joana grabbed my arm before I could hit the button.

"It's probably best to leave him be. He's said what he needed to say; let's just focus on supporting him through this," said Joana.

I nodded. Silence filled the room immediately, an empty void where I wished there had been none. I wanted to hear his voice once more and tell him he had nothing to apologise for, nothing to be sorry about. But I knew Joana was right. It would only become confusing for everyone, specifically Harper, who thought she was in control. She would know that we were talking without her involvement. It might even lead her to believe we were plotting behind her back, agreeing to something with the Verax, and possibly affecting the outcome of this mission.

I would just have to sit with these emotions and hold on to them until he was safely back aboard the carrier. The need to tell him he might also be stuck in space, stranded, unable to go home, erupted through a sickening feeling in the back of my throat. His sister was pregnant, and he had promised to go home and help. But that would never happen, at least not in time for the birth. How long would it take for an anchor to serve its purpose?

The airlock doors opened, and Em walked back into our temporary human bridge.

I pulled myself away from those thoughts. Maybe there would be time for self-centred happiness when this was all over.

"Where is Forest?" I asked.

"On bridge, with Leaders. Expert pilot, Leaders want close," replied Em. She approached me and continued, *"Question. What is 'hat and A'ex?"*

I didn't know what to make of this question. I wasn't sure if Em was asking about our friendship, our relationship, or, in general, how mating rituals worked in the human species.

"Why?"

"Strong feeling in A'ex. But good feeling."

"Yes," I said. I couldn't muster much more than that right now.

"Why?" asked Em.

"Because…" I sighed. *"No matter. Save Earth,"* I replied, turning away from her.

"We're all ready down here. We're watching, and we'll be here to advise," Harper's voice crackled. The delay felt much shorter, twenty seconds at most.

"Roger that," replied Nat over the radio. "We're in position. These guys are readying the mimic white hole. Looks like it might take a few minutes to set up."

I had nothing to add to their exchange. My eyes rested on the small ship that had stagnated and balanced in Earth's mid-orbit. Their engines still roared, I could tell from the virtual recreation, presumably to maintain their location in orbit.

"*Earth is… New word*," Em started.

I pulled up the whiteboard on the hologram and wrote it down. It always felt good to expand my vocabulary, but right now, I didn't feel like it. Emerald never stopped, never ceased to help me with the language, but it meant that my mind could never rest. Sometimes, I felt like I only wanted to experience this one thing at a time—this plan, in this moment, for instance, to make sure it worked, make sure Nat came out safe. A break. No more words. No more work. Only this safety, and then I would sleep, and then I could get back to work when I felt ready.

"*Earth is beautiful*," concluded Em.

It took me by surprise. Of all the things I didn't think Em would say… I looked at it myself, and though the hologram had dimmed some of its natural colours, its bright blue still shone past the pixels. The curves of the continents were ingrained in my mind. Continents I would never experience again unless I got off this carrier. The betrayal still stung, and below that, further still, lay a deep sadness at the possibility of never feeling the ground beneath my feet nor the wind on my face.

"*I'm sorry*," said Em, feeling the sadness in the tether.

I took a deep breath. "*No, I'm sorry.*" It was high time I took responsibility for my own feelings. It was time for me to ask for forgiveness too. Right now, and probably until my death bed, I would be responsible for how Em felt as well.

"Question," I began, *"I stay on carrier, Leaders happy?"*

Em paused, and through the tether, I felt her confusion and minor embarrassment.

"No understand."

"Earth Leaders want Alex *stay on carrier,"* I repeated. The thought had been playing on my mind since Harper had mentioned it—that I would need to tell Em and come to some agreement with the Leaders. Now may not have been the best time to bring it up, but I felt the need for some kind of validity, some idea that I might end up safe or even welcome aboard this ship.

"I don't know," hesitated Em, and she turned her head away. The tether echoed a pang of fear and awkwardness. And so, we dropped the subject, although now I wasn't even sure Em wanted me on board, let alone the rest of the Verax. Had humans not caused enough trouble? They now wanted to push their presence on an alien vessel. I had mentioned Hagen's human greed as the downfall of the Observer, and within the next breath, Harper had pushed me to stay on board, for a little bit more human greed. It made me feel sick.

"The equipment is ready," said Nat. "They're using a robotic arm to drop the mimic in place. But it seems like they'll only drop it when they're ready to open it."

"Thank you, Nat. You're doing great; keep describing everything," replied Harper.

I shook my head. My initial happiness at hearing Harper's voice had been replaced with a disgust for any human being in power. But could I really resent someone trying their best to assure the safety of the planet? No, maybe not. But the way she spoke echoed of that condescending bullshit you'd expect from someone supervising a team, someone who wanted everyone to do their jobs in the most efficient way, no matter the costs. The truth was, Nat had no choice. Just like I had no choice in staying here. Because that's what the people in power wanted, and God forbid I'd have a say in my own future.

I looked to Em and sensed that familiar anger rise up

again. Em could feel it too, I was sure.

"Human have strong feeling. I'm sorry," I said. But I knew it would not stop here. The anger, the distrust, the resentment would continue to grow. Apologies rarely fixed things, but it was a start.

"No, I—" started Emerald. *"I make mistake. With tether. Human have strong feeling, yes. More strong than I think. But I learn too."*

I nodded in agreement. We were both learning how to deal with human emotions, but it remained unfair that Em had to learn the hard way. I knew these weren't simple feelings. In recent years, my grief had clouded my judgement, had coated my emotions in a sticky, black hue. Everything I had felt, everything I had seen, had been through a lens of depression.

"Also, I have strong feeling. I have..." I wondered if they had a word for mental illness. If they had distinctive terms for depression or anxiety or pain or grief. Were they as much of an issue in their society? Maybe they felt fewer emotions. Maybe they tethered to each other to feel more. But I had felt a range of sensations through the tether from the start, so that couldn't be true. And Em had mentioned something else before...

"I have emotional pandemic," I concluded.

Em stepped back, another human instinct she had picked up over the last couple of days. Through the tether, I felt her shock and immediate fear. She stumbled on her words. Perhaps it had been unwise to compare human depression with something they called an emotional pandemic. The words would spread species-wide fear if spoken in public.

But Em changed her posture and approached me earnestly, placing one hand on my arm.

"New word," she said. We worked together to find them. *"You get better soon. I here to help."*

When all this was over, we would have to work on grammar and conjugation. Even then, I found the words to be reassuring. It felt like I had made a new friend, someone who could help me through my grief, help me become a happier version of myself. To become someone who could be honest about my feelings, someone who could ask for forgiveness.

"The robotic arm is in place. The mimic is ready to be opened," said Nat over the radio.

My heart quickened. The moment had approached so much faster than I had anticipated.

"New word," said Em. And together, we listed all the emotions I felt in each individual moment. The differences between fear, stress, and anxiety were difficult to discern, but of course, this could be straightened out at a later date. The list of new words grew, and I realised Em was keeping me occupied until this was all over.

"The box is in place. Mimic open."

We all watched the virtual recreation with intensity; eyes peeled on the mimic itself. The movements of the other objects, the satellites, the Observer, and surrounding space debris all began to shift ever so slightly. The course correction seemed to happen in slow motion.

Beside me, Joana watched the scene unravel with vigilance, her mouth ajar and her hands pressed up against the desk, her upper body leaning in. I had never seen her this fearful. Back on the Observer, when we had been locked in that meeting room, before Em had arrived, Joana had feared for her life. But this fear looked different. It was the kind you felt when you had already looked Death in the eyes and claimed today wouldn't be the day, yet you couldn't say the same for everybody else. This fear was for Nat.

Em tapped a button, and the projected trajectory of the Observer updated. The thin ring around Earth changed and shifted as the white hole towed every object in its vicinity. The impact site adjusted from the Atlantic Ocean to Morocco to the Saharan Desert.

"Keep it steady," said Harper. Not that Nat could do anything if Harper had decided it wasn't steady enough.

Around the Observer, the satellites and space debris

warped and mutated like a wave of garbage being syphoned out. The plotted course of the Observer now stated the station would slingshot around Earth.

"Great job, people; keep it up," asserted Harper.

"The Verax are keeping it open for now," said Nat.

"Better it go in the opposite direction," confirmed Harper.

In the back of my mind, I thought to the CCTV footage I had witnessed a few days prior. To the groups of people in the Hub Bunkers, each with their own issues going on. The argument, the couple holding hands, and the anxious teen. I wondered if they were still alive. If they had somehow managed to leave, or if they had died from lack of food and water, stuck in those airtight Bunkers that seemed to be somewhat defective. How I wished I could have gone back for them… But I needed to accept that not everyone could be rescued. Saving the planet from the station crash had to count for something.

Satellites shot out of orbit, missing the frigate only by a few kilometres. The Observer slowed its fall, still primed to swing around the planet.

"The trajectory change is almost complete," I said over the radio.

"Copy that. We can see it too," replied Harper.

"Leaving the mimic open," said Nat.

There was a beauty to the scene displayed before us. The debris flung around, both pulled by the gravity of Earth, which it had been orbiting for years, and torn in the opposite direction by the white hole, like the two gravities were playing some vicious tug of war. It filled me with worry and wonder, and everything that had felt unimaginable in life, spun, here in this moment, into a never-ending cycle of hope and possibility.

My palms turned sweaty, and I noticed I had held my breath. I forced myself to take some deep inhales. But that's when I observed the debris closing in on the white hole mimic.

"Mimic can take damage?" I asked.

"A bit," replied Em.

We watched as objects twisted and turned, gaining speed. If there had been any sense in it, I would have suggested it looked like a hurricane of foreign objects, all headed towards the mimic. The ship itself sat behind the white hole.

"Oh my god, this is… too much," muttered Joana. Tears had fallen down her cheeks.

"The pilot has plotted evasive manoeuvres," crackled Nat's voice.

The Observer swung low in a final decisive movement; it almost appeared to stop as it took course in the opposite direction, towards the white hole. The hologram confirmed it too: the distance between the station and the planet increased fast.

"Hold off. Wait until the Observer gains more speed. If you close that thing too soon, we might not be out of danger just yet," shouted Harper.

"I don't have *any* control over that, ma'am," he replied.

I thought I could almost hear a smirk. Nat hung like decoration in that frigate. Sitting tight and telling the story, with no authority whatsoever. Harper believed humans were special, that they would be allowed to command another, more advanced species into doing what works best for them. She was delusional.

The Observer gained traction, but so did the space debris and satellites. Some now flung so close to the frigate, I thought I could see them clip the sides of the ship on the hologram.

"We're monitoring how Earth is being affected. The last thing we want is to shift Earth's position. Nat, I will ask you to manually deal with the situation if that happens."

"You do realise they don't explain to every stranger that boards with them how to activate or deactivate the white hole they use as engines, right?"

"Don't you dare get smart with me," replied Harper, with a voice so cutting, I thought she would end the radio communication.

Yet I couldn't help but smile.

"Apologies, ma'am, but I genuinely have no idea how to shut that box. And I'm not sure threatening a group of over eight-foot creatures is going to work out for me."

"The balls on that one," whispered Joana, mesmerised.

"This isn't about you, Nat. You threaten them if you have to. You're on that ship to do anything it takes to save humanity," replied Harper.

Debris had begun colliding with the white hole mimic. Although the individual pieces disappeared into it, leaving no trace on the other side. Any loose pieces hitting the box surrounding the white hole ended up jolting the robotic arm and therefore the frigate. The impacts shook them; the hologram of the ship jostled with each hit. The frigate itself would always be fine, of course. Its protective coat consisted of that mysterious metal, the same as the box surrounding the mimic. That fantastic metal no one could explain. I knew I would have to get all the information I could about it. Humanity would want to know what saved them.

But on the other hand, the ship's one weakness was exposed: its thrusters, holding it in orbit and doing damage control when any of the debris collided.

"Projected trajectory is now clear of Earth. You may start thinking about closing it," said Harper.

"Not my decision. No change in position yet," replied Nat. Behind his voice, the sound of crashing debris rattled the ship. He sounded stressed.

More satellites were pulled from their position, like a giant syphon sucking up all the crap that Earth had thrown outside its atmosphere. The big clean-up.

"In position to close the white hole. Will take evasive manoeuvres once it is closed." They were taking significant damage, evident from the clattering coming from the radio. He was unnerved. He gasped for air at times, out of fear, I imagined.

"Earth is clear. You've done everything you need to," shouted Harper.

"I'm aware of that, ma'am." He was shaken, scared even, and getting snappy.

"Get out of there now!" I cried out.

"Box closed," he grunted through the discomfort.

With the mimic away and the arm pulling the box back in, the debris shot towards the ship. They could take a few more hits, but currently, the Observer hurtled towards them.

"Evasive... manoeuvres..."

My heart sped as I heard his pain and stress and strain. The ship's robotic arm closed the distance, and they dipped out from the barrage of satellites and debris. But not quick enough. A large object, the remnants of the BioTech station, collided with the side of the arm, putting the ship in a spin.

"Nat?!" I shouted over the radio.

"Trying... to..."

The ship spun wildly. The engines fired forward, trying to regain control, but they headed straight into the debris. A large satellite hit the ship's nose, spinning them once again, more debris hitting them from the other sides.

"The mimic is gone..." he uttered. His voice strained against the G-force of the spin, alarms blaring in the background.

Em tapped the screen and found the mimic, still in its box, spinning away, closing in on Earth. Soon, the small box would enter Earth's atmosphere and crash somewhere.

"Something... is wrong..." he tried. His tone was distressed, and he kept groaning like he was in pain.

Em tapped at the screen, bringing up an engine report of the damage the frigate had taken. The thrusters had been knocked. Without an immediate repair, they would keep spinning. My heart raced uncontrollably. We knew this mission would be dangerous, but this was not how I had imagined it ending. I couldn't lose him. Not today. Not after everything.

The Observer approached faster still. And although their ship had spun enough to be out of range, it hadn't recovered itself just yet. Another piece of loose debris hit them and changed their direction. The spin had slowed down.

"Engine not working," said Em.

"Nat, are you having issues with the engine?" I asked, pressing, desperate. My heart palpitations bounced around my ribcage. Nausea crept up my throat. I knew Em would feel the sickness too.

No reply. The pilot was attempting to start the engines once more.

"What if he passed out from the spin..." said Joana. Her hand clutched her face.

"Nat, please respond," insisted Harper.

The Observer passed their location without effect, pushing its way through slower debris and hurtling towards the infinite darkness.

The frigate approached Earth, still in a spin.

"They do emergency landing," said Em.

"Harper, they're preparing for an emergency landing on Earth," I repeated. And to Em, *"What is trajectory?"*

Em tapped away, plotting their course. The familiar thin line appeared, but I couldn't see the end of it.

"Very well, we'll prepare for a landing where we can. Send us the coordinates."

"Problem," said Em. Her eyes settled on me, and I could tell. I went cold. My heart dropped. The fear crushed me; there was nothing else but this horrific guttural pain in the pit of my stomach. Nothing but this fear spreading to all my limbs. My legs threatened to give way, and I swallowed the lingering lump in my throat.

"Metal too heavy for Earth gravity. Ship crash. They die."

ALEXANDRA GAUTHIER'S DIGITAL ARCHIVE

From: *Alexandra Gauthier*

To: *Emmanuel Gauthier*

Date: *November, 27th 2047 02:34*

Location: *Drafts Folder*

Subject: *[Draft] Hi Dad*

Hi Dad,

I've been seeing a new therapist, and she asked me to try this exercise, so bear with me.

I've tried many different ones by now—the one where they get you to talk to an empty chair to purge your feelings. I've tried keeping a diary. Morning pages they call them, where first thing when you wake up, you write until there is nothing left to write. We tried going through workbooks on Cognitive Behavioural Therapy, even though the concept is outdated by now. We tried Eye Movement Desensitisation and Reprocessing, or EMDR, but it doesn't really work if you dissociate. All these different ways to process grief and trauma, and here I am. Still me. Still struggling.

I saved that email you sent me once. When I had just started at Uni, and you were trying to cheer me up. I read it a lot when you were suffering most. It cheered me up then too. Except, after a while, the words started to feel empty. It felt like I was cherishing the statement of a different man, a different father. Of course, I remember the good times. How supportive you were, how caring you had been, how you taught me to be the woman I am today, particularly after Mum died. I couldn't have asked for a better father.

But that isn't true. Because you made the last few years of my life hell. And no matter how much I re-read that email of yours, it never made a difference. And the sad thing is, even now, I know that none of it was your fault. But I can't help but blame you. Because you were also the only one to blame. Because I'm still so angry, so tired from everything that has happened.

Some days, I don't want to get out of bed. I lie there, awake most of the night, and I get so angry. I replay those moments. The moments when everything was terrible. I replay the times you said horrible things. When your behaviour was out of control. When nothing I said or did mattered. And I picture ways I could have done better. Could I have made you happier? Could I have given you everything you wanted? But every scenario ends up the same way. With me stuck in this position, feeling the feelings I have, with no way to care for myself.

And so I lie here, every night, as bitter as the last. And the truth is, nothing will ever change that. I'm happy with life now. Because I don't have to deal with your crap. So, tomorrow, when I get up, I will—

256

16

The ship plummeted.

My voice grew coarse; I hadn't stopped shouting down the radio. If only they could wake up and take control of the ship. But the G-force had knocked them all out. Em, Joana, and I watched as it had tumbled, then steadily picked up speed.

Em continued to try to get answers through the radio, some information, or help from the Leaders. But I couldn't focus on what she was saying, couldn't understand through the incessant thumping in my ears.

I kept trying. I couldn't stop, because stopping meant it was too late. "Nat, come in, please?!"

The frigate picked up heat too. In Earth's atmosphere, a plume of smoke spread in its wake. Its speed significant now — I wondered if they might not all be dead already...

"Nat Hoang, please come in," shouted Harper. Her tone showed concern, but nothing too imperative.

"Nat!" I shouted again.

But we both knew that it was in vain. Only unmitigated silence and the odd radio wave crackle escaped the frigate. My body crushed me from the inside out. I felt like tearing my ribs open to let out the pain.

Someone took a deep sigh over the radio. "Projected trajectory of the Observer has now been coursed," said Harper. "It'll shoot past Jupiter and head into deep space. Well done, team."

I froze. Confused and angry. The heartbreak soared through me.

"Is that it?!" I asked. "You're just going to abandon him?" The tremor in my voice had been completely involuntary. Fury came close to expelling out of me. This couldn't be the end.

"The mission is complete, Alex. He knew the costs."

I slammed my fist on the desk. "How can you say that?! You gave him no choice!" In the corner of my eye, I saw Emerald fall to the ground, clutching her chest.

"It's true though, isn't it? He was ex-military. He *knew* the costs," insisted Harper.

I crumbled to the ground. Tears flowing, I felt Joana's hand on my shoulder, clenching, gripping me through her own pain. I couldn't breathe, or couldn't stop breathing; it didn't matter which. My face ached from the crying, and my hands shook as I tried to hold myself up. But the weighty pain on my chest pulled me down again.

Joana slipped in behind and hugged me tight. I could feel her convulsing, trying to keep from weeping. We had lost the bravest of our group. And no one was going to do a damned thing to help him.

"Together, you stopped the biggest man-made station in orbit from crashing into Earth. You need to remember that."

But I couldn't listen to Harper anymore. None of what she said mattered. I had developed a disgust for the woman. Every word Harper uttered felt like a stab in the back, a mockery of the highest order. Everything the NASA Administrator said simply coated me in a solid sheet of wrath.

The frigate slid further into Earth's atmosphere, almost ablaze. Due to land in the Atlantic Ocean. ETA: two minutes.

"I hope it was worth it," I said through my sobs.

"I think, in time, you'll realise it was."

Em now stood at my side also. The pain in the tether must have been unbearable at this stage. But we had come together, all three of us in this moment, and mourned someone we had only just got to know.

The ship nosedived, becoming even hotter as it inched closer. The body of the ship itself had remained intact—a metal that could survive a white hole would survive the intense heat of entering a planet's atmosphere. But there was no way the people inside would. I knew what excessive G-force would do to a body. The limited blood flow, the bursting blood vessels, the brain deprived of oxygen. I couldn't shake the images. His skin freckled with blood. His body burning up in that ship. And the snap of everything once it hit the water. The final death knell.

I let myself feel it all, curled up on the floor, wishing this had never happened. Wishing I had listened to him. Wishing I had never met Emerald, and we had travelled to another Hub Bunker. All so we could spend a few extra hours together.

Joana and I fell asleep, leaning into each other. There had been no need to stay awake, no need for anyone's attention. I had had enough of Harper. Enough of that sharp, aggravating voice. Enough of someone telling me not to grieve. And after so much stress and heed, we had almost collapsed, our bodies giving up and sending us into a deep, nightmare-fuelled sleep. I had remained still in my slumber, unmoving, waking occasionally in the same position, remembering the reality, and quickly giving up again. There was no need to live right now. No need to think, to reexperience what had just happened. So, I slept some more. Silent tears slipping in my slumber.

"You know I'm not going anywhere, right?" said Joana, as she and I leaned against the far wall of the meditation room, staring into oblivion, waiting for the void to consume us. My muscles ached, but my body refused to move. It had energy for *nothing.*

"Hm?" I muttered, unaware Joana had even spoken.

"I mean, with you staying here. I'm not going anywhere. I'm not leaving you. I don't care if it means being your admin or your bodyguard or whatever it is you need me to be. I'm staying."

I tried to relish in the fact that I still had a friend by my side, but emptiness consumed me.

"Why?" I asked finally. It made no sense. Surely, the first place anyone would want to go is home. To see family and friends and to feel safe. To feel the ground beneath their feet.

"I think we need each other," she said.

And maybe that was so. Grief was a journey best travelled with a companion. I knew that well by now. We could share the path, lean on each other for support, and reminisce together. But I couldn't shake the agony plaguing me.

"Look, I know I've been really indecisive in the past, but this..." she started. "It's not fair. To leave you in this mess when I've been a part of it. You've lost one friend today—I'd be a shitty one if I left you now."

I stared ahead of me, my voice devoid of emotion. "Don't you want to see your parents?"

"I do. But we saved their asses today, and I think that might be enough. They can hold onto that for a while until we figure out what's next."

It would be nice not to be alone, or at least not the only human. It would also be nice to be able to do what I wanted. Not only had Harper grieved me, she had me trapped. Trapped *with* someone might just be a small step up from the horror of being here.

"Thank you," was all I could muster.

At long last, I managed to look at it. The flickering dot of the crash site. It blinked at me, flashing lethargically, nagging my brain to recognise it for what it was. *See me*, it kept whispering. I didn't want to. But now that I had, a new rush of emotions clasped my chest. Fury. Bitterness. Hatred.

No doubt Earth would attempt a rescue mission at some point. And Earth would have its first alien ship to dissect and first aliens to do biological tests on. Only then would they pick up Nat and give him a crappy little medal and bury him in some fake military-style funeral.

I was just as sure that someone at some point would go looking for that mimic. It would be invaluable to humans. Some mystical technology they could never understand. Of course, they would go after it.

I simmered in my anger. If it was the only thing keeping me alive, keeping me going. Maybe it was worth holding onto.

"What do you think will happen to us?" I asked, my indignation bare, for Joana to witness.

But she ignored it. Or accepted it; I wasn't sure. "I don't know. I understand why we're here. Like Harper said, about the 'anchor' to keep the Verax grounded. To make sure we stay connected to this Council. But it all sounds a bit superfluous to me…"

"Hm," I uttered again. I needed more time to think. More time to process. My eyes felt scratchy in their sockets. Sleep awaited me, somewhere.

"Alex, come in," the radio crackled. Harper again.

I felt nauseated at the sound of her voice. My hatred for her was deep-seated, embedded under layers of my being.

But I rose from the floor anyway. My back ached, and my legs shook. We still hadn't eaten.

"Alex, come in," repeated the radio.

A fresh wave of grief grabbed me. Lost promises of dinner, of Vietnamese food. My stomach grumbled, but the appetite had left.

"Yeah," I managed, speaking into the screen.

"How are you doing?"

My brow furrowed. Did she have nothing better to do? I released a sigh that I hoped would evacuate the frustration from my voice. "What do you want?"

"Alright, I know you're upset and angry, and you have

every right to be. But I need you to be alert for what I'm about to discuss with you."

I held my grip on the desk, biting my lip and swallowing my grievances. Was this what my future held? Being called, being required to answer immediately. Being *alert*.

"Go on."

"There's a shuttle coming up to you, to your vicinity," she said. "I'm sending you the coordinates now. It has some basic supplies—food, water, portable showers and toilets, bedrolls, menstrual cups, you name it. There are also a couple of laptops. You're to start work using those."

Joana and I had had half of a sleep, and Harper was already talking to us about working. Life never ended. I remembered thinking those exact words seconds after Nat had started pulling me in towards the Observer. After the one moment I could have chosen my own fate. I had been right to think it. Life never ended, until it did.

"Alex, you still there?"

"Hm," I said, leaning my head in my arm.

"We need you to translate. Come up with a dictionary of sorts, or whatever it is you do. Decipher the language fully. The UN have spoken, and they also want to speak with you privately."

"So, they're cutting out the middleman?" I replied stoically.

"Look. I don't care if you like me or not. You and I have been in touch because *you* were in trouble and called for help. You served as an intermediary after that. It's finished now, so you won't hear from me unless something similar happens again. And you better hope to God it doesn't. Did you receive the coordinates?"

"Yes, ma'am," I replied, echoing Nat's words.

I had grown numb from this conversation already—the idea of saying 'yes, ma'am' for the rest of my life, the rest of my career at the very least, was depressing. Like with Hagen, I'd have to watch my tone, watch my language, watch everything I did, out of fear it wasn't good enough, wasn't to their standard.

But I remembered what Hagen had said: '*If you want to give up, that's on you.*' The same words I had used on my father years prior. And I knew now, more than ever, that I wasn't one to give up.

No, I had had enough of that seed of doubt. I made that decision, then and there: no more doubts, no more giving up.

"Good," replied Harper. "My email, along with various other high-profile people's emails, are already registered on the laptops coming up to you. They have been prepped for a linguist like yourself, with all the software you could ask for. But if you're missing something, give someone a shout, and they'll get you anything you need. And, Alex?"

"What?"

"You're the most important person in the world right now. Since you shouted down for help, the planet has been watching. Your face is on all the news channels, the internet knows who you are, and your name is going in all the history books. Don't fuck this up."

"I..."

The call ended, and I was left with this feeling of nothingness once again. My vision went blurry, and I left my body for a second before my feet felt the ground once more.

It didn't feel real, maybe because I hadn't been exposed to it. But people knew my name now? I didn't know how to feel about that. I had never been a public-facing figure. I wasn't sure I wanted the additional pressure of dealing with this.

Joana watched me from where we had been sitting just moments before.

"Wow," she said. I couldn't tell from her expression if it was from surprise at the unwanted attention we had drawn to ourselves, or if it was surprise at Harper's arrogance. I preferred the latter.

And maybe 'wow' was the only thought we could muster between us right now. The exhaustion, the grief, the subterfuge we found ourselves trapped in—they suppressed any other emotions.

"Come on," I said. "Let's go find Em. We've got some things to discuss."

With our helmets back on and a full tank of oxygen each, we stepped out of our room for the first time since losing Nat. The hallways were much less crowded than the last time we had been here. Now that both the brief war with the droids and saving Earth from the Observer had been dealt with, the crew had gone back to their normal pace. Some Verax still swung from the ceilings—that seemed to be a normal method of transportation rather than something they only did during a crisis.

The hallway felt that much larger without the crowds of staff; the ceilings reached up high, one and a half times the size a human would need it to be. Not large enough to be oppressive, yet the difference in height left me feeling disconcerted. Like the measurements were only slightly off.

Joana and I turned into the bridge. We first spotted Forest, who was advising another Leader in front of the hologram. When Forest saw us, I thought I detected a hint of sadness or empathy in his body language.

Others fluttered around the room, assessing the damage from the war or, maybe, trying to find a way to recover the bodies of the two Verax aboard the frigate. Em and the silver Leader were discussing something at the back. Once I saw Em, I paid attention to the tether—it sang of a subtle grief, and I wondered how the Verax mourned their dead. The carrier emanated a low energy—the Verax moved slower and took their time with each movement, as though death had released a time stop. It appeared as though they mourned collectively, a possible feature of an emotionally connected species. And although the thought felt morbid in the moment, my interest in their culture only grew stronger with each passing moment.

"*Em*," I called.

Emerald took a couple of long steps over and paused in front of me.

"A'ex, *good?*" asked Em.

"*Yes.*" That wasn't the truth, and Em could probably feel the lie through the tether. "*Em, good?*"

"*No. But we continue.*" For a species like theirs, connected through a series of emotional tethers, it was impossible to lie. Perhaps even culturally wrong. I wondered if I had disrespected her with my own lie. But I couldn't face the minute intricacies of what was culturally acceptable when walking over here had taken every ounce of energy I had.

"*Question. I speak with you?*" I asked. But even now, I still wasn't actually sure how to ask this question. How could I impose on them this way? How would they take it?

"*Yes.*" She lowered herself to my height, so we were now face-to-face.

"*Earth say I stay on carrier. Question. Leaders happy?*"

Em turned around and gestured for the silver one to come closer. Em took a moment to explain the situation to the Leader in the common tongue. Although I had gained a decent amount of knowledge about their body language, I always found it difficult to read the silver Leader. They wore an impenetrable mask when it came to emotions. I asked myself if maybe the Leaders weren't tethered to anybody for fear of sharing their emotions with other creatures, potentially revealing political alliances or unethical pacts. If they allowed me to stay, I would find a semblance of excitement in this kind of work.

The silver one didn't answer in the common language, choosing instead to reply in their native one. They kept the discussion short and to the point.

Em turned to me immediately after. "*Earth share bond with Verax. Earth have ship that crash. Earth have mimic white hole. Earth have Verax technology and know we exist. A... New word.*"

As we searched for it, the silver Leader disbanded and continued to engage with others around the bridge.

"A treaty with Earth."

"What are rules of treaty?" I asked, wondering if maybe the debt mentioned earlier would factor into this pact.

"I don't know. Leader do treaty. Give to you later. You see."

"A treaty for us to look at," I repeated so that Joana could understand the conversation.

"It's expected, I guess..." she replied, her eyes switching between Em and me. Although I could see the sadness in her eyes, I could tell she felt involved, attentive—more so than when I had started translating the language. Like she had accepted she had a role here, that she was going to participate.

"What happen to droids?"

"They are enemies to Verax. They go to Council."

"What happen to droids at Council?" I asked. Secretly, I feared humans would break our own treaty. I just wanted the security of knowing what would happen if, or when, we did that.

"New word," she started. *"Justice. They tell us about Elder plans."*

The UN would want to hear this. They would want to know and be involved in all these discussions. More importantly, they would want an explanation from the Elders. And they would want some compensation. Because that's how humans were. Always thinking of the next step, a new way up the ladder.

But the thought of the Elders still troubled me. If they had managed to conquer and enslave us, embroil us on their side of the war, what would we have become? Were we going to be front-line soldiers? Or slaves intended on making their weapons of war? Perhaps something completely different? I knew so little about them, and I was desperate to find more out.

"And we stay on carrier?" I asked finally.

"Yes," replied Em.

I was flooded with relief. Through the tether, I glimpsed that same relief and a glint of eagerness too, both hidden underneath our individual versions of heartbreak.

Joana witnessed my shoulders relax, and I nodded to her. I saw her eyes sparkle with something close to hope.

"Thank you," I said. *"Question. Earth send shuttle. Equipment for* Alex *and* Joana. *Verax collect?"*

"Yes. What equipment?" asked Em.

Now was maybe not a good time to explain the concepts of human biology. The need to eat, to drink, to wash and to sleep. So, I simply repeated some of the words I had learned prior. *"Biology, technical. Human hologram."*

"Exciting," said Em, in the most human-like manner she had ever spoken. And she was; I could feel it. We would finally be working together. None of this running away from danger crap to interrupt us. We could sit down, sort out the grammar and the punctuation and the truer meanings behind words and phrases. I could ask the difficult questions without stumbling, without misinterpreting. And I felt eager to know everything.

From how their language evolved to how their species became spacefaring. I wanted to know how the Council operated, how this precious metal that could survive a white hole existed. Who were the Elders, and why did the droids work for them? What did all these thirty-six species look like? How did they all evolve on their individual planets? What did their societies grow from, and how did they end up where they are now? What other technology was out there? And would they share theirs with Earth? Did Earth have anything to give back in return? Were we even worthy of talking to them? And would we ever join the Council?

But I needed to start small. So, until the shuttle arrived, we returned to our meditation room, and I wrote down everything that had happened. I sorted my notes from the hologram machine to make it easier to transfer what I already knew into suitable programs.

I grew excited at the prospect of being able to speak to Em about anything and everything. To have conversations about sadness and grief. To truly become a friend. And to be a good one at that.

I looked to Joana, who was peering at the hologram in more detail. Right now, all I saw was the woman that had survived. That Nat had helped. He had patched up her leg. He had fixed the radio with her directions.

For some reason, everything Joana was in this moment was a painful reminder of the man that had died. It saddened me when I came to that realisation, but I hoped, with time, that I could learn to put those thoughts to one side. To cherish and respect Joana for who she was and who she could be.

In fact, I needed to be honest: I needed to allow myself the opportunity to prosper just as much. I had spent too long looking down on myself, ruminating, brooding, and depressing over all the bad things that had happened in my life, that I had forgotten what it was like to live. To feel, to get to know new people, to find pride in work. Never had I felt such a rush of adrenaline, or a sense of commitment—a stronger reason to live. And it felt sad to admit, with the deaths that had been caused in the process. But maybe I needed to allow myself this win. I felt alive, even through my grief.

It had taken a while to accept any of this. And now, as I watched Em enter this temporary human space on the Verax carrier, I looked at her—this unimaginable creature—so full of care and feeling that everything was difficult to believe. But also, everything was so much easier to believe. There was life out there in the universe. They could be friendly. They could care and build friendships. They could look out for each other, build treaties, and respect each other's spaces.

Were humans ready for any of this? I thought back to what David had said to me, stuck in the seminar room only days before. I thought about what Joana had said, sitting on the floor of Emerald's shuttle. The answer would always be 'no'. We would never be ready. But the time had arrived anyway.

And as I sat down opposite Em one more time, I said, *"Tell me everything about your species. If we find new words, be precise. I want to know everything."*

VERAX DIGITAL ARCHIVE [TRANSLATED BY GAUTHIER]

CARRIER NEWS BULLETIN:

HUMAN PLANET SAVED AND TREATY AGREED

Losses: one ship and three lives

Human losses: total unknown

One human aboard frigate dead. But station successfully redirected. Millions of casualties avoided.

Treaty with humans now in effect. Humans currently regarded as sub-species neophyte of Verax. Humans respond to Verax, despite human displeasure.

Humans not members of Council.

Two humans to stay aboard carrier, until more permanent location is found. Humans to work with Verax to translate and begin learning culture. Verax responsible for human behaviour with regards to Council.

Tests to be conducted on tether to human. Human ambassador to be declared shortly.

Closing Statement

When someone asks me how my journey started, I want them to remember I never had a choice.

Blinded by depression, I took a job on the Observer. Blinded by greed, its downfall changed my life. And blinded by fate, I chased my instincts and followed a trail in a search for knowledge. One that led me to this very moment.

I sit on the edge of this bed, the rumble of my ship below my feet, and I never question *how* I got here. I know fate played its hand. It involved me from the moment I stepped foot on that station. And for that to have happened, everything prior needed to have happened too. My upbringing, my father's death, my grief. I'm here because I was always going to be here, even if I couldn't predict I would ever make it this far.

But what you've read so far is only the start of something so much bigger. Because, further into the depths of space, the Elders waited. They saw their chance, and they took it. They decimated our planet. It took fate to put me in the right place at the right time—to keep searching for the truth. And now I know *why* they did what they did. And I know how to stop them.

If my journey taught me anything, it's that, sometimes, you find yourself at the edge of a precipice, ready to jump, but it's just not your time yet. I spent my life believing I held no worth. I would have found it so easy to let go outside the Observer. And in my darkest moment, if I hadn't trusted that life had more to offer, I would never have experienced the things I have. We have reasons to live—whether it's to love, to learn, or to do the right thing. And now, what I once thought was the easy way out is about to be the hardest thing I've ever done. Death does not come easy to those who have learned to live.

End Transcript 1.

Acknowledgements

First and foremost, I'd like to thank all the friendly people who volunteered to beta read *inter alia*: Nicole, Haley, Sav, Ash, JD, Bruno, and Kelley—I'm eternally grateful for the feedback you provided, small or big, and for the constant words of encouragement you offered me along the way. Your interest and desire to read kept me going during tough times.

I'm also grateful to those who provided extensive story feedback. Thank you to Cristina, who encouraged me to find Nat's personality and delve deeper into Alex's feelings. Thank you to Darren, who gave me the reality check I needed to cut those pesky first two chapters and get to the action sooner. I truly believe I have a better book because of you.

Next, I'd like to thank Cameron, who very generously gave up his time to answer my silly alien linguistics questions. Thanks to your answers, I rewrote two chapters that would have ended being highly unlikely and turned them into something believable (for a science-fiction book!).

I want to thank Dee for the incredible cover. You provided me with art that I will eternally be proud to have on the cover of my book. Thank you for persuading me my ideas were worthy of a beautiful cover and for your patience in my lack of decision-making. You truly captured the essence of what the book is about.

Thank you to my Creative Writing MA cohort and lecturers at the University of Hull. I applied by submitting an extract of this novel, and finishing it wouldn't have been possible without the generous feedback and encouragement I've received from peers and tutors alike. A special thank you to Caroline: seeing your book on my shelf inspired me to keep pushing through the edits. Thank you for taking the time to read through *inter alia* and line-edit the first few chapters—your advice and support became invaluable to the rest of the book.

I'd like to thank my family: Dad, your knowledge of physics and engineering helped me better understand the logic of the story, from gravity and the effects of G-force to propulsion systems and typos. I was a bit nervous when you sat me down at your dining room table, a stack of A4 pages printed from my book in one hand and a pen in the other, but each piece of feedback you offered greatly improved every scene. Mum, you received portions of text through emails over the course of two or three years. How could I ever thank someone who read through the mediocre first drafts *more than once*? You caught many of the typos and corrected my tenses and my punctuation. Your passion for reading and the English language have made me into the writer I am today. And Jack, who has promised to buy a copy of whatever I write. You constantly open my eyes to new things—this book is thanks to a piece of media you begged me to consume. Truthfully, I think I wrote this book for you.

Thank you to my husband, Miguel, who has been supporting me since the very beginning. You've sat through long rambling sessions of me trying to get a scene to work. You've listened to me talk through issues I couldn't pin-point. You've provided me endless amounts of feedback, helping me arrive at the story that is now *inter alia*. Thank you for pushing me to keep going, even when I didn't see the point of it. I'm here because of you.

And I'd like to thank Pumpkin, my cat, who provided editing services by deleting large portions of text and replacing them with a variety of letters and numbers; and Stella, my dog, who has been sitting loyally by my side since the first draft and who sleeps peacefully next to me as I type the acknowledgements to book one. Thank you for putting up with my loud music.

And thank you, dear reader, for making it this far. I couldn't have done it without you.

About the Author

A lover of the unknown and a passionate writer, S.L. Guerreiro is due to graduate with an MA in Creative Writing from the University of Hull in 2025. When she is not daydreaming about space, she is writing about it or falling in love with depictions of it. As a young girl, she grew up watching Star Wars on repeat with her brother and became enamoured with the concept of a life in the stars. Now, she seeks to explore them herself, through her novels and from the comfort of her home.

inter alia:
book two

Help Alex continue her journey
through the stars...

Join me on Kickstarter! Scan the
QR code above, or find me at
www.kickstarter.com/projects/slgue
rreiro/inter-alia-book-2